ZANE PRESENTS

DECEPTION

THE KINK, P.I. SERIES: BOOK 2

Dear Reader:

Shakir Rashaan introduced readers to his brand of erotica with his Chronicles of the Nubian Underworld series. The author, a practitioner of Atlanta's BDSM and Fetish community, offers a real-life portrayal of this world through his characters and their lifestyles.

He launched his exciting "Kink, P.I." series with *Obsession* featuring detective Dominic Law. Mystery continues to meet kinky in book two, *Deception*, in which Law and partner Ramesses team up to solve the unthinkable homicide of a submissive whose body is discovered in a dungeon. The duo follows a suspenseful trail that leads them to the unlikeliest of suspects. And along the route, Law keeps an intense pace to solve the crime while engaging in continuous sexcapades. Be sure to check out Shakir's Chronicles of the Nubian Underworld series: *The Awakening*, *Legacy* and *Tempest*.

As always, thanks for supporting myself and the Strebor Books family. We strive to bring you the most cutting-edge, out-of-the-box material on the market. You can find me on Facebook @AuthorZane or you can email me at zane@eroticanoir.com.

Blessings,

Zane

Publisher
Strebor Books
www.simonandschuster.com

ALSO BY SHAKIR RASHAAN

Obsession

Tempest

Legacy

The Awakening

ZANE PRESENTS

DECEPTION

THE KINK, P.I. SERIES: BOOK 2

A NOVEL

SHAKIR RASHAAN

SBI

STREBOR BOOKS

NEW YORK LONDON TORONTO SYDNEY

Strebor Books
P.O. Box 6505
Largo, MD 20792
http://www.streborbooks.com

This book is a work of fiction. Names, characters, places and incidents are products of the author's imagination or are used fictitiously. Any resemblance to actual events or locales or persons, living or dead, is entirely coincidental.

ISBN 978-1-59309-604-5
ISBN 978-1-4767-7591-3 (ebook)
LCCN 2015934969

First Strebor Books trade paperback edition January 2016

Cover design: www.mariondesigns.com
Cover photograph: © Keith Saunders/Keith Saunders Photos

10 9 8 7 6 5 4 3 2 1

Manufactured in the United States of America

For information regarding special discounts for bulk purchases,
please contact Simon & Schuster Special Sales at 1-866-506-1949

The Simon & Schuster Speakers Bureau can bring authors to your live event. For more information or to book an event, contact the Simon & Schuster Speakers
Bureau at 1-866-248-3049 or visit our website at www.simonspeakers.com.

You can fool some of the people all the time,
and all of the people some of the time,
but you cannot fool all of the people all the time.
—*President Abraham Lincoln*

For my Beloved…
For loving me so much that the sound of your name silences my demons.

ACKNOWLEDGMENTS

I know we've done this before, but you know it's a lot of fun doing it again, right? Okay, cool, then let's get this done. Unlike my Nubian Underworld series, this is a complete work of fiction. There are some characters that you know and love, and there are some that you have been newly introduced to.

Now that we've gotten reacquainted a bit, let's get back to it; shall we?

With *Deception*, I took a few cases and put my usual twist on them, making sure the persons would remain nameless and faceless. Well, unless you decide to look up the cases and trials that I pulled from, of course. Dom is definitely a little more polished now, and he's having to deal with a few unexpected things with one of the cases that might have you looking at Ramesses a little differently. (He hasn't gone totally corporate, at least, not entirely, you know; he has to maintain the grittiness that my readers have come to enjoy from him.) All I can say about this installment is that you might not look at a rape case the same way once you see what I have in store for you!

I have to get this part out of the way, if for no other reason than the fact that it takes a lot of people to put books together, and a lot of the times, it takes a support system to help push the artist in the direction they need to go.

As always, I couldn't have done this book without my Beloved. I think you've gotten to the point to where you know this is going to turn into something that's going to be rolling for a very long time. I love you more than life itself. ☺

To my mother and sister, I have no words to describe the love and support that you have always shown, and your acceptance of my lifestyle. Thank you for understanding, and for also keeping an open mind with the type of material that I have been creating and giving me honest critiques.

To my boss, Zane, for your continued support of my literary endeavors; I can never thank you enough for letting me roar in my own unique way. I hope to continue to give you quality heat and the passion that I have in me with each passing project.

To my editor, Charmaine, I know every so often you have those "what in the world has he done now" looks when you go through my projects. Thank you for making me look even better than I already look. You are truly a treasure to behold.

To my agent, N'Tyse, none of this professional stuff would have been possible without your help and guidance. Don't worry, He's not done with my creativity yet, so you know I've got some new stuff coming.

I'm going to end this in the usual fashion because I still have my next in the series, *Reckoning: The Kink, P.I. Series*, burning up the pages and then some (that one is going to be crazy, I'm telling you), and I know I'm missing a whole gang of folks, so just do me a favor and insert your name in this next statement:

I'd like to thank ______________________________ for the support and love. I hope to continue to put books out that you will want to tell your friends and family about.

Thank you for reading, and God Bless you.

SPECIAL NOTE TO READERS

The grammatical errors that you might see within the dialog between the characters are not oversights. This is the type of speech and text that is used in some facets of the BDSM world. As one of my submissive friends put it, "The lowercase letters in a slave's or submissive's name are a demonstration of the hierarchical relationship. It is a reminder to the submissive that he or she is the bottom part of the hierarchy, meant to be led, and the Dominant's name is always capitalized, as He or She is the Top part, meant to lead." In keeping with the essence of the series and the essence of the BDSM community, preserving the speech was paramount. It is my hope that you, the reader, will understand and appreciate the symbolism.

PROLOGUE

"Where did all these changes come from?"

I stared at some of the things that bombarded me after taking a mini vacation with Niki and Natasha. The vacation was long overdue, especially after the emotional turmoil that I went through with the aptly named "Roman Numeral" murders.

I felt rejuvenated until I saw this craziness going on, and it looked like it wasn't slowing down anytime soon.

Ramesses was in the midst of playing ground traffic controller as the different techs were moving in and out of his and my offices. He finally got a chance to look up and saw the bewildered look on my face. "It's not like I didn't text or email you, Dominic. Didn't you check at all while you were tanning and spanking ass at Hedonism?"

I chuckled at that remark. Hedonism was a damn good time; I definitely would be lying if I said that it wasn't. But the madness that I saw swirling around like organized chaos was enough to make me want to take an extra day until the smoke cleared.

"Yeah, I got the messages, man, but it looks like you're preparing for something big," I observed as I stepped over some fiber optic cable. "Did something come up while I was gone?"

Ayanna walked past me, did a quick double-take when she realized it was me she walked past, gave a quick smile and a wink and said, "Welcome back, Sir, I hope that your vacation was good to you. It looks good on you...damn."

I swear, that woman was good for the ego when you needed it the most.

"Actually, business has picked up and then some," Ramesses replied, still pointing techs in the direction that they needed to go. "And not just in the A; some of my contacts on the West Coast have seen an uptick in some of the things going on out there. I had to send a couple of the boys to handle that madness."

That was good; it meant more revenue for the business, and that was always a good thing, especially when he was spending on more equipment.

I wasn't about to lie; a year ago when I jumped into this thing with Ramesses, I didn't know what to expect or if this thing would take off in the manner that it did.

I mean, fetish-related crimes usually got handled by Special Victims, but I also began to realize that the intricacies of the crimes that were being committed and the conservative nature of the detectives investigating the crimes, I guess I wasn't as forward-thinking as my business partner.

"I'm assuming that we'll be taking this thing on a wider scale?" I asked, trying to figure out how deep this rabbit hole was about to get.

"Let's put it this way: you keep doing what you're doing, and this could turn into something bigger than anything you could imagine," Ramesses stated.

"I can imagine a lot, Kane," I said as I grinned broadly.

"Can you imagine this?" Ramesses asked as we walked into his office. He turned on the big screen—which was bigger than before I left on vacation—and watching Amenhotep on the other side of the screen via video conference caused me to find the nearest chair to sit down.

"How was your vacation, youngster?" He asked as I saw his slave, paka, busying herself around their island home. "I can tell by the look on your face that you didn't expect a lot of this when you came back."

"That's an understatement, Sir." I tried to find my voice as quickly as I could, and even that was becoming a problem. "I remember the conversation we had concerning the changes we were proposing, but I didn't think they would be put in motion so quickly."

Amenhotep laughed heartily when I said that, like I was on the outside looking in on a joke that he enjoyed. "Dominic, if you've learned nothing about Ramesses, you should know by now that once the plan is conceived, the execution happens the next day."

We all shared a laugh as I stared at my business partner. Ramesses's reputation was legendary when it came to putting something together once he got his mind set on it. Hell, that's how I ended up retiring from APD as quickly as I did; I knew things would happen fast working with him.

But *this* fast?

I guess the revenue streams were rolling a bit more fluidly than I originally thought.

"Okay, so now that things are in motion, when can I expect to be able to get back into my office?" I asked Ramesses as I finally stood up and walked toward the screen. "I do have some follow-up to do on NEBU and Liquid, you know?"

Ramesses turned in my direction, his eyes showing the no-nonsense demeanor that I was sure the contractors had to deal with for who knows how long. "Yeah, I know you do, and I'm riding shotgun while you're doing your sweeps; there have been some additions made to those locations that you need to be brought up to speed on."

I noticed one of the techs as he walked up to Ramesses and handed him a clipboard. He gave me a nod to acknowledge my presence in the disaster area before he turned his attention back to Ramesses. "The final modifications have been completed in Mr. Law's office, Mr. Alexander. We should be finished with your modifications by the end of the business day, sir."

A smile spread across his face as he signed off on the paperwork on the clipboard. He looked back at me and winked. His grin never faded as he felt the need to gloat. "Does that answer your question, young'un?"

I shook my head, stepping over the debris to make my way into my office and survey the damage. "Yeah, now let me know what new tech you've put in my office so I can try to get up to speed, please?"

ONE

The guest list was compiled so that she could go out in a blaze of glory.

This would be her swan song, and she had every intention of making this count on several levels.

She had grown sick of the politics, the game-playing, and the messy breakups that had put her in the awkward position of making friends choose sides over whom to show their loyalty.

Now, after all of that drama and wading through the muck, she'd finally found the Dominant of her dreams.

But before she rode off into the sunset with him, she wanted one last scene with all of her favorite public players, six in all, to put her in a subspace the likes of which she had never before experienced.

She knew she would probably never experience it again, either; her new Dominant had made it clear that those days were over.

Oh well, she figured, what he didn't know wouldn't hurt him.

She chose the dungeon of one of her former Dominants—the one she hadn't pissed off—and she'd definitely pissed off a lot of them in her search for her "One," including three of the players that would be in attendance for her farewell scene.

Love is a battlefield, Pat Benatar once sang, and on that battlefield there are always casualties.

She just made damn sure she wasn't one.

That mentality came with a price, though.

The price came in the form of jilted lovers that really didn't take no for an answer, close friends that couldn't stick by her when her name was being dragged through the mud after yet another Dominant "victimized" her and treated her wrong. The mess with Master Amenhotep was the coup de grace, complete with being relocated from Atlanta "for her own protection," as she was told.

She kept up with all of the people that she felt still wanted to know where she was and what she was up to, and she even found a way to sneak away from her "exile" from time to time to get her rocks off and do her own thing...until she got caught up in another fine mess that ended in a woman being murdered and a prostitution ring being busted up. That got her really put on lockdown.

Video and email surveillance, among other extreme measures, which meant that she couldn't so much as sneeze without someone over two thousand miles away knowing about it. If it wasn't for the fact that it was HIM, she would have disappeared a long time ago, where even HE wouldn't find her.

She had one friend that stuck by her; her bestie, Ayanna, who was always there to be a shoulder to lean on when she needed her, despite her boss's warnings that eventually Ayanna would eventually get caught up in something messing around with her that he wouldn't be able to get her out of.

She didn't care for her boss all that much; especially considering that the interrogation he put her through in order to find out where to find the people responsible for the woman's death was rife with bittersweet moments. While it was hot as hell, it ended with her being relocated to the desert with people that she barely even knew.

She had it all figured out...she would ask Ayanna to be with her, serving her Dominant together, like her boss's two girls were doing now, and doing so happily. She knew Ayanna would do it; they'd been through a lot together and even kept in close touch while she was in Vegas for the past year.

They would be together, loving and serving a man who overlooked it all to have her at his feet. She would provide Ayanna as an added bonus, another willful submissive that would be at his beck and call.

It would be perfect.

But until then, she had bliss that awaited her.

One by one, they arrived and took their places in the chairs that she'd positioned in a circle in the middle of the dungeon floor, surrounding a mechanical lift, where she would be suspended from during the scene. It was almost ritualistic in nature, she thought, and she found herself turned on beyond words at the possibility of being suspended and whipped simultaneously by her guests.

After all, it was the least she could do before she gave herself completely and totally to her "One." After tonight, none of them would ever see her again.

Little did she know that someone had plans to make that happen...in ways that she never saw coming.

The stinging wisps of the single-tail whips against her skin combined with the rope burns she knew she would get from all of the writhing around in the air as each of the five tails struck would surely bring her to the ecstasy that she so longingly awaited tonight.

In her head, she shouted, *faster...harder...more, please!* as her guests mercilessly continued their symphonious assault on her helplessly suspended body.

Four male Dominants and one female Dominant—an experiment with her sexuality that, in truth, she knew she never should have done since she wasn't sincere about being in a relationship with her—were giving her trophies that she would cherish long after the marks faded away.

Her body jerked with each strike, taking her closer to the edge and into the abyss of subspace, feeling the familiar euphoria of flight. This time, the feeling was much more intense than she ever thought was possible, and she envisioned seeing the welts and scratches that would surely reveal themselves.

She couldn't wait to show Ayanna what she had endured tonight. *She would be so jealous!*

She was slightly disappointed that all of the players weren't able to make it; well, actually, only one of the six was unable, and she wanted him more than anything. She figured that his responsibilities in the community kept him from seeing about her one last time.

That, and the fact that she never got up enough nerve to send the email invitation to him, including a few words that she only meant for him to read.

She could always find him at NEBU if push came to shove and she needed to get a fix. He always looked out for her, even in the light of what she'd done—out of fear, not malice—to his mentor. He would hopefully understand why she needed to do this—he *had* to.

She felt her skin burning as the bindings around her wrists and ankles made their painful presence known to her, but she was too far gone to care. A few more kisses of the whips and she would be in the clouds, higher than any drug could ever take her.

So high, in fact, that she never noticed that she was being lowered from the suspension and her bindings skillfully removed.

Now came the fun part…

She wasn't sure if the glassy look in her eyes gave her away, but she barely made out the order to "bring her some water and some fruit" that came from the one that carried her over to the area in the dungeon where the aftercare and cool-down could be administered.

She'd gotten through the scene in one piece, and without using the agreed-upon safeword also. The pride that she felt that she'd taken all they could throw at her and she took it like a trooper.

If she could only tell her "One," though, it would have been perfect. She didn't want to keep any secrets from him, but there was not much choice in the matter.

She knew that he would never understand; he was old-school D/s and he didn't partake in a lot of the public play atmospheres that Atlanta had to offer, and usually when he did, it was only with his submissive. Rarely did he ever allow any others to touch what belonged to him, which was why she had to do this one last scene before she petitioned for acquisition.

Besides, she would heal up in time before he returned home from overseas on a business acquisition anyway, so she could get away with murder.

She felt safe in the arms of the Dominant that cared for her during the aftercare, and as her senses began to return to her, she heard the voices wishing everyone farewell for the evening, and the Dominant that she was still wrapped up with told the rest that they would lock up the place before heading home.

She smiled, thinking of the greed and hunger that suddenly came to the surface, leaving her horny and wanting to fuck. She always loved sex during subspace; it made her multi-orgasmic and put her body in slut mode. Having the Dominant she was with made the possibilities even stronger that she could cap this night off right, even though another Dominant threatened to ruin the moment with perverted fantasies of videotaping the event for "posterity."

Yeah, like there was a snowball's chance in hell of that ever happening.

The one she wanted to fuck cleverly told the other Dominant that what they were about to do was not for an audience, and bid them goodbye. Soon, it was only the two of them.

Her pussy was on fire and she needed desperately to have a long hose to put it out. Not to mention the sex was nasty and kinky as hell, so she couldn't wait to see what she would be made to do after all this time.

Imagine her delicious surprise to hear chains being pulled out of the corner near where they lay.

As the chains were being locked into place, her eyes focused on the menacing member that protruded out just inches away from her throbbing lips.

She purred as she lay splayed across the gynecological table with her legs in the stirrups, locked down by the chains wrapped around her already swollen ankles and wrists. She knew it would take her right back into subspace, and she was ready to take the express route.

"Damn, you're fucking me so good, get that pussy, baby!" she screamed with what little volume she had from the screaming she'd done during the earlier scene. The coldness of the steel against her flesh combined with the heat being generated between them became the recipe for a climax that could possibly render her unconscious.

If she only realized that someone was watching…

Sliding inside her while she was already slippery felt like heaven for her. This was what she had been waiting for all night; the only thing left was to get the wave of orgasms that was sure to come the moment that her throat was grabbed.

Her lover kept pumping in and out of her at a seemingly endless pace. Her breathing quickened, trying her best to brace for each down-stroke that seemed to push deeper and deeper inside her core.

She longed to touch, but the chains would not allow it, as she knew it couldn't be any other way, nor would she want it any other way. To be helpless and in the hands of a sadist and not know what would come next in this tryst was a dream come true.

She was so wet that she didn't notice that her lover had begun the assault on her tender asshole; the slickness of her juices all over that thick shaft made penetration a complete ease of motion.

"*That's it, baby, fuck my ass!*" she growled, realizing that her primal instincts made themselves known, smelling the pheromones emanating from the continued union of their sweat-drenched bodies.

If this pace kept up, she would surely pass out.

Hearing the tiger-like growling as her body endured the savage fucking that she begged to continue, her eyes widened with delight as she felt the right hand of her lover begin to close around her throat. Her climax would be imminent, and there would be nothing that she could do to stop it once it arrived.

Not that she would stop it, of course, unless she was commanded to do so until her lover reached the pinnacle first.

She gasped as her eyes rolled in the back of her head, feeling the pressure of the back of her head against the headrest. Her lover didn't miss a beat the entire time, which saddened her in a way; there would never be a repeat performance.

She wanted to delay the end, but her lover's grip around her throat made that nearly impossible. She wondered, even in her highly aroused state and while still getting her brains fucked out, how many women had that hand choked out before she happily succumbed to its expertly tight grip.

The fact that that grip was adorned in a leather-clad glove only pushed her deeper into the abyss.

She'd experienced breath play before during sex, and with the one she was with now, she had no doubt that she would not be in harm's way because she'd done it before with blissful results.

Seeing such a beautiful face before blacking out wasn't so bad, she figured. She could always float in the fantasies that she would have while she was under.

She never even flinched when she began to see stars and felt that she was slipping into the darkness. She knew she would only be there for a few moments, only to be brought back into the light.

As she stared one last time at her lover before she closed her eyes to travel to that blissful space between pain and pleasure, she took comfort in knowing that it would be the first thing she saw the moment she returned from the abyss.

There was only one problem…

She never returned.

TWO

"Dom, I have a Jane Doe at Inner Sanctum that I think you might be interested in checking out," Natasha was on the phone explaining.

"Go ahead, Natasha." I had Ramesses in the truck with me as we pulled out of NEBU on a routine security sweep. The call was a slight bit unexpected, but she didn't call unless it was important. "Ramesses is with me as well."

"Good, because this one's a bit unusual, Sir," she replied back, trying to maintain her discipline and professionalism at the same time. "The Jane Doe was chained down; looks like asphyxiation is the cause of death, but we won't know until the M.E. gets the body for the autopsy."

"Anything else that sets out as extraordinary?" Ramesses asked once I put the phone on speaker. "Is there anything on the scene that the other detectives might be overlooking?"

"No, Sir, I don't think so, but that's why I'm requesting the firm's services, Sir," Natasha answered again, sounding like she was on the move around the crime scene. "Lieu thinks that your expertise might help with the investigation. That and the fact that it's at one of the fetish clubs, she thought it might be a good idea to secure the firm."

"All right, my lovely, tell your Lieu that we will be on the scene in the next fifteen or so," I told her before hanging up the phone.

It was a bright and sunny, late-summer morning in Atlanta, and

I thought I would be able to do a quick check with my business partner before getting in some football on the tube before Natasha got home from work. Niki was already at the spot, taking care of the domestic duties just in case I decided to have the fellas over to watch the college players do some damage.

This phone call wasn't exactly what I'd expected to get from either of my girls, but this is what we do.

"What do you think, Dom?" Ramesses was stroking his beard again; it was what he usually did when his wheels were turning.

"Natasha wouldn't have called unless there was something there that the other detectives on scene wouldn't have picked up on," I told him. "And since the locale is at Inner Sanctum, there's no telling what may have gone down out there."

Inner Sanctum was a rival, well, establishment on the east side. I say establishment loosely because, unlike the other dungeon that has a more reputable following and does things above board, this place usually gets used by folks that want to be, shall we say, unsupervised.

It wasn't always like that, but in the last year since they went under new management, it's become less like a dungeon and more like a cum dump depot. Etiquette wasn't adhered to, and damn near anything went; there was very little rule enforcement.

To give you an idea of what I mean, let me give you a quick rundown on dungeon etiquette:

No playing without a dungeon monitor in house.

No bodily fluids.

No open sexual acts on the premises.

The problem with Inner Sanctum was that they shirked those rules in order to compete with the larger clubs, including NEBU. Between that and the membership rates blatantly placed lower than everyone else, it became a hotbed for all kinds of crazy shit.

Coming from a kinkster, that's saying a lot!

"You do have a point, Dom." Ramesses was still stroking his beard. I got the sense that he was disturbed about something after the call was over. "There might be some clues or some residue that might not tip off the detectives that we might pick up on."

"Are you all right, Kane?" I asked solemnly. I rarely ever used his real name unless I wanted to get his attention, and I hoped this would be enough to do it.

Mission accomplished.

He snapped out of the daze he was in and gave me a look like he'd been caught thinking about something he shouldn't have been…or something he didn't want to entertain. "Nothing yet, but I have a bad feeling it might be something…and something big."

The place looked like the third level of hell.

How in the world people tried to get their flow on in here, I'd never know, but we weren't here for the acoustics and the ambiance; the stench of a dead body permeating the building was a clear reminder of that.

We were greeted by the detectives as soon as we stepped foot inside the dungeon area. Natasha wasn't far behind, trying to mask her happiness to see me with the stoic demeanor of professionalism. She greeted us with the customary handshake, ready to make the proper introductions. "Mr. Law, Mr. Alexander, thank you for coming. This is my partner, Detective Cross. Cross, these gentlemen were requested by Lieu to consult on the case."

Detective Cross gave us the once-over like we had infringed on her personal space, despite the fact that we were at least five feet away from her. "So, you're the kink squad, huh?"

Ramesses stopped in his tracks, looked at me for a moment or two, trying to get a gauge on the situation. I didn't do anything more than give a "Kanye shrug" and nodded in his direction. It was only a matter of time before he would flip the tables on her, and I wanted to witness the carnage after the earthquake rumbled.

Detective Cross was a statuesque female: Amazon. The way she carried herself, you already knew she was a lesbian, but she had enough curves and softness to go along with that hard edge to her personality that threw the fellas off if they tried to approach her to holla.

She was Natasha's new partner in DeKalb County; she had transferred from Fulton County—and my old precinct—after some changes at the top brought in some new people that she wasn't comfortable with. Cross looked like she was a rookie to all of the types of crimes that we deal with, and Ramesses knew it.

"I take it you have a problem with that, Detective Cross?" Ramesses interjected, but never lost his cool. "Do we really wanna play 'my dick is bigger than yours' today? I believe we've got less than seventy-two hours to get this figured out before the trail goes cold, yes?"

To my amazement, Detective Cross backed down. "Very well, Mr. Alexander, follow me."

We walked down the hallway, following the scent of the odor into the dungeon area. The other crime scene investigators were busy tagging and bagging evidence, trying to get the area cleared as quickly as possible. As we got closer to where the victim was located, I had a sudden sense of dread overwhelm me. Usually when that happened, it wasn't a good thing by any stretch of the imagination.

Ramesses must have sensed it, too, but the moment he saw the body, he stopped dead in his tracks, frozen by the immediate recognition of who the victim was.

At first glance, I couldn't make the identification, but the closer we go, the more I understood why my partner had such a hard time moving toward the body.

Seeing the perfectly tanned skin, the tattoos that revealed a dove and a python, which probably explained the complexity that encapsulated who she was as a person, and the light-gray eyes that were absolutely unmistakable the moment you saw them, it became clear that this case was not going to be easy to handle on certain emotional levels.

safi, one of Amenhotep's former slaves, lay dead on a gynecological table, her legs still tied down on the stirrups, and her wrists tied down above her head.

Damn.

I thought she was supposed to be out of state? And what really had me confused was how did she creep back into Atlanta and Ramesses not know about it?

I saw my partner move slowly over to her lifeless body, a growing scowl spreading across his face as it looked for a moment that he would rip the bounds from her extremities and personally carry her to the gurney himself.

I felt the rising anger in his eyes, and I tried my best to figure out if I could stop him, even with the way he was feeling at the moment. Before I could get to him to take him down a couple of notches, he stopped himself. The look he gave Natasha's partner was intense enough to burn through steel. "Detective Cross, is there a particular reason why the vic hasn't been placed on a gurney yet?"

As long as I'd been on the force before leaving, I'd never seen a civilian punk a detective.

I guess there's a first time for everything.

Detective Cross looked like she was ready to chop off the heads of the persons that hadn't secured the body before they'd arrived.

She motioned for a couple of the technicians to remove the body, and then engaged in a stare-down with Ramesses, almost daring him to say something else.

Ramesses was undeterred by the show of insolence from the detective, and all Natasha and I could do was let this play out, for fear that our respective partners would snap and take this to the next level.

Once the body was in the process of being moved, Natasha began the rundown on what they found when they got there. "The owner found the body about seven this morning and called the police shortly thereafter. Her neck had been broken; the M.E. estimates the time of death around two a.m. There were signs of vaginal penetration as well as the markings that look like they came from a whip or several whips; we're not sure yet, but those occurred before the sexual encounter on the gyno table."

"Yeah, it looks like someone really got their sick-ass rocks off before the killer took her out," Detective Cross blurted out. "What in the world would make a woman want to subject herself to something like this?"

Cue the scratch of the record at that exact moment.

Ramesses knee-jerked immediately, turning around and focusing on the source of the remark. "Excuse *me?*"

She looked up and saw eyes staring in her direction.

Natasha looked like she really wanted to hide at that moment.

I wanted to smirk for a minute, but I should have been feeling sorry for the poor woman. Ramesses was ready to go in for the kill, but I decided against it; she had it coming to her and there was no sense in giving a warning. I didn't know her like that, and she needed to be baptized.

Detective Cross's body language betrayed her the moment she turned to face Ramesses; she realized she'd stepped over the line and should have kept her mouth shut and her comments in her head. She tried to stand tall, but her eyes gave her away, and we all knew it.

Ramesses invaded her personal space quickly, walking to her and nearly facing her nose to nose. When she tried to step back to create some space, he gripped her wrists tightly, keeping her in place. Their eyes locked forcefully, and the moment I saw that, I already knew what would happen next, and Natasha did, too.

Detective Cross's eyes fluttered, trying to show her defiance and anger at Ramesses putting his hands on her. "Step away from me, and take your hands off me."

Ramesses flashed a grin back at her, knowing he'd been down this road before. "I don't think so. Besides, from the way you're shaking, you don't want me to let go of you anyway."

"Who the fuck do you think you are?"

"Stick around, detective; you'll find out soon enough."

Resistance was futile, and she would find that out soon.

For those that hadn't picked up on this dance, allow me to clue you in on something when it comes to women: the ones that made the most noise about what they couldn't believe another woman would or wouldn't do, chances were, they were already secretly wishing that someone would do it to them.

As their eyes continued the stare-down, something curious happened: Detective Cross slowly licked her lips and moved close enough to, if Ramesses allowed it, kiss him. She tried to move closer, but he stonewalled her, making it clear that he was the one in control, not her. Her eyes lowered, her free hand tracing the words on her badge that hung around her neck.

If it weren't for the fact that we were in the middle of a crime scene, that shit would be hot right now. I watched a grown-ass woman reduced to a love-struck teenager in a matter of minutes.

Ramesses looked like he hadn't even broken a sweat. "Now, shall we continue?"

"Yes, Sir," she answered, looking completely mesmerized the entire time. "I'm sorry for my outburst. It won't happen again."

"See that it doesn't, or the consequences will be worse."

I swear I needed to develop that touch soon. My girls would be the better for it.

"Any prints on the table or anywhere in the room?" I asked Natasha, trying to keep things on the professional tip as much as possible. I looked in her eyes, and I already knew that what had happened between them had her as turned on as I was.

"According to forensics, a lot of them, but they won't know for sure until they get the results from the lab testing," she replied, flipping her notepad to check the other notes that she wrote down before we got there. "I also recognized at least two different types of whip marks on her body."

Detective Cross raised her eyebrow at that assessment and then backed down immediately once she got a glimpse of the scowl on Ramesses's face. Natasha grinned a bit, which put a mental note for me to check on later today when she wasn't around her partner.

"What do you mean two different whips, Tasha?" Detective Cross asked. "How did you figure out it was more than one?"

I grinned as I saw Natasha straighten her jacket. "Because the marks are not consistent with a single player, Trisha; I've seen two separate whips in motion, and the patterns that I've witnessed are consistent with at least two players simultaneously."

Detective Cross raised her eyebrow, a slight smirk spreading across her lips. "Hmm, there's more that you've not told me, Tasha, and I have a feeling that things could get more interesting from here on out."

I wasn't completely impressed, and Ramesses was absolutely

turned off by her. I would admit that she had some potential, but I wasn't about to admit that in light of the mess that she'd created already.

"Good work, detective, so that means we can check out some of the munch groups, see if anyone knew anything." Ramesses was stoic as he turned to leave. "Detective Cross, we will keep you and Natasha in the loop, of course, to let you know what we've found."

"You are more than welcome to call me Trish, Sir, if it is all the same to you." Detective Cross all but served her ass on a silver platter for him to take.

I honestly didn't know what would happen next; he'd been completely unpredictable over the past hour. That was not like Ramesses to be that way; he's too measured, too ice-cold calculating to all of a sudden start acting like he didn't know which end was up.

All order was restored in the universe when he turned around, flashed a grin at the detective, and calmly stated, "To be real, detective, it's probably not in your best interest for us to be on a first-name basis. I don't think you could handle the road you'd go down if you did."

"Maybe I might want to know? I'm a big girl; I can handle a little slap and grind." She flashed her own mischievous grin, trying to continue the cat-and-mouse banter. "What makes you think I couldn't handle it?"

"The reason I *know* you couldn't handle it is simple: you think you have control, and you thrive on the power struggle until you decide that you want to acquiesce. You won't have a choice in the matter once you make your choice, and it will be the last choice you make, trust me." He regarded her body language again, knowing that he had her dead to rights. "That Amazon act might work with regular dudes on the street, but in my world, you would be trouble, and you would fail trying to be something you're not."

Out of the corner of my eye, I saw Natasha stifling a laugh. Deep down, she knew that Ramesses was right. Trish would be too much work, and her mouth would get her into too much trouble. There were some who didn't mind having a brat for a submissive, but she was going after the wrong one.

Neferterri would have her out on her ass on the first thing smoking; I was sure about it.

I already knew that I would have some interesting conversations with her and Niki tonight; there was never a dull moment over the past year. Tonight would be no exception.

Before she could come back with something else to engage Ramesses further, he headed out of the room and hit the exit before anyone could adjust to what was going on.

I caught up with him at the truck, and once I had a chance to really get a good look at him, I realized that he really wasn't himself. He had to be shook over seeing safi like that.

This business could be ruthless on your emotions. I found that out last year.

"K, are you all right?" I asked again with real concern this time. "Is there something you're not telling me right now?"

He continued to stare into the space in front of him, looking deeper in thought by the second. He shook his head a few times, stroking his beard over and over.

I wasn't worried yet, but it would be a stretch to say I wasn't concerned.

He's not acting like his usual cooler-than-a-fan self, and I needed to know why.

Ramesses flipped out his smartphone and sent a text to someone, looking like it was the last thing that he wanted to do. I suspected the message being sent was to Amenhotep on his island. He would want to know about this, regardless of how they'd parted ways.

This couldn't be easy on him; cases like this never were when it came to people you're close to. Lord knows I had my own issues last year with the case that landed in my lap. But I needed him to be Ramesses, not whoever this man was sitting beside me in my truck. The last thing I needed was to keep an eye on him while working this case.

"Yeah, Dom, I'm fine." His voice was disquieting, giving me pause over the cryptic nature of his words. This had the makings of a very complicated situation, and I wasn't sure I liked it or not. He turned toward me as I cranked the engine, waiting for the direction that we were supposed to head in. "Unfortunately, I know someone who won't be."

THREE

"So, what's the first move, partner?"

I honestly tried to figure that out for myself, much less trying to tell my business partner. Murders were difficult to deal with, especially when it came to someone that meant something to you. safi could be a pain in the ass from time to time, but she definitely grew on me.

"The beat officers are probably hitting the neighborhood, trying to figure out who knows anything, if anyone saw anything," I advised as we left the crime scene. "I would think that we might need to find out where safi was staying when she got here. It's a safe bet that she didn't stay with anyone here."

Ramesses stroked his beard as he thought over the situation. He nodded as the wheels continued to turn in his head. "Next?"

"Next thing is, we might need to track down the players that are missing from the party," I noted. "I have a funny feeling that none of them are going to want to talk until they find out that she's dead."

I turned down Memorial Drive to hit I-285 and started making tracks toward the office when Ramesses threw a monkey-wrench into that course of action. "We need to hit Buckhead."

"Why are we heading there?" I asked, confused as to what that had to do with anything. "What's in Buckhead?"

"If I remember safi's patterns well enough, there's only one place in the city that she would stay that would keep her identity from hitting my surveillance protocols," Ramesses answered back, pulling up his laptop to get some information. "Head for the W."

Wait, what the hell did he just say?

We were still in the growing pains stage of our business relationship, but I had to believe that he had enough respect for me as a friend to at least give full disclosure. "Okay, this would be about the time that you would let your partner in on what line of thinking that you're under, Sir. You know, it would inspire a little trust, and it might help me to help speculate what you might be thinking."

"Okay, kid, here's the deal." Ramesses closed his laptop, straightening up in the seat before he spoke again. "The manager at the W is a longtime member of the community, and from time to time, he allows those that might want to remain off the radar to stay at the hotel."

"Okay, I can get with that program…and you're thinking that he let safi stay at the hotel?" I wasn't a stranger to "under the table" transactions; a lot of entertainers and athletes pulled those off without a second thought. safi was neither. "Don't most hotels have a policy to take credit card transactions only? There has to be a paper trail, even if the patrons are VIP."

"That's correct, but for the right dollars, they will be willing to look the other way, with the understanding that they don't do anything stupid while in the room." Ramesses glanced out the window as we approached the W. "I know he works the evening shift, so we might be able to catch him right before shift change and see if he can let us into the room."

"Do you think he'll give up the information?" I was a bit incredulous over how this was all coming together. In all seriousness, whoever his contact was, there was no guarantee he would be so forthcoming. Not without some aggressive persuasion, of course.

"I'm sure he will try to hide behind hotel policy or something like that to set up a roadblock."

"He won't have a choice." Ramesses smirked. "I happen to know his supervisor…well."

I left a C-note with the valet to keep the truck close by. The way Ramesses walked into the lobby, I had a feeling we wouldn't be long.

We approached the front desk, and I couldn't help but notice the international flavors of the women that manned the desk. One looked Brazilian; the other two were French and Italian. That was unmistakable; all those years working the detail at Hartsfield-Jackson International taught me a lot when it came to guessing the nationalities of different women.

Why did all of the luxury hotels always seemed to have the most exotic women staffing the front desk? Was it an unwritten code in the hotel industry or something?

"Welcome to the W; my name is Marissa. How may I serve you, sir?" the young Brazilian woman spoke. Her accent dripped with a sensuality that the Brazilians were known for, and I was glad Ramesses was the one that took the point on this fishing expedition.

"Yes, Marissa, if you would, please, I need to speak to Mr. Jansen? It's of a sensitive nature." He remained calm, not giving himself away as to what he wanted. I didn't know how he was able to pull that off; I had trouble keeping my eyes from roaming all over her svelte frame.

"May I tell him who needs to see him?" She remained very polite, most certainly following the etiquette protocol that hotels usually follow. Her eyes began to give her away, though, lending to a quick attraction to a stronger personality in her presence.

"Yes, if you would please let him know that 'Mr. Ra' is here to see him." Ramesses maintained his decorum, sounding business-professional. I always admired that about him, since I couldn't flip the switch like that. I was the rough "muscle" of this outfit; if someone needed their head bashed in, that's where I came in.

Okay, I shouldn't put us both in a box like that. It's not that Ramesses couldn't put a man through a wall; he actually was taller and a slight bit bigger than I was, if you can believe that. It's half the reason he commanded such a presence when he entered a room.

Marissa smiled as she picked up the phone to dial her manager. She quietly spoke to tell him who we were here for. Her demeanor changed when she hung up the phone, her eyes conveying the difficulty of having to relay a message that we certainly didn't want to hear. "My apologies, Mr. Ra, but Mr. Jansen says he's unavailable at the moment. He has authorized me to assist in any way that I can, if you are not offended by my assistance?"

"Oh, no, my dear, not offended at all. Besides…" Ramesses leaned forward to get closer to her. (Speaking in Portuguese) *"I do not mind having a guide as beautiful and sexy as you are. We would be honored."*

That got a blush out of her, and cold stares from the other two women at the desk. I guess they had a taste for chocolate tonight, too. I figured she was impressed with the Portuguese that he'd just spoken to her.

(Speaking in Portuguese) "I am honored to serve these gentlemen well, whatever the task requires." Marissa moved from behind the desk, ignoring the shade being thrown in her direction. The moment she stood in front of us, her attention and focus sharpened. "Where would you like to go, gentlemen?"

"There was a young woman that was a guest in your hotel. Young, very attractive, extremely flirty regardless of gender; perhaps you might remember her?" I pulled a picture of safi out of my folder to show Marissa.

Marissa studied it for a brief moment before she began blushing. "Yes, sir, I have had the pleasure of seeing her. I checked her into her room at Mr. Jansen's request."

"May I ask why you're blushing, Marissa?" I asked again, picking up on the slight grin that spread across her face.

"Oh, please forgive me, sir, it's just that..." Marissa kept blushing through the statement she was stumbling through. "We had an interlude after I got off work. She's quite the sensual lover, sir."

I didn't want to alarm her, and I was sure Ramesses wanted to keep her as calm as possible, but she had to be told. "I am sorry to have to tell you this, Marissa, but she was murdered last night."

Marissa clutched her chest in dismay, grabbing Ramesses's shoulder for support as she felt faint. "Oh my goodness, that is awful news."

"Is there any way that we could possibly get into her room before the police arrive, Marissa?" Ramesses asked quietly. "We will be discreet, I promise. Not even your supervisor will know what we've done."

Marissa didn't hesitate. Once we arrived at the elevators, she slipped the key into the slot where the concierge level suites were. That tipped me off to exactly what Mr. Jansen had done on safi's behalf, and what he got out of it for himself. "I still have the key to the room, sir. I had hoped to enjoy her one more time before she headed back to Nevada."

Ramesses didn't exactly look all that pleased that safi was afforded such high-profile accommodations. He put in a call once we got up to the concierge level, speaking in a very monotone voice; needless to say, some things would be in motion soon.

We got into the room and began make the painstaking moves

to keep from disturbing it too much, as to not alert Natasha and Trish that we were here.

Ramesses put on some latex gloves and went through the suitcases with great care, so much so that I wondered if he had done some training behind my back over the last year. I checked the effects in the bathroom and the closet, making sure that I didn't move anything too far from where it sat. Nothing looked out of the ordinary, although when I came back into the living area, Ramesses was seated and looked in deep thought.

"What is it, Sir?"

"safi's laptop is missing."

"Are you sure?"

"Affirmative, Sir. I would have hoped it would be here so we could run through the contents before DeKalb got to it." Ramesses shook his head in frustration. "I wonder if Cross and Natasha got it to their boys before we could find it."

I could understand where he was coming from; the last thing anyone in the community wanted was damning evidence that the victim couldn't defend himself or herself against. If we could get to the files, they could be purged, and none would be the wiser.

Ramesses felt like he was grasping at straws with the line of questioning he was on. "Do you think it was still at the murder scene and they tagged it before we got there?"

"It is a possibility, Sir. If so, the tech boys will probably have a field day with it." I shook my head; the information that could leak…I didn't want to think about the repercussions.

I was hoping that one of my contacts in DeKalb might have gotten the evidence. I put in a quick call and left a voicemail for him to look out for the name on the evidence tag and to hold it before someone else got to it that wouldn't be as delicate with the information as he would be.

"I hope you are able to find who did this, gentlemen," Marissa stated as she wiped small tears away with the handkerchief she'd had in her pocket. "She was a lovely woman. No one deserves to have that happen to them."

"We agree on that, my dear," Ramesses replied as we headed out of the suite. "We thank you for your help; I know you took a risk by bringing us in here."

The smile on her face and a knowing wink tipped me off that her supervisor was compromised in more ways than one. Beauty did make men weak. "There's a reason why he chose me to escort you around the premises, gentlemen. I assure you, I'm in no danger of anything. The reprisal would be swift and harsh."

We were greeted by Mr. Jansen almost as soon as we got off the elevator and headed back to the atrium. "Gentlemen, I apologize for my absence. I hope Marissa was able to get things accommodated for you?"

"Yes, Marissa was a most gracious escort and took care of everything that was needed." I noticed the way he tried to gauge my facial expression, trying to figure out what he'd missed out on. Yeah, like I was going to give him the satisfaction.

"Great, and Mr. Alexander, my supervisor, Mrs. Eddington, wanted me to personally give you her respects and greetings with the hopes that the next time you're in the building that I make sure you're taken care of personally." Mr. Jansen seemed a bit on edge, and I felt the disingenuous tone in his voice. He was irritated that we had gone over his head.

He'd get over it. What he was unaware of was that his supervisor, unbeknownst to him, was a major benefactor to NEBU and was an exclusive VIP to functions that he didn't get a whiff of notice about.

Ramesses remained steadfast, polite, even in the face of the fake offer presented to us. I saw the brute underneath, slowly trying to make its appearance, as a reminder that there once was a man with a temper. "Oh, that won't be necessary, Mr. Jansen. Anytime that I'm at your hotel, I'll make sure that Marissa and the other front desk associates take care of anything that I need while I or any of my guests are staying here. I like it when I can trust the people that provide excellent customer service."

Marissa smiled, and Ramesses picked up her hand and kissed the back of her palm.

(Speaking in Portuguese) "Thank you for making us feel at home. You truly are a beautiful woman, and I will make sure you are rewarded properly for your service."

Marissa blushed again and replied as she headed back to her desk, (speaking in Portuguese), "You are very kind, sir, and it was a pleasure serving you. You are a very beautiful and sexy man, and your wife is a lucky woman. Good night."

We headed out of the hotel to the front driveway, and once we got back into the truck, I had to ask him about the exchange between him and Marissa since I didn't speak a lick worth of Portuguese.

"Sometimes it helps to be able to use many tongues to achieve the goal that was needed, Dom." The grin on Ramesses's face betrayed any ideas he had at being discreet. "Besides, a gentleman never besmirches a lady's honor, even while flirting. Just know that if we need anything here, she's definitely the new contact from now on. Some people need a reminder of their place."

Damn, it's like that?

I tried to find a way to figure out exactly what he meant by that, and the look on Mr. Jansen's face was a dead giveaway that someone—and I was not saying who—was going to rip him a new asshole for not following directions.

I guess that's what Ramesses meant by "reminder of their place."

I wasn't exactly asking for a blow-by-blow of what went on between him and Marissa, either. I've known my partner long enough to know that he would be dangerous if he used his power and influence for nefarious intent. But after watching the way that Marissa longingly looked at us as we headed out the door, I knew one thing for certain.

I needed to learn Portuguese.

FOUR

Instead of heading back to the office, Ramesses and I decided that we would shoot downtown to the Sun Dial restaurant for drinks and to bounce some more ideas on the cases off each other.

At seventy-three floors up and at the top of one of the tallest buildings in the A, it was an interesting locale to be alone with your thoughts.

We took the outside elevators up to the restaurant, which was basically in bar status on a weeknight. Not too many dinners are happening unless it was hotel guests coming in to take in the sights.

I definitely needed the sights. It might help me to figure out the pieces that I might be missing.

I ordered the usual, a Hennessy and Coke, and Ramesses opted for something with a little less strength, drinking a Caramel Apple Martini. I figured he did that more to relax than anything; he drinks harder stuff at the office.

After we got the drinks from the bartender, I picked up where we'd left off at the W to figure out what needed to be done with the case at hand. "Suspects?"

"Obviously, we have the attendees to run through first, but we need to find out who those persons are, otherwise we'll be spinning our wheels for a couple of days, and we don't have that kind of time." Ramesses downed his drink in one gulp. That's definitely not like him to do something like that.

"Look, I know this is grinding on you, Sir, and I'm sorry we found safi like we did," I quietly said to him, trying to gauge where his mind was. "What else have we missed outside of the laptop?"

"You tell me, young'un. I think that is your field of expertise, don't you think?" Ramesses shot back at me, taking me aback for a moment. He saw the look on my face for a moment and began to realize his lapse. "Dom, I'm sorry about that; my nerves are on edge. I never expected it to be her in my wildest nightmares."

I empathized with him; safi did grow on me a little bit, even though my function was surveillance and lock down protocols. Anyone that lost their life at such a young age was cause for sadness. I decided to bring back an earlier conversation we'd had before I left the force.

"Look, Kane, when we first started doing this, I told you that sometimes it wouldn't be easy, and unfortunately, this is one of those times where it won't be easy. This case may test your ability to keep your emotions under control; are you prepared to deal with that?"

"I don't know if I have the ability yet, honestly, Dominic," Ramesses answered, taking the second round as quickly as the first. "Right now, trying to get that image of safi out of my mind is what I want to happen as quickly as possible."

"Then help me figure out if we have all of the puzzle pieces, Sir," I pleaded, tapping the bartender for another round. "What have we missed that was at the crime scene?"

Ramesses stroked his beard for a moment, sipping his drink again before it seemed the light went off in his head. "Did you notice that they waited until we got there before they moved safi's body? Is that regular protocol?"

"Not to my knowledge, honestly," I answered, going through my training and what I remembered from going through the crime scenes before. "They had plenty of time to cover the bodies and get them ready to go to the M.E.'s office for autopsy. Hell, I was in shock that you punked Cross like that. Usually, the lead detective doesn't take shit from no one, so I'm trying to figure out what the hell happened."

"I don't profess to know crime scene protocol and all, but I knew something was…wrong…with having her sitting there like she was on someone's sick display or something like that." He shook his head as the image played out in his mind again. "I couldn't have that image in my head. I refuse to have that."

"Well, either way, you were in the right. They had to be on scene at least over an hour before Natasha called us, Sir," I admitted. "There was not much she could do to rebut or try to catch any type of attitude with a civilian."

"I'm not an ordinary citizen, though, Dom, and you know it." Ramesses grinned as his phone rang. "Yes, Beloved, I'm okay… yes, had a bad day at the office, really bad… I'll explain once I get home, and I won't be too late tonight. I need to get some sleep."

I tried not to laugh as he hung up the phone, but I couldn't help but be a little jealous at the same time. As much as I wasn't exactly *feeling* marital bliss or anything like that, the fact that the main woman in his life made sure that he was okay was hard not to ignore.

I watched him as he took his finger and began drawing an imaginary flow chart, using his photographic memory to plot every point that he was trying to make sense in his mind. While I liked to freestyle, which meant I usually talk things out with myself out loud, Ramesses was extremely cerebral. He rarely ever thought out loud.

Watching him work was a thing of beauty in and of itself. I was still convinced that he wasted his talents on the wrong career. But then again, who says you couldn't switch gears in the middle of a life's pursuit? Hell, I thought I would be a career law enforcement officer, and look at where I was now.

He snapped out of the cerebral trance he was in, snapping his fingers like he'd found a needle in a haystack.

"What is it, Sir? You look as if you found a missing link somewhere?" I queried.

"There was no blood, no fluids on her," he continued as his mind started to kick into overdrive. "I remembered safi was a squirter, and even if the cops found her after the fact, there would have been a marker for the CS investigators to chronicle."

"Damn, now that information I did not know about. Good eye, Sir," I acknowledged. "We might be able to find out from the M.E. if there was anything else that might give us a clue to the killer."

"We'll see how that works out, then," Ramesses replied as he signaled for the check. "In the meantime, we need to track down that laptop and figure out what might be on it. I'll see you in the morning."

FIVE

"Good morning, Sir. Here are your messages."

Hearing Ayanna's sultry voice in the mornings once I'd gotten into the office was one of my guiltiest pleasures. It never hurt that she's extremely easy on the eyes, and we had always had a delicious sexual tension between us, but I always tried to keep from mixing business with pleasure, especially now that I was the boss.

Yeah, I know what you might be thinking...what about Niki?

If you recall, Niki and I never got together until I quit the force? So, technically, I still haven't exactly broken that mantra.

So, are we good now? Okay, back to the eye-fucking, shall we?

Ayanna's not married anymore, but she's a swinger, and her new boyfriend was pretty cool about all the flirting that we put her through at work. I remember one day he called me out of the blue and said that he was glad she worked for me; she always came home and fucked his brains out the moment he hit the door.

I always had a feeling that she enjoyed the tension between us, too. She always made sure to wear different outfits that she knew accentuated the positive assets that brings all the boys to the office to make sure they checked in before hitting their assignments for the day, and I always made sure to compliment every last outfit that I arrogantly knew was meant for my benefit. I was sure her boyfriend was going to take some of the credit, but in my mind, he was a temporary measure. Ayanna was always a free spirit; if she wanted to be claimed, she would make the choice over who that would be.

She never disappointed, and today was no different. Today she wore a little, flirty black dress, which she knew was my favorite color on a woman. It wasn't tight, but it still made sure to hug those ample curves of hers, especially those hips and her chest. What I also noticed was the vibrant colors wrapped in front of the dress, with a multicolored sash that flowed down to her hemline, held down by a patent leather waist belt. And of course, her outfit wouldn't be complete without a pair of high-heels, and according to her, and my girls, the enduring hotness was Christian Louboutin.

To me, and maybe most men, heels were heels, and as long as they made them legs look good, why should we give a fuck?

"And how are you doing today, Ayanna?" I half-scanned the messages in my hand the whole time, more interested in the view from the top.

"I'm okay so far, Dom, and I'm digging the suit you got on today. Were you getting all dolled up for me?" She was in full flirt mode, flashing her light-brown eyes up at me. "Maybe you should take me out to lunch so I can make the women in the restaurant jealous?"

She was half-right. I picked out this suit, a dark blue with gray-pinstriped, three-button, single-breasted piece with my leather boots for a meeting later on at the DA's office. I wanted to look presentable, especially when I knew Niki would be at work. I watched her blush as I stared at her, my blatant attempts to raise her body temperature manifesting itself with her sudden need to grab a fan. "I don't know, have you been a good girl for me to take you out to lunch?"

"Yes, Sir, I've been more than good; I made sure that you saw this dress first before the boys did. I even stayed covered up under the desk so they wouldn't see it until after you did," Ayanna responded, sliding out from under her desk before she stood up. She did a slow twirl in the dress, making sure to show off as much of her body in the dress as possible.

Yeah, it was good to be the boss sometimes.

"I love the way that dress is hugging you...that shit is sexy, girl," I commented, making sure she saw that I stared hard at her frame. "Maybe I might need to take you out to lunch, and maybe something for dessert, too."

"Well, if I can get a hug to go on top of the way that the dress is hugging me, you might make a girl happy for the morning." Ayanna blushed as she continued teasing. She bit her bottom lip as if she didn't want to go that far with her flirting, but she kept up a good front, though. "And I have to be careful about dessert, Sir. A girl has to maintain her figure, you know."

I slipped into her personal space, whispering in her ear as my hands roamed, taking mental note of every curve and crevice. "I guess I can add a hug on top of the hugging that your dress is doing to you,"

I didn't expect her to feel so good in my arms, though. I did my best to shake the lust in my thoughts as I tried to keep from drooling over her legs and headed into my office to get an idea of how my day would flow.

Upon seeing a few messages, I already knew it would be an interesting morning. Ayanna usually took down the messages exactly as the callers gave them, and that was what had me the most concerned.

There was nothing earth-shattering about the message: *"Need help...a Dominant raped me."* In my experience, the note looked routine...until I saw something that gave me a reason to stop dead in my tracks.

I was in Ramesses's office about five minutes later. His executive assistant, Taliah, greeted me the minute I entered her space. Her voice nearly made me forget the urgency of seeing Ramesses. "Good morning, Sir, I hope things are going well so far today? You clean up really well, if I must say…usually you're rocking the jeans and boots. I like it. You should dress up more often, Sir."

I couldn't stop smiling at that compliment. Taliah had as much sex appeal as Ayanna, and that voice of hers could make a few men do some rather surly and grimy things just to be with her. It didn't hurt that she had her own natural thickness and curves that most women paid thousands of dollars to fabricate.

I needed to focus, and the halter dress she wore today definitely would affect my ability to do that.

God, I loved summertime in the A.

"Is your boss available, Taliah?" I grinned as she took in the suit-and-tie look one more time.

She unconsciously took her index finger and traced her bottom lip. She seemed to lose herself in the subtle energy exchange between us, almost reveling in it in ways I could only imagine. "You are my boss, too, remember? Not my favorite boss, of course, but you're still my boss."

Her words were lending themselves to a feminine power that I would have happily succumbed to on a normal day.

Today was far from normal.

"Okay, Taliah, is your *favorite* boss available? I have something that he really needs to see." I tried to bring it back to some sort of professional conversation. Lord knows the sexual harassment claims would be plentiful if other folks were to witness the flirting that went on around here.

Luckily for them, they wouldn't have to witness.

Taliah giggled a little, realizing my discomfort, and finally put me out of my misery.

"He's in his office, Dom, you can go ahead and see him. But I wasn't playing about the suit, though…damn."

I watched her admiring the flow as I finally made it inside of his office.

I nicknamed his office, "IT Heaven." Ramesses was the biggest techie that I knew. From the computer at one desk that he used for keeping up with the everyday operations at NEBU, to the state-of-the-art virtual computer and keyboard incorporated into the conference desk in the middle of his office, everything was wired and tapped into anything that we might have wanted or needed to solve the cases that came to us.

I dropped the message in front of him, expecting him to display the same initial shock that I had before I found myself standing in his office. He studied it for a few seconds, looking up at me in an attempt to figure out why I was so agitated. "Okay, so it's a rape case, Dom. What's the big deal? Or am I missing something? This sounds like something that would be routine for you, man."

Yeah, it might have been something routine, but I suspected that he was missing the one detail that I was certain he didn't see upon first glance. "Sir, you know the scene as well as anyone, as much as you get around and as much as we host at NEBU. You might want to look at the name again. If I think I know that name, this case will not be as routine as you think."

His eyebrow raised a slight bit as he looked back into the information on the message receipt. I knew the moment that he read across the name a second time; I saw his lips form the words *oh shit* before he looked back up at me with an incredulous expression. His eyes darted between me and the note, his growing concern becoming more evident with each passing second. "This can't be real…are you sure Ayanna heard that right?"

"I wish it weren't, but I know Ayanna; she makes very, very few mistakes." My confirmation only solidified the darkness in his eyes. "I double-checked against the database anyway, but it's not a joke, Sir."

"This week just got more interesting," he deadpanned, a sardonic smile spreading across his face. He looked up and stated matter-of-factly, "No matter what, D, this gets played by the book. No shortcuts, no creative liberties. Are we clear?"

"Crystal clear, Sir." Considering the person that owned the submissive that left the cryptically distressing message, there was no way that we would be able to get away with anything less than our most professional work.

She would expect nothing less.

I was glad to be home.

I needed release from the tension that today's events brought, and I couldn't think of a better way to do it than fucking my girls into oblivion.

Natasha was the fortunate prey this evening, since Niki had to work a little late at the office on a double homicide case. I heard her screaming out, but that didn't stop me from running through her like a wrecking ball through a condemned skyscraper.

"*Oh fuck, Sir, you're gonna blow my back out!!! Damn, it's your pussy, shit!!!*" She felt the aggression in my strokes, but I didn't care at that moment; I needed to get it off me so I could think clearly about the cases that I would have to deal with.

I had her pinned against the back of the sofa, bent over doggie style with her hands cuffed behind her back, completely at my mercy. I never gave her enough time to get out of her work clothes as I raised her skirt and ripped her thong off before slipping inside her without warning. The only thing she could do was hold on for all she was worth.

"*Can I come, please?!?!?! Please, can I come?!?!?! You're wearing this pussy out, Master!*" She continued to scream, gripping my hands for dear life as I found myself working into a comfort zone that I didn't want to come out of.

I was completely oblivious to Niki's voice in my ear, encouraging me to drill her sis into a puddle of yummy satisfaction on the plush cushions. "Give it to her, Master. Give it to her good…she's been a good girl all day today; wear her out."

I pulled out before either of them expected it, forcing Niki to her knees to suck Natasha's juices off the condom that still clung greedily to my shaft. I pulled the easy release latch on the cuffs to keep Natasha's arms from getting numb. Without missing a beat, she knelt next to Niki, pulling the condom off and alternating between kissing Niki and sharing in the oral presentation with her sis.

I was so far gone I hadn't noticed my body would soon betray me.

The growl that let loose from my throat was so loud that it bounced off the walls in the living room. I gripped the back of Niki's head to regain my balance, and I felt Natasha's hand on the small of my back to keep me from falling.

I forgot how strong they were, but I wasn't about to test that strength, either.

Looking down and seeing the grins on both of their faces, it was safe to assume that their collective mission had been accomplished.

I lay on the sofa, completely spent from the energy that I'd just exerted, watching Natasha crawl to a spot by my leg to rest while Niki walked upstairs to grab a towel and washcloths to clean ourselves off.

Upon her return, she cleaned the remnants of my juices from Natasha's chest, helping her remove the rest of her clothes before stripping down to nothing herself. I loved having them naked when we were at home.

"May I inquire what has your mind occupied, Master?" Natasha asked as she took the washcloth from Niki to clean up. "You're usually not that aggressive unless the cases have become a bit more than you thought they were."

Over the past year, they had definitely been more observant of my patterns, both as their Dominant and as a fellow law enforcement officer. No matter what I tried to do to mask my discomfort, some things simply could not be hidden. "The case that we're working on now, Natasha, seems to be a little difficult to read. Ramesses is acting stranger than usual, but considering safi was the person who was killed, I can't say I blame him for being a little off-key."

"Do you think he might know more than he's letting on?" Niki asked hesitantly as she continued wiping the sweat from my legs. "I remember the case we dealt with last year before I got promoted; you were not yourself the minute you found out who the person was behind the serial murders."

Niki had a point. I was a little more shook up than I originally let on when Simone came up as the murderer in the case we worked last year. I almost didn't want to believe it, but it was there in my face. Even more so, I didn't want to believe that I may have had something to do with the path that she had chosen to take.

Thankfully, I made peace with that a while ago, but I never thought that perhaps there might be more than just Ramesses's discomfort with the fact that even he didn't know everything that went on in the city...especially when it came to a woman that he promised to keep tabs on to keep her from trouble.

Still, I didn't want to believe that he would sidestep protocol to protect himself.

Regardless of what I wanted to believe, I had to take the suggestion under advisement and ask some hard questions of my mentor and friend. "Ramesses wouldn't breach his protocol, Niki. He's too disciplined for that."

Niki was still in the midst of her washing when she asked, "May I speak freely, Sir?"

"Yes, you may."

"I think you're allowing Master Ramesses too much wiggle room, Sir." Niki never broke from her task as she spoke. "If it were a person of interest that you thought might have information pertinent to the case, you wouldn't hesitate to question him thoroughly."

Natasha echoed Niki's sentiment. "Niki is right, Master; if it were someone else, you would have them in the cage by now, trying to find out what information they knew to help close the case quickly."

They were right; as much as I wanted to skirt around the issue and let Ramesses straighten himself out, there was no doubt that there was something that he knew, or might know, that I needed to know.

My mentor needed to unload what he knew. If he didn't, I would have to find a way to make him understand that this was business and not anything against him.

I had a case to solve.

I needed to hit the streets to see if I could find some answers. If that didn't work, I would have to grind a little deeper to get what I wanted, and the only way for me to do that was to see an old friend.

SIX

"It's been a long time, Sharpshooter."

Tori's look of surprise to see me walking into her new surroundings was definitely worth the price of admission, but she shouldn't have been too surprised. After all, ever since the "Roman Numeral" murder case that she helped with, I'd been keeping tabs on her over the past year.

My birdies kept up with her, letting me know that she'd upgraded to madam, setting up shop in the industrial district over in Tucker. She'd been doing pretty well for herself and some of the girls she took off the street, too; the word was she was able to keep some of DeKalb's finest off the trail while having some high-powered people, both male and female, helping with the cash flow at the same time in exchange for her discretion in the types of things that they were into.

I knew the quid pro quo all too well: "You watch my back, and I'll keep your secrets."

She was one of the best at it, that's for damn sure.

It was obvious to see that being at the top of the food chain agreed with her; she filled out nicely, looking ample and voluptuous for a white girl, but it suited her very well. She toned down the attire from how she was on the streets, looking very conservative in a business suit and skirt to match; even the heels were understated. It still didn't take away from her sex appeal, though, and I appreciated that.

"You're lucky I like you; I don't let anyone call me that at all," I teased as she got up to greet me. I softly kissed the back of her palm before engaging in a tight hug. "How is business?"

"Business is actually pretty good, considering the economy is still fucked up," she replied, slipping a kiss on my neck for good measure as we broke from the hug. "How is the PI business for you? I've been hearing that you and your partner have been flowing pretty well up and down the coast."

"Things have been good; I'm sure you wouldn't be too surprised at who needs the firm's services," I rebutted, lightly patting her ass as we stood in each other's personal spaces. "I see you've filled out pretty good, sexy. This work must agree with you."

"It has its moments, but I do like to get dirty from time to time." She winked as she let me in on that little detail. I sat down in one of the chairs near her desk as she tried to figure things out. "So, enough with the flirting and the sexual tension that you love to have between us. I know this isn't completely a social visit; otherwise, we'd be doing something other than talking."

"Guilty as charged, babe." I put my hands up in a defensive gesture, getting to the crux of the matter. "I need some help with a homicide; the victim was killed at the Inner Sanctum. Do you think that you can check with a few of your girls, see if they might have heard anything, seen anything at all?"

"And what makes you think that I would want to involve myself in another one of your cases?" Tori smirked, moving my hands away from my lap and sitting in the vacated space. Her perfume threatened to dull my senses quickly, and I could also tell that under the blazer she wore, there was absolutely no fabric showing underneath.

Now that's the Tori that I was used to lusting after.

I leveled with her, wrapping my arms around her waist to pull her closer. "Well, there are people on the streets that won't mind talking to you and your girls that won't touch me with a ten-foot pole. I simply need to know if the streets have been watching anything that I might need to know about."

"Now, who would be so stupid as to not touch you? All this masculine sexiness deserves to be touched as often as humanly possible." Tori continued her cat-and-mouse with me, moving in close enough to kiss me, leaving her lips tantalizingly close enough for me to do some serious damage if I didn't have anything else going on at the moment. "And for the record, I do miss touching you, Sharpshooter."

"You know, you do wonders for a man's ego. I might need to see you a little more often if I get stroked like this," I teased, feeling her squirming in my lap the entire time.

"If you come see me more often, I'll make sure that you keep coming back for more, often, if you feel me?" Tori kept up the play on words to the point where I really needed to lift her off my lap before she really found herself in trouble.

"You know I'm feeling you, Tori," I admitted, tracing her lips with my index finger and slightly shuddering when she parted those lips and began to lick my finger. "Which is why I know you won't let me down with any tips that your girls might find."

"Same ol' Sharpshooter, business before pleasure, no matter how much the pleasure would be for you." Tori sighed, lifting up from my lap. "Those two must be really special to have you not break your vow of fidelity. Are you sure there's no way I can change your mind? You know, be a part of the rotation, so to speak?"

I was sorely tempted to accept that invitation to have her whenever I wanted, but I was never one to hit and run, either. If I ended up sexing her, there would be some twisted sense of possessiveness that would be attached to her, and I really wasn't sure I wanted to possess her like that. "Things are still new with the girls, Tori."

"Well, when they aren't so new anymore, I'll be here, waiting to serve and help in any way you need me to," Tori stated, taking the back of my hand and kissing it.

"Thank you for calling, youngster. I can imagine this isn't easy for you to do right now."

I was in Ramesses's office on a video call with Amenhotep, safi's former Master. We set up the video feed because Ramesses wanted the call as personal as could be had, short of making the flight down to the island.

I already knew this would be a difficult conversation to have, but I had no idea of just how deep this might go.

"Sir, I am at a loss as to how she slipped through the safety protocols that we had in place." Ramesses looked fractured, and I couldn't blame him; I felt the same way. When you're in the business of protection and security, the last thing you want to have happen is a breach of any kind.

"Kid, safi was her own free spirit; she was going to do what she wanted to do." Amenhotep tried to sound reassuring through the video feed. "The only thing we can do now is to try and figure out who did this. Do you have any leads?"

"Nothing yet, Sir; we've allowed the authorities to start canvassing and key off the leads they receive, and we're checking the usual channels within the community to see if anyone knows anything."

"Look, youngster, no matter what you do to try and keep something contained, eventually, they will find a way to get free." Amenhotep tried to console as he spoke. I always liked that about him, in that elderly father-type way. "I'm hurting, and I'm sure Het-hotep is hurting also. The best way to ease the healing is to bring peace and justice for safi."

"He's right, Sir," I concurred, placing a hand on his shoulder in support. "We need to get whoever did this and bring them to trial."

"Then that's what we'll do." Ramesses's body language was different, and that wasn't a good sign. I felt his body shaking in anger, and that was something unusual, to say the least. "We'll get the person who did this, and I'll personally deal with him before we turn him over to the police."

"Slow down, Ramesses, that's not the way to handle it," Amenhotep cautioned. "This has to be done without emotions confusing the situation. You could blow the effort out of the water, and the killer would never be brought to trial."

This wasn't like Ramesses to develop a bloodlust; that was usually reserved for real killers and really bad people who really could not have cared less about anyone else but themselves. That's not him. "Trial is not on my mind right now. If they're lucky, trial would be the least of their problems."

"Sir, the last thing you want to do is let this person get away because we skirted protocol," I tried to appeal to his sense of logic and decorum, but I knew it was a long shot. This was really getting to him. His emotions were getting the best of him, and I needed him to think clearly. "If we fuck up, the killer goes free. There's no room for error on this."

"Listen to Dominic, Ramesses. Take your heart out of it; I'm hurting for her in ways that you cannot imagine, but I also understand that justice needs to be served. I also know that it doesn't happen overnight. Be patient…be prudent…but be efficient," Amenhotep finally counseled. "In the end, I know that this will be handled properly."

The look on Ramesses's face was incredulous, but he had no choice but to deal with the circumstances. He finally backed down as the call drew to a close. "Fine, Sir, we'll take care of this in the proper manner. At least for now…but if this doesn't happen in the manner that I see fit to get this done properly, I will handle this in the manner in which it needs to be to get the results I want. I guarantee it."

SEVEN

"We are sorry for your loss, Sir."

Being a Dominant within the Fetish/BDSM world, there are certain mystiques that you tend to pick up on. Myths, if you will, that made a Dominant a Dominant. One of those myths was that Dominants never showed weakness, regardless of the circumstances.

It was a myth that I had no problems emulating; it helped to keep things simple when it came to other Dominants and Masters, and submissives and slaves alike. It was an unwritten code that, fair or not, you knew to keep as close to the vest as possible.

Het-hotep, in my dealings with him in the past, was probably the epitome of that myth. He was a burly and large man, he looked like he probably had me by at least fifty pounds and a couple of inches, and I'm not a small man at six feet three inches and two hundred-fifty pounds. His salt-and-pepper beard lent to the transition into the twilight of his life, maybe fifty, fifty-five or so, I'd say. He commanded all eyes on him the moment he entered a room, and I didn't say that about anyone; Amenhotep was barely six feet tall and did the same thing, so it's not about the size of the man, that's for sure.

However, there were things that made even the roughest of us drop to our knees and shed tears, and loss of a loved one was one of them; I didn't care who you were or how you identified.

So, being one of the men that had to be the bearer of bad news for a fellow Dominant who was making final preparations for the burial of a slave who was his property for all of two months before her untimely demise, I was witness to the shattering of one of those myths, and it broke my heart to bear witness to it.

Tears came to my eyes as I watched Ramesses try to console Master Het-hotep, a close friend of his mentor, Amenhotep.

As I understood the depth of the situation, I began to understand why he was in such a state of shock; safi was not only going to become his by collar, but by legal binding also. The diamond engagement ring that sat on the coffee table was a testament to the union that he was prepared to endow upon her as a surprise once he returned from his trip overseas.

It had been only a day since safi's murder, and already I could see the toll that it was taking on my friend.

Meanwhile, I had my own internal battle raging.

My heart told me that he couldn't be caught up in this; there was no way he could have been.

My experience told me that no stone could be left unturned, and no matter what my feelings were on the matter, I was going to find a way to question him about why he'd been so unbalanced in the past twenty-four hours.

"I had to find out by voicemail on my cell phone, Ramesses," Master Het-hotep said through tear-streaked eyes. "I thought she was still in Nevada preparing for the move. How in the world could this have happened?"

Ramesses shook his head, wiping away his own tears. He looked completely defeated, and I didn't know what he could say to ease the pain of this loss. "Sir, I've been trying to work the back channels in Nevada where I had her stashed. No one knows when she departed, but I promise you, we will get to the bottom of things."

Master Het-hotep's eyes grew dark, causing a stark turn of the flow of the conversation. "*You promised me she would be out of harm's way! I trusted you with her life!!!*"

Ramesses was taken aback by this sudden display of anger, doing his best to adjust and not sound as aggressive. "I did what I could to make sure she was in one place, Sir. Someone helped her leave the area without alerting my fail-safes, and I will find out who breached my protocols."

I should have known a flight out to the West Coast would be coming, but there was another way to find out without calling the pilots for pre-flight prep.

Master Het-hotep calmed down almost immediately, but the anger still simmered. "You will find out who did this, Ramesses. Whatever it takes to do it, I don't care. Find her!"

That last exclamation tripped my warning senses. "Sir, I understand that you might be upset, but what made you yell for us to find 'her'? Do you have an idea of who did this?"

"Yes, I have a clue of who might have done it," he spat. "You said that they found her at Inner Sanctum? Then I bet that trick Master Jen was at the scene. She'd been trying to convince safi through emails to come back to Atlanta to be with her."

Ramesses interjected, irritated that he would make such a claim. "I had taps on all of her email addresses, Sir; that's not possible. I would have picked up on it."

Master Het-hotep stopped in mid-sentence like he'd been caught doing something he had no business doing. "Well…that is to say… there was one email account that you were not made aware of, created by my command."

My eyebrow rose immediately. "Sir, do you care to run that by us again?"

If I was prepared for a blowup, this was definitely the time for it. It was Ramesses's turn to completely lose his religion because his protocols were breached. It was the only thing that I knew that could get him to lose his composure. "*You have the unmitigated audacity to try to blame me for the murder of your property, when you breached the very security protocols I had in place to ensure that she was safe?!?!!? No wonder she found a way to skirt my protocols; she used you to do it!*"

All I could do was shake my head. safi was under constant surveillance; we made sure of that. But that surveillance was contingent upon her ability to stay within the parameters she was told to. Based on the events from yesterday, she neither listened nor complied with her instructions.

Master Het-hotep put his head in his hands again, tears flowing copiously now. "Surely you must understand, Ramesses, I needed my slave to have the freedom to speak to me without—no disrespect, Sir—prying eyes viewing what should only be between Master and slave."

Ramesses's eyes narrowed, piercing through Master Het-hotep's face. He was irritated beyond measure, trying desperately to keep what remaining calm that he had left. "And look where it's gotten you. I'll bet you the salary you made overseas that she used that exact account to email with the killer, and she found a way to hide the emails from you before you could check up and figure out what happened."

"She wouldn't have done that to me, she…" He rambled the phrase over and over again before the light switch went off in his head in a quick moment of clarity. "Her laptop…but she couldn't have, could she? She loved me; I know she did."

"Right now, we're going to start there, which means that I'm going to see what you didn't want me to see. And while we're at it, we're going to need your laptop, too," Ramesses cautioned. "If there is something that you need to tell me, you might want to tell me now before I see it for myself."

Master Het-hotep froze. He protested vehemently over the seizure of his personal laptop. "This isn't legal, Sir; you need a warrant, and that could take some time to get."

The look on Ramesses's face was priceless. He flipped out his phone and hit a speed-dial number, waiting for the call to connect. "Yes, Judge Lexington? This is Mr. Alexander, Sir. I was wondering if I could cash in on that favor you spoke of a couple of months ago for helping with that missing person's case under the table?"

Het-hotep's eyes widened upon hearing the judge's name. I was a bit perplexed that Ramesses had one of the superior court judges at such close proximity, too, but I wasn't about to allow my facial expressions to give me away. He slumped against the back of the couch, resigned to not make this any messier than it had to be. "Okay, take the laptop. You win."

Now I couldn't wait to see what was on safi's computer when we got to the PD, and the added prospect of going through Het-hotep's laptop, too? Considering the computer forensics specialist assigned to the case was a personal friend of mine, the things that we would find would not exactly become a matter of public record, but they could with the right amount of outside pressure.

Het-hotep knew it, and he knew that we knew it. The fear in his eyes conveyed as much.

"For your sake, you better hope that she doesn't have anything incriminating on that laptop, Sir. I won't be able to help you if there is," Ramesses warned before we headed out of the house to allow him to continue to grieve.

Yeah, this was going to be a very interesting afternoon, indeed.

We were inside the central offices of the DeKalb County Police Department, going through the computer files with the computer forensics technician in his office. And it was all I could do to keep from making fun of the faces that this dude was making in reaction to the files that were on safi's and Het-hotep's computers.

The tech, Ty, was a personal friend of mine from my days on the force, even though he worked in DeKalb and I was in Fulton, at the time. He was a slim dude—you know how techies tended to be—but he kept himself in good shape in case there was a problem that needed to be handled that didn't require an IQ near two-hundred. In his job, he'd seen a lot, and I do mean a *lot*, so I knew that I could somewhat trust him with the information that he was going to be exposed to and not leak it out to the media outlets.

Ty moved with an efficiency that came with years of experience on the job. He knew exactly where to look and exactly what files would hold the most viable information pertinent to the case. Every so often, I saw a smirk spread across his face, and I could understand why. Most people only get to read about this in trashy romance books and the like.

It was an education of sorts for Ramesses, too. He had never been through something so pervasive in his life, and I knew he had to be stewing about some of the files that the technician searched through. I felt the Fourth Amendment argument coming a mile away. But the thing that Ramesses had to remember was that Master Het-hotep was a person of interest since he was romantically linked to safi. Even though we were going through her computer, everything that he'd ever sent her could be used against him.

All of it was old hat to me, although it still made me more squeamish to go through this part of the investigation than any crime scene ever could. You uncovered more intimate knowledge about a person from their computers than any other way possible. So, it made me no less squeamish when we started rolling through the older files from decades gone by, before the Internet came to prominence. I saw kinks on this man's computer that would make the most extreme of us blush and say to themselves, "I could never do that!"

It felt like I was going through the Middle Ages of kink or something, but then again, I had to realize that my frame of reference was from the early twenty-first century to present day.

Ramesses even gave up a shudder or two from time to time, which let me know I wasn't the only one who could remain immune to the images for too much longer.

Seeing the images of the things that Master Het-hotep was doing when he was a younger dude were no less crazy to say the least, and I tried to envision what the attraction was to this dude for safi, but I wasn't a female, either.

I'd spare you the details of what I saw because I just had lunch, okay? But let's say there was some extremely vivid medical play going on, for starters.

Going through the email files were nothing short of a lesson in the cliché, "what's done in the dark." Every email that Master Het-hotep thought he'd have in confidence was there to be seen, and different references to Ramesses were particularly of notice.

Needless to say, my partner was not pleased at all.

In a few emails, there were potshots taken at him from Master Het-hotep, calling him a unilateral control freak, and he couldn't understand why safi showed such reverence to a man who was linked to her former Master.

To her credit, safi defended Ramesses at every turn, even getting into a virtual shouting match in a few emails. But it still didn't absolve her of complete guilt, as her orders were to inform him if she were to ever change her methods of communications and provide passwords when they did.

"What about the name that Het-hotep yelled out; Master Jen, I think is the name?" I asked Ty to look up for me.

After a quick search on the laptop's hard drive, Ty shook his head. "No dice, D, there's no mention of a Master Jen anywhere on her laptop."

Well, that was a dead end, but what would make him yell out that name in anger?

I made a mental note to check up on that a little later; it might prove useful later in the investigation.

We continued to look over her email files, and the thing that caught me off guard a bit was the email drafts that never got sent in the days before her death. They stuck out like sore thumbs. "Pull those up for me; there might be something there."

Among the drafts was an email addressed to Ramesses that was originally drafted a couple of days before the homicide. Ramesses's eyes widened for a moment or two, and we had the tech click on the draft to see its contents.

What we read felt like a bomb was going to go off:

My dearest Ramesses,

i know that receiving this email from a foreign account will be a breach of protocol, but i need You to understand that i really didn't want to overstep Your authority over me.

i am sending this email to You (which will be erased and placed on my laptop so that He will not see) with the hopes that You will be a guest at a farewell party for me in Atlanta in the next few weeks. i want to get every fantasy and desire out of my system before i give myself completely to my Master.

In case You needed me to spell it out for You, my dear Sir, You are one of the desires that i desperately need to get out of my system, although i feel a sense of betrayal in admitting to You that i don't think i'll ever get

You out of my system, as You have always watched over me, even when i did not deserve it. i may be out of line by saying this, my Sir, but i had fallen in love with You, and by some measure, i will always be in love with You.

i sincerely hope You will grace me with Your presence, and i dream nightly of Your hands caressing my body one last time.

Until then, my Pharaoh

His bella cagna (formerly safi)

The shit got thick…real quick.

The bomb that Niki and Natasha had warned me about dropped with the yield of a forty-kiloton bomb: *he* was supposed to be there that night??

I couldn't believe what I was reading, and the pieces still weren't fitting together the way that I needed them to. Something was missing, and I needed to know from him what it was. After all, he was nearly obsessive about making sure safi was well taken care of. He wouldn't have done that for anyone else except for Neferterri and the girls. On the other hand, it explained why Ramesses had been so off-kilter since we'd found out safi was the victim. Perhaps he had deeper feelings than he led any of us to believe.

It also explained why safi was so quick and so fervent in her defense of Ramesses. Thanks to that email, the cards were on the table in terms of her love for him.

I guess that mystique really did have its benefits. After all, he was the Great One…he worked to get to this point. It wasn't like he was given the pedestal everyone wanted to put him on. I could only imagine the pressure that he was under when Het-hotep came at him with the accusations that he didn't do enough.

I knew differently.

She was safer than the gold in Fort Knox.

However, warning flags were sounding off in my head, and I

didn't like where the deductions were taking me. "You were supposed to be there? Don't you think that would be information that you would want to inform your partner of?"

"Relax, Dom, I know that this looks bad, but if you slow down long enough to recall, this was in her email draft folder." I read his facial expressions, and this shook him, probably more than even he wanted to let on. "If you want, once we get back to the office, I'll let you examine my accounts, for your piece of mind. I'll even let your computer forensics bloodhound here do the sweep for you."

Ty, seemingly unfazed by all of the things going on, inserted, "Honestly, gentlemen, it looks to me like this young lady that you're speaking about plotted to keep all of this from her lover... Master...whatever he was."

"Explain, Ty," Ramesses inquired. "I'm all ears for any explanation right now."

"Well, Mr. Alexander, while you two were discussing the severity of the letter in making you a person of interest, I pulled the files in her laptop, and I found the exact letter in a doc file, verbatim. The only thing she didn't do was actually send the email, for whatever reasons." He pulled up the document to show a side-by-side view. "I would imagine she planned to sneak in, handle her business, and then head back without anyone being the wiser. Perhaps she had second thoughts about emailing you because of the fact that you would have discouraged her from coming?"

Knowing safi's history, that definitely sounded like her usual M.O. If she could find a way to skirt around and get her way while still giving the appearance that she was following protocol, she would definitely find it. The only problem with that scenario was she wanted Ramesses there, too; at least, initially speaking. It didn't make any sense that she would want the one person on the planet to know that she had openly disobeyed his protocols.

Nothing was making sense.

Ramesses continued to scan through all of the other emails that did get sent out, and all of them made mention of a "special guest" that would take the gathering into a whole other level of intensity. Someone who she'd hoped would be in attendance.

He shook his head in frustration. I could tell he couldn't tie the loose ends together, either. "Thank you, this helps things a little bit. Is there anything else that we might have to go on?"

"Yes, as a matter of fact, there is," Ty continued. "You mentioned that the victim's lover yelled out that you needed to get 'her'; is that correct?"

"Yes."

"Well, there is an email exchange that safi erased that I was able to retrieve from the IP address archives," Ty offered. "It's pretty juicy stuff, Mr. Alexander."

"Is it to this 'Master Jen' person that we were told about?"

"No, sir, but from the way the emails were going back and forth, I wouldn't be shocked if she weren't a close associate of that person."

"Do me a favor and send the information that you have to this email address so we can work things out from there and check the lead," I told him as we walked out of the room. "If you find anything else, let Detective Cross or Detective Reddick know, just to keep things on the level."

"Will do, D." Ty gave me pound before we left, then shook Ramesses's hand. "Mr. Alexander, if you ever need an IT guy to do some underground work for you, I have no problems getting my hands dirty."

Ramesses smiled for the first time since yesterday. "I will definitely keep you in mind, my friend. I have a feeling I might be taking you up on that offer soon."

EIGHT

We took a quick detour to look in on Niki since we were still on the fly. I hadn't had a chance to really get a look at her new digs since the promotion.

Her executive assistant showed us in and told us that ADA Santiago would be with us in a moment. She had a briefing with the DA on a new case that popped up earlier this morning.

I had to admit, there was a bit of pride and a desire to puff out my chest because both of the women in my life were successful in their individual careers. Especially Niki, who seemed to have been taking to her new assistant district attorney title like a duck took to water.

Ramesses took a look around the office also, getting a lay of the land. "Very nice indeed. It seems the government is hard at work sparing no expense on the décor."

I laughed out loud at that understatement, but I couldn't help but agree with the assessment. Her office was as nice as mine, with the lacquered desks and the spacious area that allowed for a separate sitting area near the window. Even the computer system looked updated.

My girl was moving up in the world.

I honestly wasn't sure she would get to this point a year ago. After I left the force, she took a spot as a lead detective in DeKalb County. She left our old precinct, I assumed because she didn't want to be bothered once I was gone.

I remembered the DA was hot on trying to get her on the payroll downtown. I think his name was Barnes or something like that.

He and I had a conversation before I retired. It wasn't a pleasant conversation; I could promise you that. Words were exchanged, idle threats were made, and I basically made it clear that I was no one's puppet.

I had hopes that when Niki made the move back into Fulton that she wouldn't have to deal with his arrogant ass. In the past year, she never gave me a clue that she was dealing with him. After all, the DA's office was large, so they might not even cross paths all that much.

The way I remembered how he ran the office, no one really got a chance to see him anyway. I made a note to ask her about that soon.

After about ten minutes of Ramesses and me bantering back and forth about all things government corruption, Niki finally appeared in her office, along with another gentleman who walked closely with her.

Upon sight, she smiled brightly as she kissed me and hugged Ramesses as she made the impromptu introductions. She looked a bit unnerved, despite her happiness to see us. "Mr. Alexander, Dominic, this is ADA Jason Matthews. Jason, this is my boyfriend, Dominic, and his business partner, Mr. Alexander."

Ramesses picked up on her irritation almost immediately. "Are you all right, Niki? You look a little perturbed."

"Yes, Sir, I am, to be honest," Niki responded as she shifted her weight, leaning against the desk. "We just finished briefing with the DA, and he's not as upset about this case that was brought to our attention."

Jason chimed in, trying to stifle a chuckle. "C'mon, Nikia, it's a man claiming that he's been raped, and by a woman. You mean to tell me that it's something that we should really work with any real zest? I mean, it's not like it was a woman being raped."

That irked me. A victim was a victim, period. I thought about placing myself in the conversation, but I had a feeling that my submissive had things well in hand to the point to where all I needed to do was sit down and enjoy the proverbial popcorn as the fireworks flew.

"Jason, a man can be raped. We don't even have all the facts yet, and you're treating this like he could have overpowered her or something?" Niki countered. "Why should we have any less respect for the victim because he's male?"

"Because you can't rape the willing," Jason shot back, "unless the woman looks like a complete dog or something."

I really wasn't digging this dude, and I was one more snide remark away from putting him in his place.

"Maybe if you run the case by us, we might be able to help?" Ramesses asked, looking at me like the case that they received and the message that was left earlier yesterday might have some similarities.

Upon hearing the legal name of the victim, I exhaled slowly.

"The victim says that he was in session with a Mistress. He was on loan from his current 'owner' as he stated." Niki turned and grabbed her legal pad from behind her on the desk and began reading from the notes. "In the middle of the session, the Mistress does something that he didn't consent to, and when he tries to say no, she continues, ignoring him. In my book, that's rape."

"Yeah, that is rape, Jason," I chimed in, not liking his attitude at all.

"Have you seen the 'Mistress' that he was in session with?" Jason asked, shoving the visual advertisement in my hand. "Can you sit there and say that you would claim you were raped by a woman as gorgeous as she is?"

I took a look at the woman in the advertisement, and Jason was right: she was drop-dead gorgeous. She also reminded me of one of the Dominas that attend some of the parties at NEBU from time to time. I made another mental note to check the database once we got back to the office.

"I don't think you get it, Jason," I interjected. "This man, according to the notes, was willing to go through the session up to the point where his boundaries were violated. If the roles were reversed, you would be losing your mind right now."

"All I'm saying is, that woman right there can 'rape' me anytime," he replied, winking in Niki's direction.

Niki shook for a moment, visibly irritated by Jason's subtle jabs at her. I saw her grip the edge of her desk, contemplating her next move.

I began to take a step in Jason's direction, as I didn't like where that subconscious flirting was going. Ramesses gripped my shoulder and shook his head silently. "Let it play out, Dom."

"Yeah, easy for you to say, Iceberg Slim. This isn't shamise or sajira doing this in front of you," I retorted. "What do you want me to do; sit here and not do anything?"

"You'd be amazed at what my girls have done in front of me, kid." Ramesses smirked. "And yes, that's exactly what I expect you to do. Trust me, let it play out. You might like the results."

I decided to trust his instincts, even if my own instincts were to make Jason's balls a permanent fixture on the walls of her office.

I watched Niki as she glanced back at me and gave me a slight wink and a nod before she turned her attention back to Jason. She took an interesting approach, one that I don't think any of us expected. She startled him as her voice took on a commanding tone. "*On your knees, bitch!*"

"What the fuck?" he protested as immediately putting his hands in the air by his head. "What kind of bullshit are you pulling, Nikia?"

"Don't play with me; you know you've wanted to taste this pussy ever since we'd been paired together; now, *get...on...your...knees!*"

"Oh okay, I get it; you wanna role-play? Okay, we can play." Jason thought he was playing along, until Niki bent him over the table, ripped his hands behind his back and put the handcuffs on him. Jason wasn't ready for that move, but he did something I didn't think any of us were prepared for; he acquiesced immediately.

"Now, will you be a good little boy for me?" Niki asked as she licked his ear.

"Yes, ma'am, I will be," Jason replied softly.

"Good, and if you're a good boy, I might just let you taste this good pussy. Would you like that, pet?" she cooed again, tugging on the cuffs to make sure he couldn't get loose.

"Yes, ma'am, I would."

"Good."

I didn't know whether to laugh or stay pissed off at the display going on in front of me. Niki had this man eating out of the palm of her hand, and probably other things if she'd allowed it. Or for that matter, if I allowed her to allow it.

Ramesses grinned from ear to ear, and I found that I couldn't resist smirking, either. I watched Niki as she made Jason her willing bitch in the middle of the day, and in a law enforcement building, no less.

She moved her hands from his back, down to his waist, moving to his buttocks, where she gave a good squeeze to keep him aroused, reaching her destination at his crotch, massaging him until a grin spread across her face when she got the reaction she wanted out of him.

"Oh my, is that all for me?" she asked, giving Jason a good swat across his cheeks.

"Yes, ma'am, it's yours."

"Mmmmm, damn, maybe I might keep you around after all." Niki kept the impromptu scene going.

If I were a lesser man, I would have stopped her right there; jealousy would have long taken over.

What a difference a year makes.

I glanced over at Ramesses, and he winked, giving a silent gesture of, *Let's see where this thing ends up.*

In the next moment, Niki quickly pulled a small baton out of her desk drawer and began to massage the space between Jason's legs.

Needless to say, the role-play was over for him. "Okay, Niki, enough is enough; joke's over, you made your point."

He struggled against the baton caressing his scrotum, and it wasn't until he tried to move his arms to stop her that he remembered he was still handcuffed and helpless. The response to his statement was a slap in the face.

"Did I tell you that you could speak to me?!?!" Niki raged, poking him deeper with the baton. *"I should fuck your ass with this baton just for even breathing in my direction!"*

"Niki, what's gotten into you?" Jason continued to protest, which got him slapped again. It was a good thing he was a dark-skinned brother, or he would have had to explain a few things to some people.

He tried desperately to get out of the cuffs, his face showing genuine panic as he began to realize that Niki could do anything that she wanted to him and all he could do was take it.

"Okay, baby, I think the rookie has had enough. You may release him," I commanded. "You still have to work with him, you know?"

"Yes, Sir, as you command," Niki replied as she took the key to release the cuffs. "But only because you commanded it, my Master."

"So, ADA Matthews, would you like to file attempted rape charges on ADA Santiago?" Ramesses tried to stifle a chuckle as he asked the question. "I have no problems being a material witness, as I'm sure you might need one, you know?"

"Y'all are some sick people; do you know that?" Jason howled, turning in Niki's direction. "What in the fuck made you do that, Nikia?"

"Well, you said it yourself, you can't rape the willing," Niki responded, handing him a hand towel to wipe the sweat off of his face. "You were willing until the situation no longer was in your favor. When that happened, you were ready to tell me to stop; weren't you?"

Jason took a little time to calm down so that he could think a bit. "Okay, Nikia, you made your point. I shouldn't have been short-sighted about it."

"Thank you, so that means we can go back to the DA and let him know that this case is worthy of investigating further?" Niki asked him, placing the baton back into the desk drawer.

"Yes, it's worth a second look. And for the record, gentlemen, your reputation precedes you. I was hoping you would be able to get with SVU on this particular case, on a consult, of course," Jason suggested.

"Well, considering the special nature of the case, I think it would be to the advantage of the DA's office to consult with your detectives on this case," Ramesses agreed. "We will be happy to assist."

As Jason began to make his way out to his office to move on to other business, Niki blurted out as she stared as his crotch again, "Oh, and by the way, Jason…if we weren't working together, you could get it."

The moment Jason left, Ramesses tried to find the first chair he could and doubled over in laughter. "I swear to the gods that was the funniest thing I've ever seen!"

Niki took a bow, a smirk spreading across her lips. "It was my pleasure to provide entertainment today, Sir. It was an off-the-cuff moment, pun intended."

"Speaking of cuffs, I thought you didn't have cuffs anymore?" I asked, stroking my goatee with an inquisitive look on my face. "Those don't look like department issue, at least not Fulton County department issue."

Niki blushed, moving toward me to gauge my demeanor. She dropped to her knees and kissed the back of my palm in an attempt to placate me before speaking. "I'm sorry, my Master, I borrowed these from Natasha when I discussed the case with her earlier this morning before work. I beg your forgiveness for not discussing the possession of the cuffs."

I wanted to punish her, and every instinct told me that I should, but when I looked in Ramesses's direction to pose the question, he shook his head as he straightened his suit coat. "It's better they ask forgiveness than to ask permission sometimes, Dom. She had to make the adjustment on the fly. I would consider something light this time around, but I'm sure she won't let this happen again."

Niki blushed when she heard those words. She looked up at me for a brief moment to steal a glance before dropping her eyes to the floor again. I took my fingers and lifted her chin, giving her a quick kiss across her lips. "You are forgiven, this time. I know it won't happen again."

"Thank you, my Master."

I switched out of my D/s mode to figure out what needed to happen from my partner. We needed to get back to work. "Now that we've had time to hit the comedy circuit, what did you have in mind in terms of the next move to make?"

"I have an idea, Dom, but I can tell you this much…she's a real piece of work."

"Keep your wits about you around her, understood?"

Ramesses and I were heading to the house of a Domina by the name of Mistress Taboo, one of the persons that safi was speaking with by email. She was a regular at NEBU, but she wasn't there this past weekend. Considering the information that we received from Ty that led us to her as one of the people at the farewell party that Ramesses was almost invited to, we figured she might have been willing to be of some help.

She lived in the northwest corner of the city, in a town called Dallas. No, not Dallas, Texas, but Dallas, Georgia. It was a smaller town, a good mix of folks of all races and economic backgrounds, and quiet enough not to draw too much attention to themselves.

I wish I could say the same thing about the woman we were going to speak with.

This...*woman*...was a real bitch, and that's being nice, if calling her a bitch was being nice. Hell, she would have taken it as a compliment. How safi came to even having any type of attraction to this woman was beyond my comprehension.

Mistress Taboo was what I termed, "a man truly trapped in a woman's body." Not only was that man trapped, but he was determined to make sure everyone knew it. Taboo's body resembled that of those female bodybuilders that you see in those national competitions, and she had the butch attitude to match. She challenged any male in authority for shits and giggles, but despite all of that, she seemed to "respect" Ramesses and didn't pull that type of nonsense at NEBU.

Whether or not that had a lot to do with the behavior clauses that trigger the breach of contract fine is anyone's guess. Either that, or because she's been after Neferterri, shamise and sajira for the longest, she might not want to mess up her golden opportunity to scene with and fuck any or all of them.

From the way that Ramesses's demeanor changed to something more hard-edged when we turned into her subdivision, I had a sneaky suspicion that I needed to do the same thing.

"Ramesses, well, this is an unexpected pleasure," Taboo quipped upon opening the door.

"To what do I owe the honor of Atlanta's chosen one?"

"Taboo, spare me the sarcasm, please?" Ramesses shot back, keeping his eyes transfixed onto hers. "My partner and I have business to discuss with you, if you don't mind answering a few questions?"

"Certainly, dear…make yourself at home." Taboo turned and walked toward the great room in her home. "What exactly is the business that you have with me?"

"safi has been murdered," I answered for him, perturbed that my presence had not been acknowledged. "We would like to ask you some questions regarding your attendance at a get-together at Inner Sanctum the night before last."

Taboo snapped around as if she didn't expect to hear my voice. She tilted her head to the side and then gave a smirk and huffed, "Ramesses, you really should train your apprentices better; they should know better than to speak to a lady in that manner."

"Taboo, I need you to focus, *bruh*." Ramesses sneered, catching her off guard and causing me to turn a side-eye for a moment. "My apprentice understands how to speak to a lady; I'm a bit disturbed that the lady didn't have the common courtesy, as a lady *should*, to recognize when gentlemen are in her presence."

"Touché, my dear Ramesses, I do apologize." Taboo stated dismissively, continuing to walk toward the couch and placing chairs in the middle of the great room. "Won't you please have a seat?

As your associate said earlier, safi was murdered? What a shame… that's simply horrid."

I chimed back in, wanting to get to the heart of the matter. "Can you help us with some information, Mistress Taboo? We have reason to believe that someone at the get-together may have had something to do with safi's murder."

"Mmmmm, such directness, you are one of Ramesses's finer projects." Taboo licked her lips at me as she replied, "Let me guess, you would like to know the other players at the party?"

"Yes, Ma'am, that would be helpful." I tried to stay neutral rather than let my disdain show through, but her indifference to a member of the fetish community being murdered was of particular irritation. You would think a woman that had a belief in Female Supremacy would be a bit more broken up about one of the women that she could have "converted" had wound up dead. "And if you know of a woman named Master Jen, it would be helpful to the case."

"And so polite, too…you could teach your Mentor a thing or two about that." She continued her playful banter.

The banter stopped the minute she saw me take my SIG-Sauer off my shoulder harness and place it onto the coffee table in front of me.

"Oh, I'm sorry, I needed to get comfortable," I said as I winked at her. *Two can play that game, bitch.* "Now, you were saying about the other guests at the party?"

"Hmmm, okay, I see how this is going to play…there were four other people at the party including me, and I'm sure Ramesses knows them: Master Cypher, Master Altar, Master Osiris and Sir Xavier." Taboo rattled off the names without a moment of forethought. "Master Jen is another name that I go by in other circles outside of the city from time to time. But there are a few people who actually know that information, so that leads me to believe that Het-hotep decided to point the finger in my direction, I would guess."

She put that statement in the air as more of a subtle attempt to inform us that we were barking up the wrong tree, in a manner of speaking; while she did her best to ensure we no longer considered a suspect, I also sensed she was a bit irritated that Het-hotep would throw her under the bus like that.

I tried to jog my memory, but I could have sworn that Osiris was still in Vegas when we'd spoken to him over the weekend to make sure everything was still rolling smoothly at Deshret, the sister location to NEBU. Then again, same-day flights weren't too far-fetched, especially if you had the capital to do it at moment's notice.

Ramesses sat stone-faced. If he was thinking what I was thinking, I'm sure his blood had to be boiling by now. After all, it was Osiris who was supposed to be one of the persons that ensured that safi was on lock in Vegas to begin with.

This case was getting deeper by the minute.

Taboo studied our expressions, no doubt gauging what to say next to fuel her own curiosities. "I can tell by your faces that some of the guests were not who you were expecting. The question now becomes why that is so."

"The last I checked, you were not on the payroll," Ramesses snapped as he stood to leave. "Do us a favor and make sure you're in town for the next few days. I'm sure there will be follow up questions that the detectives we are helping with this case will want to ask you."

"Oh, I'm not going anywhere any time soon." Taboo laughed as a mischievous smile spread across her face. "In fact, if you're not too busy, maybe you two could stick around and watch me break in a couple of boys that should be coming over any moment now."

"No, I think we'll pass on that, Taboo," I answered for the both of us. "Besides, we're at work right now. You know? The thing you're supposed to be doing, too?"

"Why work when there are willing slave boys that have no problems footing the bill for a Goddess such as myself?" she scoffed, looking me up and down like I was supposed to be the dessert to the main course she had lined up. "It's such a shame that all that talent has gone to waste because of that Dominant mind of yours. You would have made an excellent Alpha slave."

"Sorry to disappoint you, dear, but that definitely is *not* on the menu," I shot back, giving her a glare that should have stepped her back a few feet, but it shouldn't have surprised me that it didn't. I was definitely not the one to try like that; it didn't matter to me who the fuck she thought she was, I'd drop her like the man she was trying to be. "Besides, regardless of what you think, not every man was made to bow at your feet, you know?"

"That's why I said it was talent gone to waste…physical tools and all." She laughed at her inside joke. "But it's always nice enough to fantasize every now and then. Good luck trying to figure out why one of your brethren snuck into your domain in the middle of the night. *Ciao.*"

NINE

I headed back to the office while Ramesses went home to check on Neferterri and the family. I didn't mind too much; I needed some time to myself to figure out how the two cases would work themselves out in my mind.

Ownership had its privileges, of course. After all, he's the one signing the paychecks.

When I got inside the building and made my way to my office, I found Ayanna in tears at her desk. It wasn't like her to be that upset about anything. The last time was when her father passed away about six months ago, so I knew it had to be something serious.

"Are you okay?" I asked as I moved around to the side of her desk.

"Yes...well, no...I'm..." Ayanna stuttered, trying to get the words out between sobs. "I just received word about safi. Is it true? Is she dead?"

I had hoped that word of mouth hadn't gotten back to her yet. I was hoping to be able to tell her myself. I guess it was only a matter of time. They were very close friends. I nodded, allowing her to press her face against my chest and continue to get her grief out of her system.

Taliah heard the cries and rushed in to see if everything was okay. "Sir, is Ayanna okay? She didn't seem like herself this morning when she came in."

"I'll be okay, Taliah; thanks for checking in on me." Ayanna seemed to calm down a little, flashing a small smile as she snuck her arms around the small of my back. "I'm okay now."

I subconsciously placed my hand in her hair as she said that, watching her eyes as she looked up at me. I saw something there that I didn't want to acknowledge, and she didn't shy away, either.

Taliah smiled before she headed back to her desk, doing her best to not make it seem like she caught on to whatever she thought she saw. "I'll catch up with you later at lunch, Ayanna. The usual spot?"

Ayanna nodded, watching her sway as she disappeared into the other area of the building toward Ramesses's office.

"Do you want to use my restroom to try and fix your face?" I asked her, noticing the streaks of mascara on her face. I couldn't tear myself away from her eyes despite her disheveled look, and I wasn't sure exactly why.

"Yes, but I want to confess something first. If I had known that she was in any danger, I would have told you first, Dom, I swear." Ayanna's intensity had me off-balance. "I knew she was in Atlanta. She begged me to keep it a secret because she didn't want Ramesses upset."

My eyes widened when I heard that, and she could sense the questions arising in me, so she continued her purge. "I know Ramesses's anger when his protocols are breached, and I know how you can be when the protections that are put in place are circumvented. I didn't want you to be disappointed in me, Sir. I don't ever want to disappoint you."

She wiped her eyes to remove the mascara smudges, but she never left my presence. To say that it made me more than a little nervous would be an understatement. The last thing that I wanted to do was compromise our working relationship, but there was something between us brewing quickly, and it was only a matter of time before something would trigger it.

Ayanna cast her eyes down, avoiding my gaze as she leaned against the front of my desk.

"Ayanna, what is on your mind? I can feel the conflict within you; let it go," I told her, lifting her chin to make her meet my stare.

"You are what's on my mind, Dom," Ayanna finally managed to say. "The past year has been one of the most eye-opening experiences of my life, watching you and Ramesses working the type of cases that you do, and I've learned a lot. Taliah has also. I want to serve you, and not only at work, either."

My whole world stopped in that instant.

I already had my hands full with Niki and Natasha, and while I had learned a lot from Ramesses with regard to handling multiple submissives, I had no real intentions of having another one serve me.

And yet, here we were, with my secretary nearly exposing herself and her feelings, waiting for me to respond.

"Ayanna, are you sure you know what you're saying?" I tried to deflect the attraction that was quickly building inside me. This would complicate things on a major league scale, and I knew that, but I couldn't help wanting her, too.

Okay, you remember what I said about mixing business with pleasure? You're simply going to have to forgive me for breaking my rules.

Ayanna moved in closer, and I kissed her without hesitation. Before we both knew it, she was on top of my desk with her skirt hiked up to her hips, trying desperately to unbuckle my belt and feel what she'd been fantasizing about the entire time.

I was surprised to find out that she wore no panties, not even a thong or G-string. I fought the urge to suspect that she might have been plotting this moment for some time, and the mixed emotions I had of wanting her and feeling guilty for wanting her only fueled the intensity to take her as quickly and as hard as our bodies would allow.

"Dom...oh my God, Dom...take it...take it, please..." she whispered trying not to arouse Taliah's suspicions of what we were doing in my office.

The condom wrapper couldn't come off quick enough.

Ayanna wrapped her legs around my waist, using my tie to help balance herself on the desk. Her eyes flashed every time I stroked her, begging me to make her mine with each passing second.

She was already mine. I already knew she would be.

I slid her off the desk and bent her over, pushing the skirt over her hips so I could enter her again. This time, there was no doubt in my mind as to my purpose of blowing her back out. I wanted her to feel me even after I slid out of her.

"Yours, Daddy...yours...all yours..." she screamed, bracing for the force of the impact as we vibrated against the heavy oak desk.

I raged as I felt my body burning, readying for the eruption that would soon arrive. I lost myself in the volcano, urging my body to wait for a few more minutes.

Ayanna grabbed for my wrists as I gripped her hips tightly, trembling violently as she came. She grinded her hips deep, forcing my own shockwave as I released hard while still stroking her.

Sweat caused my shirt to cling to my skin as I struggled to pull out of her. My legs betrayed me as I collapsed onto the chair that sat near the front of the desk.

Ayanna still lay on the top of the desk, her ass still exposed as I managed to pull my pants up where I sat, trying to make sense of what had just happened.

"It will be our secret, Sir," Ayanna finally said as she lifted from the desk and straightened out her outfit. That freshly fucked look of her hair would be hard to conceal, and we both knew it. "I won't tell a soul."

You would think that betraying my submissives by fucking a

woman behind their backs would have been at the forefront of my mind, but I was focused on other matters, like finding out what Ayanna knew and working it into the case without arousing suspicion that she was involved in any way.

I'd deal with the consequences of what happened today later. Right now, business needed to be handled first.

"Your secret is safe with me, Ayanna," I replied, knowing that keeping that secret would make matters worse if it ever came to light. "But I need to know everything you know, right here, right now."

As she began to recount all the details that she knew, I felt the need to protect her from being involved in this case, but was I willing to withhold knowledge of a material witness to do so?

I got the text from Ramesses as soon as I finished interviewing Ayanna about safi's case.

I exhaled. I didn't like what the text read, and more importantly, where we had to go as a result of it.

Mistress Sinsual just found out about the rape of her boi. Needless to say, she was incensed that nothing had been done yet.

This would be a difficult meeting, to say the least.

I told him I would meet him at her home in Smyrna.

I put my truck on cruise control, thinking back to what had quickly occurred between Ayanna and me.

I wasn't sure if I wanted to admit or not that it was something I had been wanting for at least the past six months. We had been bantering back and forth, putting as much tension between us as we could, and hoping to find out what would happen if space and opportunity would occupy the same moment in time.

She felt so good it was scary.

Almost as good as Niki or Natasha…*almost.*

I didn't want to give up my newest guilty pleasure at all, but eventually I would need to explain to the girls that I did take her.

Natasha probably wouldn't be as irritated as Niki would be, but that's because Niki and I had a longer history together. That and that legendary Puerto Rican temper of hers was liable to flare wild and free.

I also found myself in a quandary; I needed to seek Ramesses's counsel regarding how to handle this situation. Mixing business with pleasure at the job was not something that I wasn't sure he would condone, let alone guide me through, but if he found out through someone else, it could cause a bigger issue of trust between us. He trusted me to run the business the way I saw fit with very minimal oversight on his part because he and Neferterri have a variety of businesses that are a part of the empire. The last thing I wanted to do was betray that trust.

As I got closer to Sin's home, I found my senses were heightened. I was expecting more than what Ramesses let on. Any time Sin was upset about anything, it was never considered a normal set of circumstances. Once I got there, watching Sin's body language as she stood toe-to-toe with him was clear indication that this would be no ordinary interview of a victim.

"I know the bitch that did this, Ramesses; what the hell is taking so long to bring her in?" Sinsual gruffly asked Ramesses as I walked up on the exchange. "What good are you if you can't put two and two together and put this sorry excuse for a Dominant behind bars?"

"Sin, I think you're not seeing anything but red right now," Ramesses assessed calmly. "It's the reason that we're here now, so we can speak to tiger and find out what exactly happened."

"You and Dom won't get a whiff of tiger until I get some assurances that this trick is dealt with." Sinsual was completely losing her decorum by the moment, and it was a side of her that I'd never seen before.

I stood there for a moment, trying to figure out how to approach things. *So, the prim-and-proper one can get dirty when she wants to.* The thought was rather comical in my head, but I knew better than to let it show outwardly, for fear that she would snap in my direction.

"I cannot get the DA's office to name a suspect and arrest him or her at the drop of a hat, Sin; it doesn't work like that," Ramesses continued, showing his frustration more than usual. Sin usually took at least a half-hour to forty-five minutes before he started to take matters into his own hands to calm things down. "The last thing we want to do is erode the relationship we have with them right now."

"I am afraid he is correct, ma'am." I heard voices behind me that didn't sound like the usual fetch teams that were on the company dime. That unnerved me to no end. "We send greetings from the DA's office, Mr. Alexander, Mr. Law. Detective Tanner, and my partner, Detective Bryson, SVU. We're here to take the point on this investigation now."

I had no way of knowing how long he had been there. For all I knew, Bryson and Tanner could have already been here when Tanner texted me earlier, trying to gain access to tiger through his Mistress. Seeing these detectives from SVU was a slight crimp in plans also. The only thing I could do was roll with the punches. I was prepared to be whatever backup I could be at that time, regardless of who was there.

"Ma'am, if I could ask a question," Detective Tanner interjected into the conversation before she stonewalled him. "If I can talk to the assistant DA's and see if they could get us to pick up this suspect, would it persuade you to let us speak to the victim?"

"Detective, I don't—" Ramesses protested.

"Sir, I'm sure the last thing that this lovely young woman would want is to have a pair of detectives that would not be as delicate in this particular situation as we would be." He stared in our direction, quickly winking at Ramesses to tip him off that he may be pulling a fast one.

"Detective, your 'pull' in the DA's office means very little to me." Sin brushed him off quickly. "I have already talked to Niki, and she's looking into it for me already. I should hear from her within the next hour or so. You two are nothing more than consultants, and I need results now!"

I felt the irritation on my partner. Ramesses was about as blunt as I'd ever seen him at any time. "We are going to speak to tiger before we leave this porch; are we clear, Sin?"

I didn't know if it was the extra bass in his voice or the sheer volume in his tone, but Sinsual took a step back like she thought Ramesses would haul off and hit her if his command wasn't followed. I nervously looked in his direction, and the scowl he had on his face looked like it could melt metal. He was showing a new level of aggression that was truly beginning to worry me.

Detective Bryson looked slightly amused at what was happening in front of him. He looked the part of a grizzled, veteran flat-foot who needed to be put out to pasture. He slowly waltzed in front of Sin and flashed a small grin before he spoke. "Ma'am, please, we are not, nor have we ever been, your enemy. I understand your frustrations, I truly do. It was all I could do to keep from breaking a few necks last year when we heard about the case with Dom's ex-wife. We need your help, ma'am. He is the only one that can help us get to the bottom of things."

Sinsual took a look at me, at Ramesses, over at the two detectives, and a smirk slipped across her face like she figured out what was going on. "Oh, I get it now, the old 'good cop, bad cop' routine, huh? I never thought that would ever work on me, but I guess it depends on the cops involved. Okay, Dom, I'll let you see him, but I will be in the room."

"Actually, no you won't, Ma'am." I did my best to exercise as much tact as possible, but she needed to know that she was not in charge. "I mean no disrespect, but I don't want the interview tainted by your influence."

"I don't think my influence—"

"Dom's right, Sin," Ramesses interrupted. "He has no ties to tiger at all, so there won't be any pressure on him to try and 'fabricate' anything."

"I hate to say it, considering these two are not exactly 'hard-core detectives,' but they have a point, ma'am." Detective Tanner surprisingly sided with us. "If he has a good rapport with him, it might help the investigation move more smoothly."

Sin exhaled hard, staring at the ceiling of the porch. She took one look in our direction and shook her head, the proverbial question dancing around in her head, taunting her. "Why is it that the two of you are constantly making me feel more uncomfortable every time I see you?"

"Because we're good at what we do, on several different levels," I replied, stepping toward Sinsual to place a kiss on the back of her palm. "I won't damage him any more than he already is."

"You had better be aware of that when you speak to him," she cautioned, her voice gaining a measure of seriousness. "My boi may be submissive, but he's not meek. He's embarrassed by this turn of events more than anything."

I could empathize with him. I had dealt with one other rape case where the man was the one that was raped, and that was when I was new on the force back in the nineties. I had a hard time believing that, as much as we men heard the word "no" when it came to approaching a woman for a date or sex, a man would turn down sex from a woman, unless she really turned him off on every level imaginable.

By the time I was done with that case back then, the woman had received two years in jail and another five on probation, and she'd gotten off lucky because the judges in Georgia were just getting used to the "Seven Deadly Sins" law that required a mandatory twenty-five-to-life for cases like rape. Fast-forward to present day and the judges were more than comfortable with the spirit and the letter of that law.

I didn't want to be this woman when we found out who she was.

I followed Sinsual to the bedroom that tiger was holed up in. For me to say that he looked a shell of the submissive that I was used to interacting with was putting it mildly. He was completely shuttered in, under the covers, not drawing much attention to himself, exhibiting the very traumatic symptoms that rape victims showed in the days after the assault.

It damn near broke my heart to see him like that. Regardless of gender, rape cases were always the most difficult to deal with because of the raw emotional damage that has been done.

"tiger, precious, I need you to talk to Sir, please? He's here to try and find out what happened and help catch them, okay?" Sinsual tried to softly persuade him. I'd never seen her so tender, so loving before. "Are you up to talking now?"

tiger never spoke a single word; he only weakly nodded in her direction before he turned his head away from us again.

Sinsual quietly nodded, and when she turned to face me, there were visible tears in her eyes and she was trembling. Her voice cracked as she left the room. "Take care of my boi, Dom; I am begging you."

I was not prepared for this side of Sinsual. For the past year, she'd always been a hard ass when it came to me, no doubt because I was still training under Ramesses and she regarded me as not yet on her level, as it were. I wasn't yet ready to believe that her view of me had changed, but the weight of Ramesses's words hit home the minute that she left the room: *do this by the book, no shortcuts.*

I finally turned my attention to tiger, steeling myself against whatever I would be facing with my first statement to him, with the hopes of getting him to open up. "tiger, I cannot imagine what you're going through, nor am I going to try to. Whatever you tell me, I will not repeat a word of it; you have my word as a Dominant and as a law enforcement officer."

"I trusted that…*woman*, Sir." He sat up in the bed, feeling for a glass of water that was placed on the nightstand for him. He took a few sips before he measured his words again. "I made it clear my Mistress had certain parameters once we began."

"Help me understand what happened, okay?" I kept the tone light and nonjudgmental, trying to keep him talking. "What exactly were your parameters while you were in her care?"

"I was there in a domestic service capacity, Sir." tiger regarded my question for a moment, nodding slightly once he understood that I wasn't asking out of ignorance. "It isn't uncommon for a Mistress to secure the services of another Mistress's slave, and this particular Mistress has held me in high regard, as I was told by Ma'am, for quite a long time."

I quickly noted down the important details in shorthand to keep up with his flow. The way the words were coming, it would only be a matter of time before the trickle would become a raging rapid.

"I was flattered that she would want me to serve her, but ultimately it was up to Ma'am to decide, as it is her will," tiger recounted. "She met with her and nailed down the parameters that I was to be operated under, and it was agreed upon then. She reluctantly agreed to have me scantily clad in a pair of leather briefs for the service also."

"So were you to be used sexually after performing your domestic service?" I continued to scribble, still trying my best to keep up. "Considering the request was made to have you wear such revealing clothing."

"Absolutely not!" he snapped, catching me off guard. Realizing that his anger was about to get the best of him, he closed his eyes and slowed his breathing. "Sir, I apologize for the outburst; my Ma'am trained me better than that."

I waved my hand, dismissing the transgression as nothing more than a slight faux pas. "No, it's fine, tiger, continue, please."

"I sidestepped the advances that she kept making, saying how fine I was, how she would love to have me serve her full time." He rattled off the encounter like it had happened hours ago. "I politely accepted her compliments of me with the addition that my Ma'am likes it when her bois are in good shape. Then out of the blue, she tried to kiss me."

"What happened next?"

"I quickly stopped what I was doing and prepared to leave. She stopped me at the door, apologizing for being so forward and asking me to stay and finish." tiger's statement was intended to be matter-of-fact, but I sensed something under the monotone responses. "When I told her no, she snapped."

"How so?" I asked, trying to talk as little as possible but continuing the flow with bridge questions.

"She hit me with something, which knocked me to the ground." He rubbed a spot on the back of his head, the subtle reminder that the event was all too real. "By the time I got my bearings, she was already on top of me, closing some zip cuffs on my wrists behind my back."

So that explains how he was unable to overpower her. I saw the tears begin to flow from his eyes, and there was no way I would have been able to keep my composure at that moment. I was so incensed I was ready to break out the door and go on a personal manhunt.

"She yelled in my ear that she was going to take what she wanted; she didn't give a fuck if Ma'am gave permission or not." He was visibly shaken now, and there was nothing anyone could do about it. "She slicked lube around my asshole and entered me before I had a chance to scream out. She took me on the floor at her front door."

It was all I could do to keep from wanting to rip this woman to shreds myself. tiger was well built, definitely, but he was all of five feet five inches and could be taken down by a larger person in a heartbeat. Not without a struggle, of course.

"What happened after she was done?" I continued the questions to get what I needed, regardless of how difficult it was for either of us.

"She took the cuffs off and told me how good I was," he spat, disgusted with the words that came out of his mouth. "Then she tried to threaten to tell Ma'am that I had disobeyed her if I tried to tell Ma'am about the sex we had."

My blood boiled at that point. Blackmail, too?

"I cleaned up and grabbed my things and headed home as quickly as I could," tiger finally concluded. "I left a voicemail for Ma'am when I got home to let her know that I'd been raped, and then called and spoke to Ayanna to tell her what happened before I lost my nerve."

"I want to commend you on your bravery in coming forward with this, tiger," I said in earnest. "We will do everything in our power to make sure this woman pays for what she's done to you."

I finally stood to leave, and as I walked out the door, tiger uttered, "One more thing, Sir, that I forgot to mention. I got a phone message after I got home that was somewhat cryptic and might help."

"What's that, tiger?"

"The voice on the message said, 'you weren't the first, but you could be the last. We can put her away if we stick together.'"

TEN

"I hope you don't mind, but your executive secretary told me it was okay to come in."

My surprise in observing Tori walking through the door to my office this morning must have been evident on my face. I honestly hadn't expected to see her for at least another day after asking her to find out some information for me on safi's murder. Not that I wasn't pleased to see her, but I had to readjust my focus—among other things since Ayanna and I were flirting over text messages—so that she wouldn't get the wrong idea about the bulge in my pants and think it was for her to take advantage.

The mood I was in, I might have let her anyway.

I rose slowly to offer the chair in front of my desk to sit. I was still somewhat aroused, so it made it difficult to be chivalrous and not be vulgar. "Yes, of course, I'm definitely pleasantly surprised to see you. You have some information for me regarding my request?"

"Yes, of course I do, sexy, but you already knew that the minute I walked in." Tori smirked as she looked around my office to soak in the surroundings. "You've definitely moved up in the world, Sharpshooter. I didn't expect you to be laid up like an upgraded version of Shaft. You got a girl tingling, to say the least."

I tried to bypass the flirting, trying to get into investigative mode, pulling a pen from the inside of my suit jacket and situating the legal pad that was already on my desk. "I figured you would be impressed, but time's working against me, Tori. What did you find out?"

She leaned back in the chair and crossed her legs, letting her skirt rise to dangerously sexy levels. I wasn't immune to her charms, or her body, and my eyes widened as I allowed them to follow every inch until the fabric of the skirt let me know that she had gone commando for this visit.

"See something you like, babe?" She allowed a slick smile spreading across her face. "You know you can get it; all you have to do is lock the door behind us and take it."

"Yes, I do, but that can wait until later." I shook myself out of the trance I was under.

"Yeah, yeah, I know, the case...or should I say, cases, now." She pulled that out of the blue, confusing me for a brief moment. She smiled, giving me the idea that she was deciding whether to continue to torture me or not before her expression turned serious. "I got an interesting visit from someone that I didn't expect to see, and she was rather pissed that I was connected to you."

Yeah, she had the advantage on me, and I wasn't sure if I liked her having that edge on me. I needed her to go ahead and put me out of my misery before this visit began to lose its luster. "You have me at a disadvantage, babe; who are you referring to?"

"Mistress Edge." Tori's body language closed up tightly, her arms folded across her chest as she lightly kicked the toe of her shoe against my desk.

Who in the fuck is Mistress Edge? I stared across my desk at her, trying my best to sound like I knew who she was referring to, but nothing could have been further from the truth at that moment. The confusion faded in seconds once I realized Mistress Edge was the woman who tiger was referring to, but the unfortunate part was that Tori found out that information in a not-so-pleasant manner. That wasn't the case I was worried about, but it took priority whether I liked it or not. "Why did she come to visit you? Isn't that breaking some unwritten code or something? I don't remember you mentioning anyone that you worked with by that name, at least not the last I checked."

"We aren't friends; in fact, we're not exactly warm and fuzzy with each other, either. That's why the visit was so interesting." Tori's facial expression changed in the blink of an eye, and her body stiffened like she was preparing for a fight. "She came by to try and keep me from saying anything to the cops about her rape case."

"What in the world? How in the world does she know that we're on to her?" I didn't like where this was going, and I tried to think two steps ahead to figure out what answer she was going to give me.

"I don't know anything about her pending case, but she has ears in some of the precincts, some cops that she does freebies for, and someone leaked the information to her. She somehow knows my connection to you, and she tried to put two and two together." Tori shook her head, a look of disgust was plastered across her face. "She's threatening to expose me, Dominic. She's been talking to one of the reporters at the *AJC* to let her know of my clientele. I got a call from him asking some pervasive questions earlier today that made me nervous; no one else in the game has the guts to pull a stunt like that."

I wasn't thrilled by the leak, and I was determined to figure out its source. I was not in the mood to deal with bullshit coming out of the PD. I snapped my pen in half, causing Tori to flinch for a moment. "She's bluffing, babe, and you know it, but if you want me to do some digging to find out if she's got something hard on you, I have no problems handling that."

After everything that had happened last year, my senses were on edge and my anger couldn't have flowed any more freely. That bitch had some nerve trying to intimidate anyone that was connected to me in any way. I'd bury the bitch before that happened, especially when she was in the same fucking business (pun intended) that Tori was in. All this over wanting to have her way and not get busted over something that she knows she did?

I was oblivious to Tori's body language as she twitched and squirmed in her seat. She was turned on; she felt the heat on me, and the concern that I had for her well-being was something that she hadn't seen before.

"Careful, detective, you might have a girl thinking that you actually care about her." Tori grinned as she lifted her leg and rested it against the front of my desk. "Not that I think you love me or anything, but it is comforting to know that a real man has your back when you need him."

"I'd be crazy to say that I'm not attracted to you, Tori. In fact, bending you over my desk right now and wearing that ass out is in the forefront of my mind because I need to get this aggression off me," I admitted, grabbing another pen out of my desk drawer. "Once I have a chance to get at least one of these cases wrapped up, I might need to revisit that thought with you, and not in a business capacity."

"I'll tell you what you want to know, Dom," Tori cut me off in the midst of my rant. "We can talk about that other thing between us later, preferably when I'm not in such constricting clothing."

I nodded, a new pen at the ready as I watched her adjust in her seat and pull her skirt down closer to her knees. I wanted as much information as she could give me, and considering her sources were rather thorough, it was bound to be a very lengthy conversation. "Fair enough. Now, what did you find out about the murder case?"

"The party at Inner Sanctum almost didn't happen. The organizer called about six hours before the party was supposed to begin and told the owner she wanted to cancel since all of the attendees were not going to be there."

"Who was the missing attendee? It must have been someone with a lot of juice to have her want to cancel the whole thing?"

Ayanna rushed into the office, breaking the flow of the conversation. She did a quick double-take at the sight of Tori's near-topless body in my office, and for a moment I thought she might have said something or tried to get territorial. A quick half-smile spread before she remembered the reason why she was rushed in the first place. "Sir, Ramesses is yelling in his office. Taliah felt it was something that you needed to be aware of and possibly help with, if possible."

Ayanna's face looked serious, and considering that Ramesses never yelled while at the office, this was something to see about. I stood quickly, heading for the door, tossing a quick phrase in their direction, more concerned about the pressing issue I had to deal with. "Tori, if you don't mind, I need to handle this right now. Ayanna will see you out."

"Sure, babe, you know where to find me if and when you need me," Tori shouted at me before I disappeared down the hall. "And you will need me."

ELEVEN

"You breached my protocols!"

The yelling became more intense the closer I got to his office. I'd never heard him this animated before, and this included our younger days when he was a lot more hotheaded than he was now.

I came rushing into Ramesses's reception area after Ayanna came to get me. Taliah confirmed it when I got there, telling me that the video call that he was engaged in with Master Osiris was getting fiery. I did what I could to figure out what I could do to calm the situation, but Ramesses was already in full fire-and-brimstone mode, going at it with Osiris like he was one of the investigators who botched a report or something.

I guess the honorifics and protocols were out the window once a person was murdered.

This morning was getting more interesting by the second.

"Ramesses, I understand you're upset, but who were we to interfere in the connection between Master and slave?" Osiris tried to keep his tone level. I saw it in his expression. He did not recognize the man on the other side of the video conferencing screen.

Quite frankly, I didn't, either.

"I don't care how deep the connection was, Het-hotep was out of the country when safi got down here, and she was intent on getting into some trouble." Ramesses never once took it down a notch, his eyes narrowing as he continued to berate Osiris. "If you won't tell me who breached my protocols, I'll be on the first thing smoking to Vegas to find out for myself."

I ain't gonna lie, I wanted to stop him, but I had no choice but to let this play out. He was still my mentor, and there was no cause to embarrass him in front of another member of the Society of the Masters of Honor and Enlightenment, better known in the Fetish communities as *Neb'net Maa'-kheru.*

Still, I had to find a way to slow this freight train down before some real damage was inflicted. He was two steps shy of being completely out of control, and he was not one to let his emotions get to him like this, but that's exactly what was happening in front of me and Osiris.

Something had to give, and it wasn't going to be Ramesses.

I think Osiris got that indication also; his body language changed to that of resignation. He braced himself before he spoke, realizing what the consequences would be once he uttered his confession. "Ramesses, that is unnecessary; I breached your protocols to make sure that safi got to Atlanta without your knowledge."

The proverbial "shit" just hit the proverbial "fan" with the utterance of those words.

"You did what?!" Ramesses glowered. He was livid, rubbing his temples to figure out the next course of action to take. "What in God's name possessed you to do that, Osiris?"

"You've forgotten the oath you took, Ramesses. No one should ever put himself above the Society; you know this." Osiris's cold stare was enough to turn the temperature in the office a few degrees cooler. He straightened himself in his chair and continued. "I don't know where your thirst for power is coming from, but this isn't the Ramesses that I know. You would have never put any of us in the positions that we were in if—"

"If what, Osiris?" Ramesses shot back, leaning against his desk with his arms crossed in defiance. "If Amenhotep were still here? Well, I've got news for you, Sir. He is in the Caribbean, enjoying His life down there; meanwhile, the rest of us still have to take care of His interests stateside."

"I didn't say that, Ramesses." Osiris tried to back down, realizing his near-mistake.

"Something's going on with you, Brother. I can see it, and so can your business partner."

Ramesses spun to his left, getting a glimpse of me being in the room with him for the first time. I simply leaned against the doorway, poker-faced the whole time, but my body language obviously betrayed me. I straightened up for a moment once it looked like he wanted some sort of explanation from me, so, I gave it to him. "I know that safi meant a lot to you, Ramesses. I'd grown fond of her over the time she was here with us. But she belonged to Hethotep, which meant your protocols were secondary to what he deemed fit for his slave."

"It's amazing how everyone wants to throw protocols and chains of command and all when it's convenient," Ramesses scoffed. "But I wonder if anyone has told you guys up in Vegas that safi was killed the same night she got in to Atlanta, or should I just watch your face now since you were one of the last to see her alive? Or for that matter, that you were one of the ones who laid hands on her one last time?"

Osiris didn't give an inch on his reaction…yet. It was only a matter of time before he would crack. No one could receive news like that and still be able to remain emotionless, especially if he professed to care about safi the way he said he did.

The gauntlet had been thrown down at Osiris's feet, and the horrified look on his face as the severity of Ramesses's response spoke volumes of the weight that his decision had placed on his shoulders.

"Yeah, I know you were *here*, Sir." Ramesses continued his onslaught like Osiris were some newbie that didn't understand the rules. "So, how was she? Did you get hard enough to want to fuck her when she screamed at the sting of your single-tail? Did you fuck your slave the moment you got off the plane later that night? *Tell me*, Sir; I'm all ears."

I waited for the silence to break, and Osiris finally put us out of our misery, but his stubbornness in this incident began to shine through in a way that I didn't think that a Dominant—and a seasoned one with the respect that Osiris had earned and commanded—would have ever let come to the surface. Considering he was caught dead to rights, it was a curious response, that's for sure.

"If you want someone to blame for the breach, then I will take the blame. I'm sorry that something so…unfortunate…happened to safi, but none of us could have foreseen the consequences." Osiris tried to reason with him. "Yes, I was there to partake in the celebration, but as I understand it, you were supposed to be there, too, Sir. The way you're reacting, it's almost like you're regretting some decision that you made a few days ago."

Ramesses took a crystal vase that happened to be nearby and threw it down against the floor in a fit of flashed rage.

"I think I hit a nerve," Osiris observed, letting a slight smile escape. I didn't find it particularly funny, and apparently the poor attempt at dry humor wasn't lost on Ramesses, either.

"You can try to rationalize your mistake all you want, but the truth is that a young woman—a baby, she was only twenty-three, goddamn it—would still be alive right now if you'd stuck to MY protocols. I knew what she was capable of if she got the chance to breach them, *not you.* On top of that, you violated your own protocols to get a chance to sample pussy that didn't belong to you and head back home before another Brother of the Society would be the wiser. As far as I'm concerned, you need to check *your* priorities, and figure out how you're going to live with your actions. She's dead, in part, because of YOU. Marinate on that, Brother. Her blood is on YOUR hands."

The video screen went dark before Osiris could rebut. In actuality, it was Ramesses who turned the monitor off before Osiris could say another word. He slumped down in his seat, shaking his head. He couldn't believe what had just happened.

This was the opening that I needed. He'd left me no choice in the matter. I tried to ease into this as best I could, but there was no easy approach. "Kane, you know you were completely out of line back there. You're not God, Sir, there was no way that—"

"Dominic…don't." Ramesses stonewalled me, placing his hand in a motion to stop me from speaking any further. "You can save the speech for someone who gives a damn."

"No, Sir, that is not an option, not this time." I was not about to get caught up in a lecture from him where I didn't get a chance to speak my peace. "I have watched you, for the past forty-eight hours, come completely unhinged, so much so that the people who are closest to you can see something's wrong. My God, you even berated a senior member of the Society when I've seen you handle a transgression with a helluva lot more discipline and tact. I'm surprised that Neferterri hasn't read you the riot act over your behavior, man."

Ramesses paused for a moment, still leaning against his desk, and he exhaled as he closed his eyes. He stayed like that for a couple of moments before he finally opened his eyes to wipe the tears that were threatening to well. Bringing Neferterri up sobered him…I didn't have a choice in the matter; it was the only way to get him back to some sort of sanity.

"You know, I forget how good a detective you are, always paying attention to the most inane detail. I hate that about you sometimes." Ramesses laughed at his inside joke. "Maybe I am too close to this case, Dom, but I have to see this through. After what happened to you last year, surely you can understand my need to do what needs to be done?"

He reminded me that the roles were reversed last year. I realized that Ramesses had not really had a moment to himself to grieve over safi's loss. All of this hurt, this anger…I remembered it well.

Taliah finally stuck her head in the door to survey the damage she was expecting to see after all the commotion and raised voices. "Sir, is there anything that I can get for you? Say the word, and your command is my will."

I immediately raised my eyebrow in her direction, trying hard to convince my brain that I'd heard what I thought I'd heard.

Taliah was oblivious to my stare, not even acknowledging my presence until she received the answer to her question from Ramesses. She was right; I was her boss, but I wasn't her *favorite* boss. There was more going on with them than even I realized, but I would have to worry about that later.

"Yes, little one. I need you to do two things. First, please call Osiris back and let him know that I will call him in an hour to apologize for the way I spoke. The other thing is to take Ayanna and make a quick grocery run. Your bosses need some time to get back on the same page."

"As you command, my Sir." Taliah nodded her head as she left the office.

The minute she closed the door, I allowed the incredulous look on my face to shine through. I tilted my head to the side before I turned my attention back to Ramesses. "What in the world was that—"

"I'll explain that to you later, Dom, but first, I feel the need to confess to something I should have done yesterday," Ramesses said, walking to the conference table to sit down. He motioned for me to join him so he could finish his statement. He interlaced his finger, leaning forward on the table as his eyes connected with mine. "I've been beating myself up over the past couple of days because the email draft had been haunting me, making me play the 'what if' game. I kept wondering, 'What if I had gotten that email, would I have gone to that gathering that she planned?' I didn't want to admit to anyone—least of all, myself—that I would have been weak enough to go, keep it a secret from Neferterri, the girls, and pretended like it never happened. I've been angry with myself because I couldn't look in the mirror and know that I would have made the right choice."

"Sir, with all due respect, you may be the Great One, but you're not perfect." I stood up and walked around the desk, grabbing his shoulder. "None of us are, and for you to beat yourself up over something that you couldn't have possibly had any control over is not going to do any of us any good."

The thing about Ramesses that I'd learned a long time ago when we were growing up was that he was extremely measured in his actions and words. He analyzed every angle, sometimes ad nauseam, until he knew the move he made was the right one. He was cerebral, logical, cold and calculating on levels that the next A-type personality wouldn't have had a clue about. The problem with that was when emotions fell into the equation, the one variable that he had no control over threw everything off-balance.

At the end of the day, he couldn't face the fact that he was never given a chance to know if he would have made the right decision.

Ramesses shook out of the fog he was in for a moment, like he was convincing himself that he would have time to deal with his emotions later. It looked like he flipped the switch and was back in business mode in no time. "Okay, the next person on the list is Master Cypher. What's the intel on where he is right now?"

I pulled up the files on the touch screen on top of the conference table, using my fingers to open it up so we could get the latest on Cypher's movements. I could learn to enjoy all this technology to get things done, that's for sure.

I slid the file we needed to see across the table, toward the plasma screen on the far wall, watching it pop up on the screen and re-center itself in such a way that we could read it without squinting. Damn...that was some fly shit. "It looks like according to the intel, Cypher's got a party going on later tonight. I take it we're rolling?"

"Yes, we're rolling. In fact, make sure Niki and Natasha are with you tonight. I'm texting Neferterri to get the girls ready. Cypher's not one to let the bruhs in without some pussy to display." Ramesses sounded disgusted that he even had to mention it in that manner. "I don't feel comfortable using the girls or my Beloved in this manner, but we don't have a choice."

"Consider it done, Sir. But the way you're sounding, we might need to keep some heat on us?"

"Heat would definitely need to be on the menu, Dom. Cypher usually has heavies at his parties to keep the wannabe thugs that want to hit the party muted. He lives out in Lithonia, so don't expect to do a down and back. We need to prepare like we're gonna be out there for a minute."

As we got busy on our smartphones to get the girls prepped for what was about to happen in a couple of hours, I noticed Ramesses slipped back into his contemplative mode again. "Sir, are you okay?"

Ramesses quickly snapped out of the funk, no doubt wondering if I would get on him again for slipping. "I swore to protect her, Dom, even from herself, at least until Het-hotep could claim her.

I wish I could shake the guilt on my heart right now, but I can't. And to have outside forces undermine my efforts, I don't know if I'll get over that any time soon."

"Look, man, the one thing we learned at the Academy was that you can't save them all," I told him, walking to his desk and sitting in the chair across from him again. "The only thing you can do is keep it from haunting you and work to save the ones you can."

"Yeah, I hear you, but I wasn't trying to save them all…just her," he rebutted. "Just her."

TWELVE

I stepped into Cypher's with Neferterri, Natasha and sajira around ten o'clock. I was ready to go at 10:05, and I was being generous with the other four minutes.

Let's see how I could put this without sounding too crass...I guessed you had to see how the other half lived from time to time, right?

On the outside of the house, the place was palatial. It had three levels, four if you accounted for the basement hidden in the rear of the house. It could give a few celebrity homes a run for their money. I remember Ramesses telling me a while ago that Cypher used to be a high-powered sports agent; even had some real ballers that he represented. That was before he got busted a couple of years ago in a federal underage sex sting operation.

It took a colleague to take a chance on his case and help him beat the charges, but by then, his clients dropped him, especially once the S&M play came to light. Everyone in the Fetish community shunned him, at least for a while, which was why he decided to run things out of his home. He was *persona non grata* now.

The inside looked like it was about a step above what Inner Sanctum looked like, and that was on a good day. Less is more—I think that's how the saying went—and Cypher could have stood to remember that when he decorated the place. There were swords on the walls, masks and other paraphernalia; I remembered Cypher bragging once during one of his "tours" of his house that he'd picked them up from the Congo. The furniture was white leather to match the marble floors and pristine white walls. The shit looked like he was trying to re-create something out of *Scarface* or something.

Once we got up to one of the dungeon areas on the third floor, the strong scent of sex was in the air, which I didn't mind so much. The ladies weren't quite so forgiving. Not that they were prudish about sex or anything like that, but, like I said before, we had to see how the other half lived. The look on their faces made it clear there would not be a return trip under any circumstances.

I texted Ramesses to let him know that we were on the premises, looking for Cypher. I sent another text to Niki also, to make sure in case something went down.

I would have been more comfortable having a full contingent to attend this...party...but Niki and shamise were unable to come out with us tonight. Niki was stuck at the office doing a briefing for a case the next morning, and shamise was out of town helping with Ramesses with a surprise audit at the Thebes compound in Virginia.

Talk about the pressure of keeping the members of Kemet-Ka safe and sound while we were here? Why didn't he simply have me protect the mayor or something while he was at it?

I wondered why he told me I needed to keep heat on me, and I began to understand why. It was a complete sausage fest going on in here. The dudes looked thirsty as fuck for anything that even remotely resembled an attractive woman.

Neferterri gave glaring looks at anyone that got close to either her or sajira, while I tried to keep things as close to home with Natasha as I could. We walked around the dungeon area trying to find Cypher, when he managed to walk up on us when we least expected it.

"Welcome to my home, ladies and gentleman." Cypher tried to

sound like a gracious host, but from the way Neferterri reacted, I felt the need to move forward as a shield to his bullshit. "I hope that you all are enjoying yourselves? I rarely get such elite and exquisite company these days. What brings you by here?"

It was my first time really interacting with the man, so I made sure to keep my guard up. Luckily, Neferterri didn't hide her disdain and venom as easily as her husband usually did. That made it easier for me to take a hardened stance in front of him.

"We need to ask you some questions about a gathering you attended a couple of nights ago," I queried, bringing up a brief look of confusion from Cypher.

After thinking on it a few moments, he snapped his fingers in recognition. "Oh, the thing with safi? Yeah, I wanted her to have it here instead of that hellhole at Inner Sanctum, but she said she didn't want anyone to trail where she might have been."

He was one to talk about hellholes with the way that he was keeping his "dungeon." I didn't even want to guess how the other one in the basement looked. There was no cleanup between scenes; bodily fluids were on everything. I knew sajira was a nurse at one point before she settled into accounting, and she turned her nose up every time she looked at a scening station.

"So, we got to wear that bitch out." Cypher got loose with the tongue a bit until he saw Neferterri out of the corner of his eye. "Forgive me, we had a pretty intense scene; we were all lashing her with the single tails while she was suspended above us. We only had about ten minutes before she had to be lowered to keep her limbs from losing circulation."

"What happened after you left? Who was still there?"

"Let's see, there was some woman there with her, and she was pulling safi out of subspace so they could fuck," Cypher recalled with a slick smile on his face. "I asked if they wanted me to videotape it like I did the scene and they both flatly told me no."

I saw the look on Neferterri's face. She was not happy about the way Cypher recounted that night and it showed. I wasn't exactly thrilled over his cavalier attitude and indifference over his version of the events, so I figured he needed to be aware of things. "You do realize that you have the only evidence and eyewitness account that safi was still alive, right? You were the last one to see her breathing, so that makes you a person of interest from where I'm sitting. I wonder if I should alert the detectives of what I've discovered."

"Still alive? You mean to tell me that—" Cypher's attitude changed quickly, but only for a moment. He went into complete defense mode. "I want my lawyer, since you wanna play that game."

"You aren't under arrest, Cypher; I haven't read you your rights, and neither has my submissive, who actually does have the authority to do so. Why so nervous?"

"I'm not saying another word until I have my lawyer present. Unless—" he said as he leeringly glanced in sajira's direction, "we can make an arrangement."

Neferterri balked at the suggestion quickly. "Touch her and you won't have use of your hands again," she snapped, stepping in front of sajira like a lioness guarding her pack.

Cypher looked undeterred, until he saw the laser sights of a Glock and a Sig-Sauer locked in against both sides of his neck.

To say the party came to a screeching halt would be an understatement.

A couple of Cypher's bodyguards came into the fray with their guns drawn, adding more tension to the situation. Neferterri was not fazed by the show of steel as she continued to berate Cypher for his indecent proposal. "You might want to tell your boys to lower their weapons, or some other information that you don't want to get out in the midst of all these people in here might... shall we say, slip?"

Cypher took a step back, giving the signal for the men to stand down, shaking his head at what had transpired. He gave me a look, staring at the gun still in my hand, wondering when I would holster it. The slow shake of my head told him that he was not in a position to negotiate after he crossed the line.

"You got only one way out of this, considering my baby is an officer on duty right now." The sneer across my lips was meant to ensure that my words were not meant as a bluff. "You can go downstairs and get the evidence that we need right now to further the murder investigation, or you can explain to everyone here about the illegal activity going on in here."

Cypher glowered at me, trying to stand his ground. "There's nothing going on illegal here, and you know it, Dominic. You got nothing."

"Oh, we got nothing?" The rhetoric and sarcasm dripped from my tone. I raised my voice so everyone could hear me. "He says that we got nothing on him, baby. Would you explain to the party-goers in here of the charges that could come up against them as the result of a sting operation into the illicit acts that Cypher here is promoting?"

Natasha gave a quick laugh and huffed as she began recounting the laws broken. "Sir, let's see…there's the lewd and lascivious behavior in a residential neighborhood, operating without a business license, operating without a liquor license, aggravated assault, possession of a concealed weapon, assault with a deadly weapon…need I go on, Master?"

By the time she was done rattling off the list, Cypher noticed people tiptoeing out of the house, some without clothes at all, as they saw our weapons still drawn and pointed at him. "You win, dammit. Tell these people that there's not a problem. Okay, I'm sorry that I came at the young lady the wrong way; I swear."

I kept my gun drawn on him as I waved him to move and grab the package that he so willingly "volunteered" to give up. I followed him down the stairs as I heard Natasha addressing the crowd that there was no issue and they were free to continue what they were doing.

"I ought to make you pay for what you did in there," Cypher threatened as I escorted him down to his office to open the safe. "You tried to embarrass me in front of my people. That comes with a price, bruh."

"I'll make sure to leave an invoice so you can address that with the owner of the company." I laughed out loud. He was dead serious about his "threat" and all I could do was stand there with the bullet in the chamber, trying to figure out exactly why he felt the need to come for me like that. "I'm sure he'll be more than happy to discuss it with you."

Cypher cursed and spat, knowing that I had the upper hand on him. The last thing he wanted to do was deal with Ramesses, especially after he had just come at sajira wrong and strong. There were some things you simply didn't do.

We made our way back to the main level to the front door, where Neferterri and the girls were waiting. I nodded that I had the disc, and Natasha finally holstered her weapon at that point.

"Are we done here?" Neferterri still had anger in her, and I couldn't blame her. If he had come at Natasha wrong, I probably would be still pressed to put him through a wall.

"Yes, my Lady, we are done here."

"Good." Without warning, Neferterri quickly took one of the wooden bats off the wall and took a swing, hitting Cypher on the side of the knee. He yelled out in pain as he dropped to his knees, holding his arm up in defense as Neferterri took another swing to his ribcage.

"That's for trying to disrespect me and my girl!" Neferterri blasted. "I ought to break your jaw for even letting the words come out of your mouth, you sick sonofabitch!"

I wanted to laugh so badly my stomach hurt. He looked like the bitch he was as Neferterri wailed on him like she was chopping down a tree. Wherever he tried to block, she found a new spot to hit. The instinct to stop her from beating him to a broken pulp was there; I simply didn't act on it. My priority was to ensure that she and sajira were able to enter and exit without a hair being harmed on their heads. Mission accomplished on that front.

"You're not gonna stop her from hitting me?!" Cypher yelled at us as he cowered into a corner by the door. Neferterri dropped the bat at his feet and headed out with sajira in tow. "This is complete bullshit! You can't do this!"

"I think she just did, bruh." I gripped Natasha's hand to lead her out of the door. "I think you are better off not pressing charges, either. You don't want someone else to bring the rain, do you?"

Cypher shook his head, holding his knee as he tried to survey the damage. "Just go. I don't want to see any of you anymore."

"You go on and enjoy the rest of your party, okay?" Natasha said with sarcasm dripping from her lips. "I'm sure there are plenty of bitches to go around tonight."

"Go to hell!" Cypher screamed, still wincing in pain from where Neferterri hit him.

"Sorry, I only follow the commands of my Master, bitch," Natasha uttered. She released my grip and pulled her gun again, this time walking up on Cypher and pressing the barrel to his temple. "Besides, someone's gotta hold the door for us when we get there. Do you want me to make the travel arrangements right now?"

Cypher violently shook his head no.

"Good, that's what I thought…oh, and by the way, my partner

and I will be back with a warrant in the morning to pick this place apart. Good night."

We never made it home.

The beauty of having a truck was that if the mood hit you, simply pull over to the side of the road and make use of the bed of that truck.

I ripped the cloth cover off the bed and shoved her into it before she could say a word. It was a good thing she wore a short dress to the party; all I needed to do was hike it up over her ample hips and wear her out.

"Fuck me, Master, please! Hurt me, spank me, I was a bad girl tonight!" Natasha yelled into the night air as she reached behind her to grab my hands.

"Who do you belong to, slut?" I yelled out.

"I belong to you, Master!" she screamed, reacting to her hair being pulled as I pounded into her with no remorse. "Oh my God, please, Master, fuck your pussy!"

The cars were whizzing by as we went at it, not caring if someone stopped long enough to find out exactly what we were doing. I had to have her right then and there.

I spanked her ass so hard that I could feel the heat from her skin. My hands were pulsating from the skin slapping, but she felt so silky smooth and wet that I couldn't have cared less if I broke a finger while I stroked her into oblivion.

Her screams became inaudible guttural moans and sexy coos as I felt her walls squeezing me tight, letting me know that she was coming any moment. Rather than trying to say the words, an ear-piercing screech came out of her, which would have caught me off guard normally, but I was high on the sex and completely in the moment, and I had no intentions of coming out of it.

I flattened her on her stomach and continued to drill down into her, wrapping my hand around her neck to close off her airway. I knew she would come again soon after, but this time she wouldn't be able to scream until I released her throat to allow her to scream.

This time when she came, her body shook violently, and she fought me to take my hand off her throat. I released her a few seconds later, watching her taking much needed breaths as the orgasms continued to take siege over her body.

"Oooooooooooohhhhhhhh fuuuuccckk…mmmmmm…ohhhh shhhhhhiiiiiiii!!!" Natasha tried her best to say or scream or anything, but her body was not having it.

I felt raindrops falling as I continued stroking her deep, feeling the crest coming fast and relentlessly. I pulled out of her and rolled her over on her back, taking the condom off so I could unleash my own storm to match the one that began to make its presence known.

She instinctively took my shaft and began stroking me, pulling the wave closer with each fervent caress.

"Oh fuck, Tasha, I'm gonna…shitttttt!!!" I bellowed from deep as the last image before I closed my eyes to ride the crashing climax was Natasha basking in the stream of my essence flowing all over her chest, rubbing it into her skin, dropping her top to massage her breasts and lick them slowly.

We got out of the bed of the truck quickly as the storm raged harder, getting into the cabin to dry out as best as we could.

"Thank you, Master; I hope I pleased you." Natasha never lost her discipline or protocol of thanking me after either a play scene or sex interlude.

"I'll tell you this much," I panted, trying to catch my breath. "I'll never look at a rainstorm the same way again."

THIRTEEN

"I have a facial match, Daddy."

I didn't know how I felt about Ayanna calling me that, but it felt good as hell to hear it; I'll admit that much. I was outside of a Publix near the office, waiting inside the truck to pick up the image she'd found. "Send the image to me, baby."

As I saw the image downloading into my laptop, my mind drifted back to the encounter in my office with her. I had to try to make some sense of how and why that had happened. It's not like I wasn't happy with my girls, but the attraction and connection could not be denied.

I was conflicted about telling the girls that Ayanna and I had been intimate also.

I texted Ramesses to let him know that I needed guidance for something lifestyle-related the minute the private plane touched down from D.C. I didn't need this hanging over my head when cases were still hanging in the balance.

"The image download should be complete, Daddy," Ayanna cooed over the phone, warming my blood even more. "Is there anything else that I can take care of for you?"

"Yes, Ayanna, I need you to clear out my schedule for about two hours later today. There's something that we need to discuss," I told her, knowing that I needed to focus more intensely. "Find a restaurant where we can have lunch."

"As you command, Sir." Her voice dripped of honey as she hung up the phone.

I focused my attention to the image that was in front of me of the woman being accused of rape. Jason was right: she was gorgeous, even without makeup. It finally clicked in my mind that I did know her from my interactions with her at NEBU; Mistress Edge was her name.

I realized there was another reason I knew of her; she used to be a member of NEBU last year, but she terminated her membership due to personal reasons. If I remembered it correctly, she had to move out of town for a little while to build money until she could come back to the A. Other rumors had it that she swindled a lot of people while she was here. I didn't pay any of it any mind as long as shamise told us that her accounts were clear and up to date at NEBU. At least on that front, there were no improprieties to concern myself over. The simpler, the better.

I got word through my usual channels that Edge was living in Midtown, which was interesting to me; I honestly didn't remember it being her style to live in such a "rainbow" type of area. But then again, I've learned never to take things at face value. She was an eclectic woman as it were to begin with, so she would fit right at home near Little Five Points.

I found her condo over in the new Atlantic Station area, which had me wondering exactly how much money had she been stacking to afford to live over here.

"Who is it?" she asked after I rapped on the door.

"Detective Law, ma'am," I answered, trying to sound professional. "I need to ask some questions about an incident a couple of nights ago, if I may?"

The door slowly opened, and Edge appeared wrapped in a towel and little else. Not exactly the way that I expected her to receive company, but it wasn't like I was complaining. Her body hugged that towel nicely, and I couldn't help wondering for a brief moment why tiger would refuse such a stunningly attractive woman.

"Come in, detective, I remember you," she said, trying to hold on to the towel as if she didn't want me to see the goods. The way that I remembered it, her outfits left very little to the imagination anyway.

Not to sound conceited or anything, but if you've seen one, you've seen them all.

I sat down on the couch and found myself a little surprised when Edge slid right beside me, turning her body toward me and crossing her legs to close the opening between us.

Okay...this could get interesting. "Thank you for agreeing to talk with me, ma'am."

"Please, 'ma'am' is so formal. You can call me Kacie," she interrupted, flashing her eyes at me. "As good as you sound, you can call me whatever you like."

Kacie was trying to throw me off balance, and she was doing a damn good job at it for a moment. She tried to be slick by letting the towel hang open a little at a time, like it would get me to focus on her body than the reason I was there.

That would work for a lesser dude that wasn't getting any, but I'm well taken care of, fuck you very much.

Still, I wouldn't have minded to have her pinned under me, taking her the way I took Niki and Natasha.

Focus, Dom...I know those legs are begging to be spread open, but that's not what we came here for. I tried my best to keep my mind from wandering, but she wasn't making it easy.

She could feel my eyes all over her, and she took full advantage of the situation, letting the towel drop away from her chest, exposing her fully naked body for the benefit of my visual enjoyment. "See anything you like, detective? I don't normally bottom in my sessions, but for you, I am more than willing and able to make a damn good exception in this case. I know you want it, take it. I won't even charge you for it; this is pleasure only."

Wait a minute. Did she sit there and try to say this was a freebie?

That sobered me up quick. I was no one's charity case.

That one phrase reminded me of the reason I was there, and it definitely wasn't to turn her into a personal whore, so I straightened up as best as my body would let me and stuck to my interrogation.

"Kacie, there's a gentleman that you had in your charge a couple of days ago. He was the property of Mistress Sinsual. Do you remember securing his domestic services that evening?" I kept my distance as I opened her up to this line of questioning. She had to know what was coming, and I wanted to make sure that I was prepared for the outburst that was sure to come. Guilty people do it all the time.

"Yes, I remember that gorgeous piece of ass," Kacie gushed, and for a moment I thought I saw her blushing like she had been caught in a quick flashback. "So, my sexy detective, what seems to be the trouble?"

"I'll cut to the chase: Sin's slave has leveled rape charges against you, saying that you accosted him after he refused your sexual advances."

Sure enough, Kacie's cheeks flushed quickly, and her eyes narrowed, which gave me the indication that I had found the right nerve to hit. She readjusted her towel to cover herself. Oh well, so much for the peep show. "That poor excuse of a slave...I did not rape him! He couldn't handle the fact that he enjoyed being fucked by me and his guilt made him pull this shit!"

"Kacie, I need to know your side of the story so I can help you." I tried the "be your friend" tactic to keep her calm. "You want my help, don't you?"

"I ain't telling you shit, Dom," she fired back. "For all I know you're probably trying to box me in, too."

"That might have been true if I was a cop, but I'm not anymore." I tried to reassure her, but she was in full rant mode.

"That pussy was there for the taking! He should have been happy that a gorgeous Goddess like me even wanted to have him at all!" she continued ranting, letting her towel slip off her. "I know it because you haven't been able to take your eyes off me since you got here! If you want some, why don't you come get some? Be a man about it, take me!"

The next thing I knew, I heard commotion outside of her door, and it sounded like there was as much arguing going on out there as there was between Kacie and me. I distinctly heard Niki's voice outside of the door. "APD! We have a warrant to search the premises."

Kacie didn't flinch. She ran for the door and opened it without regard for the fact that she was stark naked. She was both surprised and relieved to see her lawyer present along with Detective Bryson and Detective Tanner.

How in the hell did they manage to be here? I never gave them the heads-up that I would be here in the first place.

I was also surprised to see Niki accompanying the officers. That wasn't standard operating procedure, either.

Something's amiss; I could feel it. The fucked-up part was, it wasn't a good feeling for me to have; it always meant that someone was nosing around where they shouldn't have been.

I hated it when I detected a leak. I hated it even more when I couldn't find out where that leak was coming from. But I had a sneaking suspicion that I would find the answers sooner rather than later. That was the next thing on my to-do list.

However, I had immediate business to take care of, and seeing the KAP lawyer (that's a kink-aware professional for those not in the know) tipped me off as to why she had to make the adjustment.

She was wide open a moment ago; now she wanted to act like I had an STI or something.

"My client will have no further comment at this time." He was a slightly built man, definitely metrosexual, but I wouldn't stretch to call him gay, although the mannerisms were there. "I want to know why a law enforcement consultant is here with my client, possibly violating her Fifth Amendment rights."

"Sorry, my friend, you're barking up the wrong tree," I protested, adjusting my belt and pants for effect to give the impression that I was dealing in post-coital cleanup. "Kacie and I were just getting started with something kinda sexy when you barged in."

"That's a lie, Dominic, and you know it!" she countered, forgetting that she was still naked with her body on full display, including protruding nipples that hinted at excitement of what was to come. "You were trying to get me to admit that I raped someone!"

Click.

"That pussy was there for the taking! He should have been happy that a gorgeous Goddess like me even wanted to have him at all!" her voice repeated from the voice recording on my cellphone. *"I know it because you haven't been able to take your eyes off me since you got here! If you want some, why don't you come get some? Be a man about it, take me!"*

"What the fuck?!?" Kacie clutched her chest, realizing for the first time that she might be caught up. "That's not what I meant; I swear it!"

"That would be for the DA to decide." Niki smirked, completely amused that she had been gifted a confession for her case. "Officers, please search the condo for any other evidence that we can use."

"You son of a bitch, you set me up!" Kacie tried to lunge at me, only to have an officer stand in her way to hold her.

I turned to the KAP lawyer, trying to contain my laughter. She was doing too much. "You might want to advise your client to put on some clothes and remain silent during this search. The warrant is righteous, and she gave probable cause with her statement."

He shook his head and replied, "You know you were wrong for putting her in this situation, Law. I don't care how slick it was, you should know better as a former law enforcement official."

"Please, spare me the bullshit." It became obvious that he had no more love for me than I did for him at that moment. "Your client is guilty, and I have no problems doing what needs to be done to prove it."

"Spoken like a true cop." Niki walked in on our brief pissing contest. "If I know you, I know that you will be turning over the contents of that recording to my office ASAP; isn't that right, detective?"

The special tone on my cell phone that let me know that an email had been received went off. I picked up the phone off my case and read it before showing it to Niki and then the KAP lawyer.

Just got the recording, Law, and it has been sent to the defendant's attorney just now, the message read on my phone from Jason's cell phone number.

About a second later, his phone beeped, and when he checked it, his shoulders slumped.

Check.

"I take it everything is in order?" I asked.

"Yes, Sir, I believe it is in order." Niki winked at me before he could catch on. "Jason and I will see you back at the office to review the recording, to make sure that there were no improprieties going on that might have violated the defendant's rights."

"I look forward to it."

"I can't wait, either," she whispered to me as we walked to my truck. "I'll take any excuse to see my Master."

As she walked me to the truck before heading back to the search,

Niki caught me by surprise by confessing something I wasn't aware of. "Is it wrong of me to have secretly wanted to catch you fucking her? The thought of it has me wet as hell right now, if I am allowed to say so, Master."

"*See anything you like, detective?*" I played back the earlier part of the conversation when Kacie tried her best to serve the pussy on a platter. "*I don't normally bottom in my sessions, but for you, I am more than willing and able to make a damn good exception in this case. I know you want it, take it.*"

"Damn, what I wouldn't have given to be in the room while she was trying to seduce you." Niki showed off a never before seen voyeuristic side of herself that was both a shock to me and an amazingly wonderful stroke of luck.

"If you're a good girl, I might make something like that happen for you soon," I teased back, lightly kissing her on the lips. "Now, get to work; you have a case to close and prosecute."

"So, you're the one that Santiago's been seeing, huh?" I heard Bryson in the background as I watched them approach. "I should have known she'd go for a buster like you."

"Wow, a buster, you say?" I got out of my truck to face him. I saw Tanner out of the corner of my eye walking toward us. I wasn't in the mood for a dick-slinging contest when I already had the prize to be won anyway. "Interesting point of view coming from a married man. I wonder what your wife would say about you lusting after another woman. Aren't you a newlywed?"

"Bryson, ease back on the P.I., man." Tanner tried to play peacemaker, but he should have known that that wouldn't work. For some reason, Bryson had to get whatever he needed off his chest. "He's good at what he does, why are you giving him a hard time?"

"Because he gave up the shield to be a joke, and he took a woman that was supposed to be MY wife," Bryson retorted as he shook

Tanner off. "You had the sweet spot at your old precinct, man. How could you give up on your brothers like that, and for some pussy? I pulled your file, too, Law, and you had things on the fast track. The DA's office all but handed the keys to your spoiled ass, golden boy, and you give it all up for MY girlfriend."

That information surged through me like a transformer blew up. Niki was with *him* before we got together?

"Look, Bryson, your beef is not with me; it's with Niki, all right?" I backed off for a minute, trying to reassess the situation because emotions had gotten involved. "I can understand you wanting to be pissed with me for leaving the force…you're not the first…but Niki made her choice, and I had nothing to do with it."

"Whatever, Law, I'm over it, and once we can get this case over with, I'll be rid of you again." Bryson continued spitting with a disdain that I couldn't come to grips to understand. "As far as I'm concerned, you shouldn't have been brought in on this case anyway. You're already bending the laws and rights you swore to protect, and all for a quick buck? Traitor."

"Okay, that's enough," Tanner shouted. "Law, don't worry about him; he's a little pissed off because you beat us here."

"Well, detective, please let your partner know, since he seems to be a little non-communicative right now, that there were things that he was not privy to then when I left." I shot a glance in Bryson's direction. "As far as Niki goes, he's got to make peace with that; it's none of my business because it happened before we got together."

"Look, we all want the same thing here. We have a case to put to sleep, so let's skip the ego tripping and get back to that, all right?" Tanner said it for the two of us to hear.

"I'm good if he's good," I replied, extending my hand.

"I'm good…for now." Bryson shook my hand, trying to grip me tighter for a second like he was trying to get the upper hand.

Yeah, right.

"If you find out anything, clue us in on it, and we'll extend the same professional courtesy, cool?" Tanner said.

"If I got anything, I'll make sure to let you know," I responded, knowing by the look on Bryson's face and his body language that there was a snowball's chance in hell that he would keep me in the loop.

I got back in my truck and checked my watch and quickly started the engine.

I was late for an interesting lunch date.

"I hope you don't mind my being here, Sir."

Seeing Taliah at lunch with Ayanna was an unexpected twist in what I felt would be a rather transparent conversation with Ayanna.

I guess her nerves got the best of her and she needed the anchor.

I understood that, and there was no argument from me.

Having lunch with two gorgeous women while other hatin'-ass men stared and tried to figure out how I got so lucky was more than enough reason for me not to tell Taliah to go back to the office.

"No, not at all, Taliah. I figured Ayanna might have needed some company in case I was running late." I kissed them both on the cheek before sitting down.

"Yes, Sir, I will admit that I'm a little…well, a lot…nervous about what you needed to speak to me about," Ayanna quietly spoke, her shyness only drawing me in closer to feel her essence. There was a part of her that insisted that I have it, and I was more than willing to consume it.

"I don't want to put you in such a position, baby." I let the term of endearment slip on purpose because I wanted to see her blush.

She wanted to belong to me in some way or fashion; I read it in her body language.

Apparently so did Taliah, because she winked at me for a second like she already knew what had happened between us earlier in the week. "Ayanna's been quite taken with you for a while now, Sir."

"That's an understatement," Ayanna chimed in after sipping on her appletini. "Sir, I had been wanting what happened the other day to happen for the last couple of months. We'd been flirting so heavily that some days, I come home from work and I have to—"

I waited for her to finish her statement, not because I didn't get the gist of what she was telling me, but I wanted her to hear herself say it out loud. It wasn't a humiliation tactic, but the way Ayanna was blushing, you would have thought she was confessing that she cheated on me or something embarrassing as hell.

I put her out of her misery. There was no point in divulging the obvious. "Ayanna, it's okay, I think I understand now. The question is, how far are you willing to take this?"

"As far as it goes, Sir," Ayanna rebutted as I noticed her hands were trembling. "I know you have Niki and Natasha, and that doesn't bother me. I don't exactly want a boyfriend; I want what Taliah has."

Huh?

What Taliah has?

Taliah saw the confused look on my face and felt that she needed to explain. "Sir, you have only scratched the surface of how deep this world can go. What Ayanna is talking about is the relationship that I have with my Daddy and my Goddess."

"Okay, help me out, completely lost here." I tried to wrap my mind around the concept that Taliah tried to lead me into, but I had to admit, I was so used to shamise and sajira, and to a lesser degree, amani, that I didn't know there was another aspect to D/s relationships.

"Okay, Sir, what I'm talking about is that I am a part of the Leather Family. Ramesses is my Sir, and I do refer to him as Daddy sometimes, but only as a part of the Family. I am not an owned submissive of the House of Kemet-Ka, but I am in service to the House, in whatever capacity they ask of me." Taliah continued her explanation. "Taliah is not my birth name, but it is the name that I answer to because they gave it to me."

"So, what you're saying is, I can still keep Ayanna, but as a part of a Leather Family?" I replied, still scratching my head. "But I'm not even Leather, at least I think I'm not; that's Ramesses and Neferterri's thing."

Taliah smiled like she was in on the joke before I was. "My dear Dominic, sweet Sir, my Daddy has been grooming you within the concepts and principles of the Leather world. Simply let him know that you want to include Ayanna within your Leather Family, and he'll help you take care of the rest."

I felt like I had been double teamed, and I didn't get a chance to take any type of lead at all. Within the Leather world, as I remembered Amenhotep and Ramesses explaining to me, there are submissives and slaves who do not exactly wish to be collared or owned, but enjoy the comfort and safety of a Leather Family, as they are in service to that Dominant or Master without the constraints of a relationship or union.

It seemed the most logical step, considering that it was the road that I was unknowingly heading down. Call me selfish, but I wanted Ayanna, too, and if this was a way to explain the connection, who was I to argue?

"I don't call anyone Daddy, and you have looked out for me the entire time I've worked for the company," Ayanna added, placing her hand under mine. That simple move made my fingers twitch. "I enjoy you a lot more than I think you know, and I want to continue to, for as long as it lasts."

My phone sounded off with the specific chime that alerted me that Niki was calling.

"Talk to me, Niki," I answered as my demeanor changed quickly. She never called me unless it was something that needed my immediate attention. Natasha's the same way.

This phone call was no different.

"We've got Edge in the cage; thought you might want to sit in and see the show."

FOURTEEN

"You are some piece of work."

Kacie sat in the chair across from the detective assigned to the case, Detective Sharpe. He definitely dressed the part that his last name suggested. Good build, looked about six feet two inches, impeccably well kempt, and he commanded a presence from the moment that he walked into the interrogation room.

I didn't like him already.

It had nothing to do with the fact that he was around Niki; that didn't bother me. He was ex-military, so that wasn't it, either. It was his detail that bothered me.

He was a sniper in the Marine Corps.

That meant he was trained to be sneaky, and he never got dirty, not in terms of combat on the field type of dirty.

That was what got under my skin. I couldn't trust a man who couldn't get dirty.

Niki seemed to be quite enamored with him, though, and I didn't know how to feel about that. It wasn't jealousy in that she found favor with a dude from the office, but I hoped that some of my disdain would rub off on her, considering she belonged to me.

I needed to talk to Ramesses to figure out how he managed to have shamise and sajira on the same page like that.

I shook off my thoughts to concentrate on the exchange that was going on between interrogator and suspect.

"Thank you for the compliment; I do try to keep myself in some decent shape." Sharpe's sarcastic retort was evident as he leaned in close to Kacie to emphasize his point. "We have what we need on you, Kacie, so why don't you do us a favor and explain what really went down? I could get the ADA to ease back a bit on the charges, maybe plea it down to a misdemeanor. She and I are tight like that."

I heard a small giggle escape Niki's lips, and I shot a look at her. *What the hell did he mean by that?*

Her eyes darted away for a moment. After a few moments, she moved closer to me and placed a kiss on the back of my hand. That was her subtle gesture to somehow clue me in to the performance Sharpe was putting on to get Kacie to talk.

"Oh, a smooth talker, huh? Well, you might be able to charm some of the help around here, but I can smell a pussy a mile away." Kacie glared at him, flexing against the handcuffs that were fastened behind her back. "I know an Alpha male when I see one, and you're not it."

"Oh really now, and what makes you so sure you can spot an Alpha male when you see one, princess?" Sharpe inquired, sitting down in the chair across from her.

"Because I would be sloppy wet right now, the way I was with your consultant on this case, and right now, I'm as dry as the Sahara." Kacie smirked as she licked her lips. "I'm willing to bet smart money that he's behind the glass now, watching the whole thing."

Niki's smile wasn't so evident when she heard that.

I whispered into her ear, "Sharpe's not the only one that can put on a show, baby. He's not in her league on this one."

"And you would know something about things being out of your league, wouldn't you, Law?" Detective Bryson chimed in as he and Detective Tanner arrived into the area. "Why don't you let real cops handle this, okay? You got us this far, but we don't need sloppy play ruining a righteous conviction."

"Ryan, you need to relax with that, okay?" Niki looked perturbed by Bryson's entrance. It was clear in her body language that she really didn't have time for the argument. "Law managed to get what we needed. It's not his fault that you and Tanner were slow on the draw."

I put my hands up to offer no debate. This wasn't about me, I saw that. Hell, Stevie Wonder saw that.

"Look, Nikia—"

"That's Ms. Santiago to you, detective," Niki snapped back.

"Ms. Santiago," Bryson began again, trying to remember his original thought. "This *consultant* can blow this whole case because of his connection to you personally."

"It didn't seem to bother you when we were fucking, now, was it?" Niki angrily whispered as her eyes glowered with a "how dare you?" glare. "If you were so worried about conflict of interest, then we should have never gotten together, now, should we?"

Bryson's stance softened as his shoulders slumped. "I was simply trying to say that this woman's lawyer is from *his community*, so he's liable to find out through the grapevine what's going on between you two."

"Unless I've missed my guess, there were other assistant district attorneys on the payroll, Ryan." Niki dropped the hammer down on him. "I can recuse myself at any time and turn the case over to any of the other seven on staff, including Jason, who is usually my second chair."

"Ms. Santiago, this doesn't have to go down like this." Bryson's demeanor seemed to change in a heartbeat. His original rough edge was all but gone now. "I don't like the effect that he has on you. He left the department to be a PI, for God's sake."

"If you must know…and it's really not your business…but the reason that Law left the force was because the DA's office favored him over me for the assistant DA position," Niki confessed.

"What?" Bryson huffed.

"You heard me," Niki continued. She crossed her arms as she leaned against the wall next to the speaker so she could hear Sharpe continuing the interrogation. "He turned in his badge because brass gave him no other choice. Either he took the spot or they were going to make it hard for him to keep his shield."

I raised my eyebrow at that revelation. Only one person knew the truth outside of me, and that person retired from the DA's office right after I'd resigned. How in the world did she find out the real reason I left?

We heard a loud bang against the table, which jolted us from the heated conversation that Niki and Bryson were engaged in.

Almost on cue, Sharpe tried to get in her face again, this time close enough that she could feel his breath on her. The stare-down continued for a few more seconds before Kacie calmly stated, "Could you be a dear and find out if my lawyer is here yet? I would hate to incriminate myself in the presence of an amateur."

Sharpe pounded on the table and left the room without another word, slamming the door on his way out.

"That bitch is going to make me hurt her!" he yelled, but not loud enough to be heard through the door.

Niki moved to calm him down. "She's pushing your buttons on purpose until her lawyer gets here, Sharpe; don't play to her games."

"I don't think that wait will be too long anymore. Michael Tripp, I will be representing Ms. Porter." The KAP lawyer introduced himself as he walked in. He took a look around, recognizing everyone around him. "I believe we all know each other from the incident at her condo?"

"There was no 'incident,' as you put it," I protested, keeping the calmness in my voice to avoid any problems. "It's not my fault your client has a penchant for wanting to turn a trick at the drop of a hat."

"Mr. Law, your reputation precedes you." He nodded in my direction before he continued. "I'm not particularly thrilled with the tactics that you pulled to get my client to confess to something she didn't do, but there's not much I can do about that right now."

"If you're trying to pull a Fourth challenge, you're cracking me up." I shook my head rebutting. "Your client couldn't help herself around me, admit it. You saw it yourself. She was naked in her house, trying to seduce me, and you have the recording from my phone."

"Yes, I do, and I plan to dissect it to find out what you said to get her to pop," Michael responded as he narrowed his eyes in my direction. He leaned in and whispered low enough for my ears to hear him. "You know your so-called victim asked for it and got scared. Don't let your personal feelings get in the way of justice."

If we were on the street, he would be picking himself off the ground and in dire need of medical attention. I was mindful of my emotions, especially around Niki. He wanted to goad me into a fight, trying to get me to manhandle him so he could get me kicked off the case and get his client off.

He had another thing coming if he thought he could catch me in something so amateurish. Those hotheaded days were long gone.

"I believe you have a client to help unglue the foot from her mouth?" I shooed him into the interrogation room by himself to confer with his client before turning my attention to Sharpe. He was in a corner, using a stress ball and closing his eyes so he could re-center himself. I leaned against the opposite wall to give him a quick pep talk. I felt I owed it to him to try and help him as much as I could.

"Keep it calm; don't get rattled because she's going to want to have you off-balance the entire time," I told him. "Keep the convo tight; she responds to that better than to try and be her friend. She's already figured you're not a lifestyle Dominant, so the more you try to overpower, the more she'll laugh and try to emasculate you."

Sharpe shot me a look like he was ready to kill me.

"I got this, Law," Sharpe snapped back, catching a quick attitude. "I've dealt with harder criminals than this bitch."

In my mind I couldn't help but blurt, *you're gonna blow this case, rookie.* The only thing I could do was watch things unfurl and hope that he didn't shut her down.

"What happened on the night in question?"

"I fucked him after he took care of domestic chores around my condo."

"Tell me how you took him."

"Why should I?"

"Why shouldn't you; you said you have nothing to hide, right?"

I watched this exchange, seeing the angle of the questioning change at least twice as Sharpe tried and failed to get Kacie to crack. Michael sat there in his chair, waiting to stonewall him if he got out of line.

I didn't envy Sharpe's position. I'd been there several times over the years. Once a suspect "lawyers up," it's like prying an oyster open to get to the pearl.

He was determined to get to the pearl.

"Look, there are rules that we adhere to in the BDSM world." Kacie looked like she wanted to put this to an end as soon as possible. She was tired of playing games and was ready to lecture. "When a boi is commanded to follow a directive, he follows it, no questions asked."

"That sounds like coercion to me, Kacie," Sharpe pointed out, and correctly, too, but it was the wrong time to pull that card, and I knew what would come next. "So, did you take that ass because he was obligated to give it to you; since you're a 'Goddess' and all, don't you get paid to do what you do to him?"

"Ease back, detective." Michael sneered. "Her profession has nothing to do with this case."

"Oh, I beg to differ." Sharpe glared at Michael, the expression on his face giving rise to the incredulity of her lawyer's interference in "his" interrogation. "She thinks she's entitled to any man that comes in her direction. I simply want to find out what made this one so special? Since you say you can have any man you want, right?"

Consider the hot-button pressed at that exact moment. Kacie was at the point of eruption, and it showed all over her face. "Look at me, you sorry excuse of a Y chromosome! Men kill to be at my feet! I'm not to be treated like some cheap hooker off the fucking street!"

I didn't know if he did that on purpose or what, but Sharpe got her to open as wide as the Mississippi River. "Maybe he might know what he's doing after all."

Niki grinned, looking up at me for a few moments before returning to the action at hand. "He's a good detective, Sir. Not as good as we were, but he's good."

"That boi loved every minute of it," Kacie continued to talk, despite her lawyer's poking to shut her down. It was obvious her ego was in full swing by now. "I even got it—"

"That's it! This line of questioning is over!" Michael barked, grabbing his things before standing. "Get her over to booking so that she can post bond. We'll see you in court."

As the officers escorted Kacie to the car to take her to booking, I asked them to stop so I could speak to her for a brief moment. "Do you really want to go down this road, Kacie? What are you trying to prove here? You can't win if you go down this road. Don't you care who you burn?"

I wanted her to slow down and think. Call me soft, but there was something about her that made me want to at least help her out of the hole she'd dug for herself. There's no way, there's no happy ending if she continued without remorse. At the very least, she could plea bargain if she showed some contrition.

She was having none of that. She snarled at me as she struggled against the officer's grip, a last act of defiance to let me know how this would end. "No, I don't give a fuck, and I really don't care about anyone in the 'community,' like there is such a fucking thing. I didn't do shit, and it will come out in court. I'll have that boi looking like a slut by the time I get through talking to my lawyer."

"You're not going to like how this ends, Kacie. Just plead out; you'll be out in a year at the most." I warned her a final time, hopeful that the switch would turn on.

"Fuck you!" she spat as she was walked away from me.

Oh well, you couldn't blame a bruh for trying.

I played the last five minutes of the interrogation in my head for a moment before the images began to fade away. Those thoughts intermingled with the revelation that Niki kept hidden until today, about my real reason for leaving the force. My emotions were mixed, fluctuating between confusion and indifference as the images continued to play themselves out, the audio lending the proper soundtrack to give me exactly what I needed to figure out if there was something that might have been missed in the final moments during the confusion.

Niki looked at me curiously as she entered my personal space.

She tried to figure out where my mind was, wondering if I was freestyling silently or not. "There's a piece missing, isn't it, Sir?"

I nodded, trying to figure out what that piece was. I had to focus, so I pushed the other thoughts in my head concerning Niki to the background so that I could think clearly enough to figure out the missing link that could finish this case.

The last part that Kacie had blurted before her lawyer stopped her was interesting to hear, to say the least.

I even got it...wait a fucking minute!

Could she have been that stupid?

Nah, there's no way.

The last thing that tiger had said to me before we'd ended our conversation came ringing in like a church bell.

That was the piece that I missed.

You weren't the first, but you could be the last. We can put her away if we stick together.

I needed to get back into her condo.

Something got hidden in plain sight.

FIFTEEN

"What the fuck is she doing here?"

I sat in my office as I watched Kacie and Tori lock eyes with each other, and Tori had the nerve to cop an attitude. Last time I checked, I wasn't married, and the women in my life, my secretary included, didn't check me like that, so I knew something was amiss with the fire I saw in Tori's eyes.

I wasn't sure if I wanted to be pissed or not, but she was definitely in need of a reality check. "Tori, I don't think popping in on me out of the blue like this was a good idea, Kacie was visiting with me because she was about to make her case a little easier on herself; weren't you, Kacie?"

I honestly saw Kacie soften up for a moment. Well, until she saw Tori stroll through the door.

Call me weak or whatever, I'm not worrying myself with that, but there was something about this case that struck me differently. Yeah, sure, it's still a rape case, there was no denying that, but the problem with rape cases sometimes was that it was not always in black and white.

This case had about four shades of gray all over it.

To be real, I probably wouldn't have had this kind of leeway if I were still on the force. Hell, it was one of the perks of the position. If it weren't for the fact that one of the victims involved in this case was the slave of a very influential Dominant in the kink community, I would have cut a helluva lot of corners and made it all look like an accident.

But, I gotta play by the boss's rules, and that meant trying to find every legal angle I could to take care of this case.

I presented a pretty strong case, if I did say so myself: get Kacie to plea out, covertly help in getting the charges reduced so that she wouldn't have to do the max, although I did leave out the part about her doing five to seven anyway, and everyone would be happy.

Case closed.

Too bad Tori decided she had to see me today. Her mere presence was enough to throw a monkey wrench into my plans.

The moment that Kacie shut down, my chances for wrapping up this case dwindled to slim and none.

"On second thought, Dom, I think I'll take my chances in court," Kacie said as she stood up from where she sat for the prior couple of hours. "Besides, I can't trust you as long as you're connected to *her*."

"What the fuck ever, trick," Tori spat.

"Kacie, is there any way that you could reconsider your decision?" I asked, honestly hoping that she could see the forest instead of the trees.

"Nope, sorry, sexy, you almost had me there, too," Kacie replied, shaking her head as she licked her lips. "It would have been fun, and I'm almost tempted to make her watch…almost."

I let her walk out of the door. There was no point in trying to look desperate. What I put on the table was a good scenario for her to work, but now she's on her own, and I didn't think she's going to like where that ended up.

That was not in my circle of concern, as Niki loved to say.

I turned my attention to Tori, and the look on her face told me everything I needed to know. She was shook, and I rarely have, if ever, seen her look this shaken.

"Who needs to bleed?" I was already in attack mode, and it was only a matter of who needed to feel the pain and which direction I needed to attack.

"There was this goon that showed up at my door this morning," Tori began to explain as I handed her a handkerchief from my suit pocket. "He grabbed my neck before I could react to him, said that I needed to watch myself if I planned on helping you with any cases from here on out."

"You said that he got you at the house, yes?" I asked, allowing my wheels to turn quickly.

"Yes."

"Pull up your surveillance cameras," I ordered, offering her my chair so she could tap into her surveillance system at her office.

The funny thing about heavies or goons was that they really weren't too bright. They were only worried about getting the objective taken care of; they really didn't pay attention to the details...like figuring out if their mark was exposed or if they happened to have any security on hand or anything like that. This fool made things too fucking easy for me.

On the camera playback, there was a guy, looked about six feet eight inches and as solid as a brick wall. He definitely would be the type to shake Tori up, all right.

But I thought I was gonna have to shake him up a little bit.

I quickly put his face up against the database to find out who he was. After a few seconds, his profile came up, including his rap sheet. His name was Trill. He was connected to a small-time wannabe gangster by the name of Vega. I really didn't feel like getting my hands dirty, but I had to know what I was dealing with and why Vega wanted Tori canceled out.

I scanned through the rap sheet, and for the most part, I didn't see anything that would cause me room for alarm, but I was still irked because he decided to pick on a woman.

That was one thing I could not tolerate, and he needed to be dealt with. But I also knew that delicacy needed to be employed also. After all, I was a businessman now.

I put in a call to a couple of "ghosts" that I hadn't called on in a couple of years. I didn't call on them unless the task I had for them was something that required precision removal of trash that had become a nuisance to either me or someone close to me.

Trash removal was definitely on the menu.

"Dominic, I don't want you to put yourself out there for me," Tori explained, softly rubbing my shoulder.

"Oh no, this has to be handled, and quickly," I replied. I was so busy trying to get this dude that I didn't realize that she'd leaned in closer to my ear.

"Thank you, D. I know I give you a hard time, but I knew I could count on you to help me," she remarked as she turned my head and kissed me deeply.

"Tori—" I uttered as I tried to protest, but she kept kissing me, and I didn't refuse her. I honestly didn't want to. However, I was getting to the point to where juggling all these women—even though they all knew about each other—was going to be the death of me if I didn't get a handle on it sometime soon.

I'm not complaining by a long shot, but I knew that eventually something had to give, and someone was going to want more than where they currently were positioned.

I wasn't about to worry about that right then. My focus was solely on taking care of the matter at hand, and doing so quietly and without the cops being called to handle the mess.

"Come on, Sharpshooter, we've been down this road before, and I told you I don't give a fuck about the women in your life, as long as I get mine," Tori retorted, frustrated that she was being rebuffed again. "A girl can only take so much before she starts to get fed up."

"Look, Tori, when I get your situation handled, I will have no problems wearing you out to your heart's content, okay?" I compromised. There was no sense in throwing away good pussy being thrown at you without remorse or regret, right?

"That's more like it, babe." Tori grinned. "Damn it, just the thought of what these rough hands of yours might do to ol' boy. You got me wet thinking about it."

The phone rang before she could get back into whatever groove she was trying to flow into. "Law."

"J-Roc...who's the mark?"

"Vega's heavy...you know him?"

"Yeah, we know him...won't be an easy hit, though, but we got you," J-Roc replied.

"Good, I want this handled quick and quiet, feel me?"

"Yeah, you know how we do, D." He laughed. "You want in on it? Sounds personal from the way you sounded on the message."

I thought about it, and I realized that while I have to keep things on the level, it didn't mean that I didn't have to keep my hands clean all the time. Besides, I was beginning to miss being in the field a little bit, and this was exactly the thing I needed to keep the itch manageable.

Besides, what Ramesses didn't know wouldn't kill him.

"I'm in. Let me know when and where, and we can do this."

SIXTEEN

I needed some downtime. These cases were becoming a pain in the ass.

I decided to take Niki out to Liquid for the Fetish Night that Neferterri hosted in the middle of the week. She got the male strippers to role play with the women while the kinksters mixed in with the hard-core BDSM crowd that loved using the dungeon area that one of the local companies in the community puts together and breaks down in the course of an evening.

I needed to wear my baby out tonight, and get some much needed stress and aggression off my chest.

I checked in with the bouncers to make sure things were on the level and told them I would be here as a patron only, not in any official capacity so they could do their thing without thinking I was grading them out or something.

Niki made sure to dress less for the occasion, and she did not disappoint with the leather baby doll dress that she wore. She was naked underneath the outfit, as I'd specified.

I love it when they follow instructions.

I found Neferterri in the owner's booth above the VIP section near where the dungeon area had been set up. We made our way up, finding shamise in her kneeling position, out of the view of the attendees.

Niki followed suit, dropping to her knees and crawling to the chair next to where Neferterri sat and assumed her kneeling position, never once saying a word.

Neferterri grinned. "Good girl, it looks like the training has been coming along well, Dom."

"Yes, both girls have been doing quite well with shamise's and sajira's instruction and guidance." I gave credit where credit was due; it had nothing to do with me.

Neferterri tapped her hip, and shamise crawled over and kneeled by her. I could see the wistful smile on her face as she was being stroked by her owner. "your Daddy and I are proud of the job you've done with Dom's girls, baby girl. I might let you scene with one of the dungeon masters tonight. Would you like that?"

"Yes, my Goddess," shamise quietly replied as she purred with content with the personal stroking and petting that she immensely enjoyed. The look on her face was priceless. "If it pleases you to observe me in such a capacity?"

"Yes, my precious, I would love to, absolutely," she replied before turning her attention to me. "So, Dom, what brings you out on this special evening? I would have thought you wanted to take a break tonight."

"Actually, m'Lady, I am taking a breather tonight," I assured her, sneaking a look at Niki as I spoke. "I needed to clear my head, and a certain sexy bitch needs to get her fix tonight."

"Well, there's no better way to do that than tonight." Neferterri gloated. "Besides, with Ramesses at home with the kids, I plan to relax and enjoy the evening myself."

"Then I will leave you to it, Ma'am." I tapped my hip to beckon Niki to me.

Once we left the booth, I saw a workbench open up to be used, as someone was cleaning off the fluids before the next person used it.

"Take the bench," I commanded as Niki walked over and straddled the top, resting her knees on the flanks to the sides of the top cushion.

I lifted the dress to expose her naked ass, deciding against strapping her down for the scene. The mental bondage of whispering in her ear that she shouldn't lift or suffer the consequences would be stimulating enough for her. I learned that trick from Ramesses when he and sajira scened once at NEBU.

"Are you ready, slave?"

"Yes, my Master."

"Count off as I strike you," I commanded again.

"*One*, Sir...*two*, Sir...*three*, Sir," she yelled after my hands connected with her ass cheeks. She rotated and grinded her hips with every smack I laid on her, which enticed me to smack her harder. I noticed the crowd that formed as the barehanded spanking scene we performed became the center of attention. Not what I had in mind, but I wasn't about to stop my groove because everyone else wanted to stop and gawk.

"*Eight*, Sir...*nine*, Sir...*ten*, Sir," she continued, letting a moan escape with each number she counted. I felt her skin heat up, and the reddish hue that formed excited me as I wanted to leave marks in the shape of my handprints on both of her cheeks.

As I was about to really get into a rhythm with the music that was playing, I heard one of the bodyguards yell for assistance. I snapped out of my zone and rushed toward where the problem seemed to be, completely forgetting that I left Niki on the bench.

I got over to the space where the incident occurred, and the bouncers had both men held up and apart from each other, subduing them to keep from rushing each other again.

"What's the trouble, gentlemen? You know there is no fighting inside this establishment," I queried.

"This jackass tried to use my knives on his slave!" the accuser yelled out over the music.

I felt Niki's hand caressing my shoulder to alert me to her presence, and I grabbed her hand to keep my aggression in check.

"I never touched your shit, partner!" the other man yelled back. "You better be glad anyone wanted to play with your dull-ass shit, playa!"

"All right, cool it!" I found myself having to yell over the music, too. "Let's take this somewhere private and quieter so we can get this all straightened out."

"Naw, that's all right, I'm blazing the spot," the one making the accusations said. "It was fun until this dumbass fucked over protocol."

I took a quick picture with my cell phone to get a facial recognition on both of them, using the link with the computers at the office to get a quicker match. Neferterri doesn't allow anyone on the premises without membership and ID.

A couple of seconds later, the match came up, and I called them both by names left on the membership listings.

"Sir Pyrrhic and Sir Magic, yes?" I called out, and it shut them down quick. "That's what I thought. If you both follow me so we can squash this and these good folks can go back to their enjoyment, please?"

* * *

"You were there that night, so talk."

I stalled for about twenty minutes as I sent a text to Natasha to get over to Liquid with her partner so they could question Sir Pyrrhic themselves.

Come to find out, when I hit the Liquid database for facial recognition, it tripped the other databases at NEBU, Deshret and the Thebes compounds simultaneously. Pyrrhic's name popped up immediately, which had me cross-reference against the email list for the party that night. That match made me stall long enough to get Natasha and Trish here.

"I don't know what you're talking about." Pyrrhic tried to blow off the initial statement from Trish.

I stayed in the back, keeping Niki at my side, enjoying the second interrogation that I didn't have to do today as it unfolded.

Trish leaned in closely enough for Pyrrhic to get a good look at her chest as it sat prominently in front of him. "We've got your email as a part of a list for a submissive known as safi. We know she emailed you to join a farewell party; we picked up your IP address from our computer forensics team an hour ago."

I knew she was lying about the computer forensics team because they were still trying to figure it out, but he didn't have to know all that. Besides, he didn't look too bright anyway. It was a matter of time before he'd start singing.

"Look, we have you dead to rights; just tell us what you know and we can make it easy for you," Natasha chimed in. "We'll even tell the ADA that you were cooperative."

"ADA, what the hell? Am I a suspect or something?" Pyrrhic panicked, his eyes darting from Trish to Natasha and back. "Look, all I did was help the slut fulfill her last fantasy before she gave herself to that washed up Het-hotep, okay? That's all I did."

"I don't buy it," I interjected for a moment. "safi said in the email to you all that you should let bygones be bygones and do this one last thing with her. That tells me that you might have had an ax to grind with her for her to say that to any of you."

"Look, safi screwed me over, but I didn't kill her." Pyrrhic was in flat-out denial mode. Whatever it took to take the heat off him, he was willing to do it.

"Who said anyone was killed?" Trish started in on him. "Do you really want this to get dirty for you? I can do dirty; I have no problems at all."

Why the hell that turned me on, I'll never know.

Pyrrhic all of a sudden started singing like a caged bird with nothing left to lose. "Look, she told me she would take care of her after I left. I wanted to get sum, maybe a cream pie for the road or something kinky like that, but safi wasn't feeling it, and I left pissed off because...I mean, damn, I ain't no slouch, but why she have to drop everyone for his decrepit ass?"

"Who is she?" Natasha hammered him. "Tell us who she is."

Pyrrhic tried to shut down, but once Trish put her gun on the table with the barrel cocked back and pointed at him, he started whining again, his eyes widening in my direction. "What the fuck, man? You just gonna let them dog me like this? I thought you were supposed to be looking out for us kink folk, man?"

I was so wrapped up in Niki that I didn't really pay all that much attention to what was going on. I honestly half-heard the whole exchange. "What? Oh, you're fine, dude, you have information that they need to solve a murder; just give them what they want and you can go. Do you wanna go to jail or do you wanna go home?"

"Man, fuck it, she ain't worth this shit," Pyrrhic cursed and then closed his eyes as he tried to hold back tears.

And this was a Dominant? Really?

"Look, I stuck around for a few, you know, trying to get a sneak peek at some shit because I ain't really seen two women on the jump-off before," Pyrrhic recounted. "She was texting with someone for like five or ten minutes while safi was masturbating on the table."

"You still haven't said her name, bruh," I reprised, trying to sound like I was the instigator in the whole exchange. "Tell 'em something; there should be more."

Trish picked up her gun and pressed it under his chin, placing her foot between his legs and calmly said, "So, what's up, you gonna chirp some more or what, pretty birdie?"

I missed this part of the investigations the most. The grimy and gutter shit and being able to hide behind the shield and pretend it didn't happen.

I watched with amusement as Pyrrhic's eyes widened by the second, darting between looking down the barrel of the gun in her hand and glancing at the cleavage protruding from her blouse. Niki didn't budge from her spot at my feet, content to watch the whole scene work to its conclusion. I did notice a small smile form on her face, which tipped me off that she missed getting a little dirty, too.

Still, watching ol' boy shake was fun to witness.

"This is some bullshit, man; what the fuck happened to police harassment or some shit, huh?" Pyrrhic protested some more until he felt the point of Trish's shoe touching sensitive areas that need not be talked. "All right, all right, her name is Domina Torina. Now if you back the fuck up and let me get my phone, I can get the fucking number out of my phone, all right?"

Trish pulled back and eased the hammer down on her gun before putting it back in its holster on her shoulder. "Okay, you can get us the digits now, and you better not be lying to us, or I'll be back personally to pump your ass full of lead."

Now that was hot, and I couldn't contain myself. Hey, it's not my fault impromptu interrogations like that get my blood pumping. Watching two sexy female detectives handling business like that only made it worse on my libido.

As Pyrrhic and Trish got everything together, I called Natasha over to me. "You know it turned me on to see you grinding like you did right there."

Natasha giggled, kissing me across the lips before kissing Niki. "Why, thank you, my Master. I do love it when you're pleased with me. Now, I need to get the info that Trish pulled and see where this lead goes."

SEVENTEEN

It's three in the morning, and I sat in an unmarked unit, on a stakeout in front of Kacie's condo.

I waited there for four hours for her to come out of her place and head out for her day. I'd had birdies following her every move for the last three days to establish some sort of pattern that would give me a large enough window to slip in and slip out.

Yes, I promised Ramesses that I would do this by the book and stay within the lines, so to speak, but sometimes you can't always do that if you need to get things done.

Kacie didn't want to play fair, so why should I?

I gave a shout to Ty and kept him on the Bluetooth so he could walk me through a few things.

"What's good, D?" Ty came clear through the piece.

"Mr. Alexander wanted me to use your under-the-table services, bro. Are you up for it?"

"You know! What's the job?" Ty sounded like he was already getting the laptop jump-started, like he was waiting for this opportunity.

I loved dudes that could get rolling on the fly. But Ty was my man from way back, so I didn't expect any less from him.

"I gotta get some evidence that was hidden at the crime scene on another case we're working…video evidence. You think you can help me pull the data files?"

"Man, I didn't realize this would be that easy." Ty laughed for a moment, then got down to business. "All I need you to do is find the base station; I can take care of the rest."

"That's a bet."

I finally saw her garage door open up and her car pull out into the driveway. I took the Night-vision scopes that I had in the passenger seat to confirm that she was in the car. Once I got that out of the way, the minute she drove down the street, I got out of my truck and made my way to the side of the condo.

I put on an outfit that might have helped in case I had nosey neighbors checking for anyone that might have been messing with homes or cars. The outfit I wore gave me the look of a Georgia Power employee to keep things on the level. The way this neighborhood looked, I needed the edge in case someone got skittish.

I know what you're thinking…impersonation and illegalities and such.

I'll deal with that later, if I get caught…keyword: *if.*

I took out my cell phone and accessed one of my apps, a handy little app that I affectionately call my "all-access pass." I won't bore you with the details of how I got it, but let's say I can disarm and re-arm any wireless alarm system that's out there, simply by having the signal from my phone coordinate with the home system's signature, acting as the homeowner's phone to disarm the system.

I was in the house in less than two minutes.

"Okay, the base station should be somewhere close…somewhere where she can access it quick and still be able to hide it from plain sight." Ty coached me through the search-and-destroy mission. "Get me a camera so I can splice in and keep an eye on the perimeter while you do your thing."

With that in mind, I checked a few of the spots where I thought I saw a camera the last time I was here with Kacie. Sure enough, the camera that conveniently "disappeared" when the police arrived was suddenly in its spot, hidden in plain sight by a stack of books on a bookcase.

I guess she was that stupid after all.

I did a quick splice into the camera so that Ty could get control of the whole system. It was cool to have eyes on this setup. Ramesses was right. He might be good to use for future cases, definitely.

I made a beeline for the dungeon room in her home. I used infrared to pick up where that room was while I was on the stake-out. I was also trying to find the base station to where all of the cameras were centralized.

What? I told you we upgraded a few things.

Anyway, I started rolling through the equipment on her wall, trying to take great care not to disturb things to find the other camera. Usually with hidden cameras, the person taping tried to find the right angle to get what they want. I found that camera hidden under a whip that had been coiled in such a way that no one would ever suspect the camera was there.

I'm sure there were others, but I needed to find the base station. There could only be two places where it could be: in the master bedroom or in an office or somewhere.

"Still no sign of the station, bro. I'm going to check another spot in the house that I think it might be," I told Ty.

"Cool, I still got you on the outside perimeter, D. No activity out here," Ty said as he monitored the spliced cameras.

I took a gamble on the master bedroom because I didn't want to waste time. I wanted to be in there no longer than I had to.

Okay, Law, where the hell is the base camera? I asked myself as I quickly scanned the room. My ears heard a *click* and tipped me off to the closet area immediately.

I opened the closet door and after moving some clothes out of the way, I spotted a small door, likely big enough to hold a safe or something similar. I pulled the door open and found the source of the clicking sound I heard.

Bingo!

The base station I was looking for, complete with the split-screen monitor to watch all of the cameras at once. Looked like she had about twenty different cameras inside and outside the house, including the front foyer area where the incident with tiger had occurred.

"Gotcha, trick," I said out loud.

I slipped out of the bedroom and hurried to the window that I'd climbed in from, making sure that I reset the alarm once I got back outside.

"D, watch your six, some dude just popped up out of the blue," Ty warned quickly. "He's wearing some weird ass get-up. Watch yourself."

On my way back around to the front of the condo, I ran into one of Kacie's neighbors who happened to be heading to the front door. He must have been the one Ty was talking about.

His outfit gave him away.

Now, considering the lateness of the hour, and two men being at the same place at the same time, it was safe to imagine what the awkward opening lines to spark conversations would be. Add to the fact that the dude was wearing a men's leather corset and matching pants, and the convo would be especially fun.

I know you're dying to ask how I knew that he was her neighbor.

Well, she wasn't the only one I was observing while I was on the stakeout tonight. I didn't expect him to come calling at four in the morning, especially when his wife and kids were still asleep.

Yeah, I paid that much attention, sue me.

"Ummm, hello, who might you be?" the dude asked me, trying to hide himself like he thought I was some other vanilla dude that wouldn't understand. "I was checking to see if Kacie was home."

"Well, I'm one of the meter techs from Georgia Power," I said as I quickly pointed toward the patch on my shirt. "I'm rolling through on the monthly inspections as usual, sir."

"Oh, well, okay, then I would guess you can carry on." he dismissed me just that quickly with that statement. "It looks dark in the house. I don't think she's home."

"I'm only here to check the meters, sir. I wouldn't know what she looked like to tell you if she's home or not." I played it real thick like I was some square that didn't know anything about anything. "If you will excuse me, I'll be on my way now."

"Okay, well, enjoy the rest of your work day," he responded, relaxing because I didn't immediately gawk at his outfit. "I guess I'll check with her later on today."

"Yes, sir, have a good day," I said as I casually moved on to the next meter to act like I was checking the gauges. I could feel his eyes on me, but he never saw me go into the house, so even if he tried to snitch, he wouldn't be able to say much to her.

"That was interesting," I said through the earpiece as I heard Ty laughing hysterically over the connection. "Did you get the info that I was able to pull off the feed?"

"Bro, I even picked up the archival footage that her dumb ass left for masturbatory material." Ty scoffed. "Man, don't these people ever learn to safeguard their shit better than this?"

I laughed at that statement. Before I started up with Ramesses, I was one of those dumbasses that thought that if I deleted it and put it in the recycle bin and did a quick reboot, that it was gone forever.

I'm glad I never found out the hard way how stupid that strategy was.

"Thanks for the backup, bro. I need to get this over to the DA's office ASAP," I told Ty. "Keep your ears to the ground. There may be some more work down the line for you."

"You ain't said but a word, D," Ty replied. "Now I need to get a couple of hours of sleep before work. Peace."

I called Niki soon after I saw the dude leave and go back to his house. Based on her normal routine, she would be up because she usually likes to take a long bath before going to work.

"Yes, Master, what is your command of me?" She immediately answered on the second ring.

"If I told you that the search warrant that you guys had was not wide enough to find what you needed, would you be able to go back to the DA and get a more specific warrant?" I asked.

"In a heartbeat, Master," she replied sharply. "Tell me what you found."

"I can show you better than I can tell you when you get that warrant," I told her. "And I mean literally speaking, of course. Now, if you would excuse me, baby girl, I have some unfinished business to handle with the other case. I have a big fish to fry."

"Yes, Master, I understand," Niki cooed over the phone. "Happy hunting, as your Mentor would say."

EIGHTEEN

"Dominic Law. What the fuck are you doing here? You're out of your jurisdiction, partner."

I stood in Vega's office inside of a warehouse that he used as a chop shop with J-Roc at my side, acting as my heavy to combat Trill if things went south.

I looked around at all the cars being sliced up and prepared for the parts sale and I wanted to vomit. APD would give me a commendation for reporting this place, but Vega's lawyers would have the charges overturned in court because I wasn't an officer anymore, and there was no probable cause for me to be there to report it in the first place.

That didn't mean I wouldn't drop a dime anonymously, of course. How I found out about the place didn't have to be anyone's business but my own. J-Roc, however, was my ear to the streets, and his contacts tipped him off to where Vega would be.

Trill never left Vega's side except when he was taking care of some work for his employer. The birds that I kept around the area kept watch over their every movement, making sure to let us know when the right moment was to have this meeting.

Some of the employees that were handling the work were from my old neighborhood. I nodded at each one of them as we passed by on the way to Vega's office. A lot of them knew I wasn't a cop anymore, and they tipped the others that were grabbing for the heat that I wasn't here for them.

I was here for Vega.

From the look in Vega's eyes and the scowl on his face, things had the potential to go south, and with the quickness if we weren't careful.

Considering that J-Roc was as large as Trill made no never mind to me. I could have him singing a permanent lullaby if he thought he wanted to get the drop on me.

I was nobody's fool, either. Trill was carrying some heat of his own, and he would not hesitate to use it. We both needed to be aware of that.

Vega reminded me of Money Mike from the movie *Friday After Next*, except he was nowhere near as funny and had a Napoleonic complex for the ages. I didn't take him for granted, though. The smallest men usually carried the most lethal weapons on them.

"It's amazing who knows your name when you do a quick Q&A with some folks on the street." I cracked a smirk as Vega leaned back in his chair. "Is it okay to sit down, or is this going to take a quick second and I won't need to sit?"

"Oh, by all means, my brother, have a seat," Vega replied, his eyes on me the entire time. "Your bodyguard can take a load off, too. I'm sure his feet have to be tired from having to protect you twenty-four-seven."

Now, who was he kidding? Did I really look like the bitch that he saw in the mirror or something?

J-Roc laughed to himself and replied, "No thanks, bruh, I got a lot more stamina than you think."

Vega cut a side-glance back at J-Roc and then got down to business. "So, Law, what brings you by here? Considering you don't bang heads for the police anymore, I would have figured that you wouldn't want to be bothered with the likes of us upwardly mobile criminal types."

Katt Williams? I think not.

He laughed at his own joke, and Trill laughed right along with him, but after a few seconds of watching the deadpan looks on our faces, his expression changed within seconds. "Okay, so you're not into comedy, so you must be here on some business that I don't know about. So, out with it, Law, I'm a busy man."

"Tori Glover," I simply stated, leaving no room for mumbling.

"And that bitch means what to me?" Vega asked, looking irritated. "I don't know anyone by that name. You fucking her or something, because if this is what this shit is about, I got enough bitches on my own not to worry about new pussy."

"It means you will not have your errand boy delivering messages at her doorstep again, are we clear?" I commanded, giving a look up at Trill, who looked away for a minute after realizing that he'd been caught. "You really should train your muscle a little better. More stealth, less 'bull in a china shop,' you feel me?"

Vega looked at Trill and shook his head. "That bitch was sticking her nose into business that wasn't hers," he quipped, staring directly at me. "And don't take my hospitality for weakness, either, punk. I'll have you sliced and diced before you set one foot up outta here if you come with demands again, okay?"

I really hated it when I had to prove a point, but I had to put this wannabe gangster in his place.

"You sound like because I'm not a cop anymore that I don't have resources." I flashed a grin at him that seemed to make him flinch a little bit. I grinned wider and asked, "Do you think that makes me less dangerous, or more dangerous?"

"It makes you a mark that needs to be deleted, frankly." Vega sneered as his snapped his fingers. Trill all of a sudden stepped forward, prompting J-Roc to counter his advance on me.

"Before you consider deleting anyone, I think you might want to double-check a few things, Vega." I stayed seated as I began to explain.

"What the fuck do I need to double-check, Law? You're in my warehouse, in case you forgot," Vega countered as his eyes tried to bore a hole in my chest.

"Well, the way I see it, you and your errand boy might need to ease back a few feet," I explained as I turned my head toward the door. "You see, you might wanna be careful about the men you employ."

"These are my soldiers from way back, Law; what the fuck makes you think I need to double-check them?" Vega asked, standing up from behind his desk this time. "You're the motherfucker that's caught in a sling right now, so you might wanna watch what you say."

I looked at J-Roc for a second, and all he did was grin a little after the text that he sent.

Time to drop the curtain.

"Okay, why don't you watch what I say right now," I stated as I rose up over his half-pint, sawed-off frame. "Check over my left shoulder, and tell me what you see."

Vega slid his gaze to my right, and what he saw shocked him a bit. He didn't want to admit what his eyes saw, but there was no denying the reality of the situation.

His shop was completely empty.

Even Trill paused for a moment, trying to figure out exactly what had happened.

"Now that I have your attention, let me see if I can spell this out for your dumb ass." I smiled as I leaned in closer for him to hear me. "Breathe wrong in Tori's direction again and I'll personally see to it that you disappear, got it?"

"You may think that you have the upper hand now, Law, but I promise you by the time you see me again, you'd wished you never stepped to me." Vega smiled back like he hadn't been spooked.

"Okay, you think this is a game or something? That's cool; we can play games. I'm one helluva chess player myself," I uttered as I clicked a button hidden under my watch. "You should have seen this coming in two moves. Checkmate."

All of a sudden, FBI agents stormed the area and came rushing into the office.

"What the fuck is this about?" Vega yelled as he was planted face-first onto his desk. "We haven't done anything wrong, officers!"

"Oh, I beg to differ, considering the parts lying around in your shop, bruh," I snapped, pointing the other agents in the direction of the half-chopped cars sitting in the bays and on the lifts. "After all, theft and receipt of government property is a federal offense, not to mention distribution."

"You can't get away with this! My lawyer will have me out in a week, and then I'm coming for you!" Vega yelled as the agents took him away.

"You do that, and I'll see you in about ten to fifteen, especially with your rap sheet," I yelled out after him before looking at Trill. "You might wanna plead out before your former employer does. You know what they say: the canary that sings the loudest gets the best deal."

NINETEEN

"Sir, I need a favor."

"Go ahead, Dom."

"I need Sin to bring tiger to the office, and this time I want her in the room with us."

"Is this on the level?" Ramesses asked.

"On the level, Sir. There's no choice in the matter," I replied bluntly. "Some new evidence will be coming to light soon, and I need to know what we're up against."

"Say no more, Sir, I'm on the horn in ten seconds." He quickly hung up the phone.

I was on the way into the office from the south side, doing a routine check of NEBU for the weekend events so that the boys would be prepared for the upcoming madness as usual. I was a little bit distracted because of what I'd found at Kacie's house, and I was trying to figure out how to spin this to get tiger to loosen up and not shut down on me.

Whatever Niki and her detectives found at the location would be crucial; I was certain of that. That made this next interview with tiger even more compelling.

Since I was in multitask mode, I called Natasha at her desk at the precinct to catch up on a few things on the homicide to see the latest.

"Yes, Sir, we're still waiting on the results to get back from the autopsy. The M.E. has been swamped with bodies this week," Natasha explained over the phone. "We're doing what we can to lean on the office without pissing off anyone that would get back to Cap or Lieu to chew us out."

"Any other leads that have come up right now, or are you working on the one that Pyrrhic gave up?" I queried.

"We're trying to locate the woman that he mentioned, yes, Sir," Natasha continued, clearly trying to keep things professional with other ears listening in. "She has proven to be a bit elusive, but we think we have the primary location where she will be tomorrow."

"Good, that will give me time to get this second interview done with tiger," I responded as I took the exit ramp to where the office was located.

"Yes, Sir, Trish and I will catch up with you then to handle that." Natasha wrapped up the conversation. "I'm looking forward to that scheduled meeting later this evening to take care of some tests that haven't been completed also."

I couldn't stop grinning at that last little slip-in. "So, someone's in need to complete a few more tests, yes?"

"Yes, Sir, things have been a little soft lately, and they could use a little tightening up," she teased. "I would hope that a few marks will help also, but I want to make sure that is agreeable so that I can prepare for whatever marks are given for the tests I would undergo. I also want to make sure that the usual audience is present."

"Consider it done, and let me know when you're able to locate Torina," I finally uttered as I hung up.

I got the call back from Ramesses almost as soon as I hung up the cell with Natasha. "Looks like Sin beat us to the punch, Dom," he said, sounding perturbed. "Taliah said she's been waiting for us to find out what the latest is on the investigation."

"Is that a good thing or a bad thing?" I had to ask. Sin's behavior can be completely unpredictable when she wants things her way and feels out of control. Not a good look when patience and prudence was the name of the game.

"I guess we'll find out when we get there. Taliah didn't sound distressed, so, be prepared for anything."

I got there a slight bit behind Ramesses, as I saw him escorting them to the main conference room. I would have preferred the "cage" for interrogations and such, but I didn't want to spook tiger at all. He was still the victim in all of this, and I didn't want him thinking he would be put on trial.

"Thank you for waiting for us; we were on the way in to meet up with you," Ramesses lied through his teeth. He sat down at the conference table and invited Sin and tiger to join us. "There are some more questions that Dom and I need to ask tiger, and Dom has requested that you be here for the follow-up, Sin."

Upon hearing that, I saw two different reactions.

Sin was relieved that she wouldn't be kept out of the loop this time around. The first time around was hard on her, especially when I'd told her I wouldn't divulge anything from that talk.

tiger reacted completely different from his Mistress. His eyes darted from me to Ramesses, trying to figure out why Sin wouldn't be isolated this time. I needed to see his reaction to confirm what I already suspected.

I hated when I was right.

I lit into tiger before he could get comfortable. "How dare you try to hide behind your station!"

Sin was taken aback by my rough edge. "Dom, what is the meaning of this? Why are you berating him like this?"

"Because he's not telling everything, and I can't help him if he can't tell us everything, right here and right now." I kept up my routine to keep Ramesses off guard also so that Sin wouldn't catch on to the slight misdirection. It was for tiger's own good, whether he wanted to believe it or not.

Ramesses tried to settle the room down, completely oblivious to what I had done. "Sin, I trust Dominic, and if he says there's something missing from the puzzle, then he's got to find the pieces. Let him go to work."

I knew I would have to explain myself after they'd gone, but for now, he would have to let me take the point on this one and provide the wingman support.

"What else happened that night, tiger, and no BS this time; I'll know if you're lying to me."

tiger remained steadfast in his denial; that much I expected from him. "I was raped that night. She dropped me with one of the wooden paddles. What else do you need, Sir?"

"I need the other part that you're trying to leave out because your Mistress is here, tiger." I dug in on him, leaning over the table for effect. "Either you can tell us here, or you can talk to the ADAs that are working the case. I can tell you now, neither Niki nor Jason will be half as gracious as I am."

His eyes widened, and I sensed panic in his body language. Sending another submissive to do the dirty work was a low blow, yes, but it was necessary now. There was no one to hide behind, and knowing Niki, she'd completely roll through him.

Sin looked like she'd been caught on the outside looking in and she was completely out of the loop on the insider information. "What is he talking about, tiger? What are you not saying?"

tiger's shoulders slumped, signaling that he now knew there was no other way out of this. I knew what he was dealing with, and it would be hard. He looked up at Sin as his eyes welled up with tears, and recounted the entire incident, straight with no chaser.

"I followed the protocol to the letter, at first," he began, looking more at his hands than at anyone in the room. "I did the usual stuff, different things around the house, different cleaning tasks and such, nothing out of the ordinary. Even the outfit was not exactly supposed to inspire any arousal; I just wore leather shorts."

"What happened next, tiger?" I kept asking shorter questions, as I didn't want to interrupt the flow.

"Do you really think this is necessary, gentlemen?" Sin tried to protect her slave, and I could understand where she was coming from. I would want to protect mine, too, but this was beyond any control that we had at that point.

"No, Mistress, this has to be out there. I need to make sure my conscience is clear." tiger kissed the back of Sin's hand, a silent gesture for her to realize that he would be fine.

"Continue, tiger, let's have the rest of it," I encouraged. I received a text message about a second after I spoke, and upon checking the message, I knew I needed to get the whole account. It was the only way that he would get justice of any sort.

"After I finished with the chores, Edge tasked me to run her bubble bath and to wash her," tiger explained, still looking at his hands and avoiding eye contact. "During the bath, she commanded me to arouse her while in the water. At first, I hesitated, but then she said she would tell Mistress that I disobeyed her if I didn't. With that over my head, I basically finger-fucked her to orgasm several times, while washing her at the same time."

Sin tensed up immediately, and tiger placed his hand over hers to calm her. I marveled at the way he was able to flip the power exchange, giving me a new-found respect for his station. It was difficult for me to deal with male submissives or slaves, and he single-handedly changed my perception from the weakling that I thought they were.

"After taking care of that task, I began to clean up the bathroom before going home." tiger finally began to look in my direction, as if he needed to draw some strength from me to get through the next part of what he had to say. "That's when she tried me the first time. She started to caress my body, realizing that I had gotten excited and hard from making her come so much. She whispered in my ear that I deserved a reward for being such a good boi."

"What?" Sin blurted. I placed my index finger to her lips so that tiger could keep talking.

"I immediately pulled away to try and grab a towel for her because she was still naked and soaking wet, and I had yet to dry her," tiger kept rattling off, undeterred by his Mistress's protestations. "I did my best to contain my libido while I dried her off, and she kept trying to put her hands on me the entire time, trying to keep me stimulated."

"When did all of this foreplay eventually lead you to the front door?" Ramesses needed tiger to cut to the chase. Frankly speaking, so did I, but I was obviously more willing to be patient to get to the punch line in this twisted joke.

"After I dried her off, I rushed into the foyer, where I'd left my clothing, and tried to get dressed," tiger replied to Ramesses's question. "Since the shorts didn't belong to me, I took those off before I finished putting my clothes on."

"So that's how the incident began? She found you naked in the foyer and tried to take you then?" I asked to keep him flowing since he felt that I would be able to keep him going.

"Yes, Sir, that's where it happened," he continued on, speaking like he were on auto-pilot. "She grabbed my dick and whispered in my ear that I was going to fuck her. I immediately told her that I couldn't do that because it wasn't a part of the parameters set by her and Mistress. The whole time, she kept stroking my dick, trying to keep me hard, and I couldn't help myself. I—"

"It's okay, baby, I'm not upset anymore." Sin began to realize, as we all did, that this was a power play, not rough sex. "Let it go."

"I came all over the floor," he said as he exhaled hard. The tears began soon after, but he refused to let his voice reflect what he must have been feeling inside. "She saw that, and she said that it didn't matter what my mind wanted, my body told her otherwise, and she was going to take it whether I wanted her to or not.

"I tried to struggle free, and that's when I felt the sharp pain against the back of my head." He kept his eyes fixed with mine, somehow using me as a crutch to get to the end. "I couldn't get my bearings, but I felt my arms locked behind my back, and it was then that I realized I was in trouble.

"I just let her do what she wanted." tiger shook his head, trying to shake the memories out of his mind. "I never made a sound, and she damn sure didn't care because she made enough noise for the both of us, screaming and coming all crazy and shit. If I had known that she was trying to set me up for the bullshit, I would have left out naked and dressed in my car.

"She finally cut the binds off my wrists and sat in the corner to come down from her high from fucking me." He looked as if he was ready to wretch as he got the final parts of the account out of his mouth. "As I left, she mentioned that she would tell Mistress that I was a good boi for her, good to the last climax."

"I'll kill her," Sin flatly stated. "You better hope the cops get to her before I do."

"Sin, let us handle this." I locked eyes with her. "It won't help matters if you go off half-cocked. That's what she wants you to do, trust me."

"I don't care, Dom; that bitch will pay by MY hand." Sin wouldn't be deterred, and she was getting more animated by the second. "I'll deal with the consequences after, but this shit has to be dealt with."

"So, tell me, what about tiger?" Ramesses asked. "Do you think coming for the person that did this on his behalf will help him heal? Do you think some get back and taking the consequences will do him any good when you're behind bars?"

Ramesses walked over to Sin and grabbed her by the shoulders. "Understand that I know this shit is not easy for me, either. You're part of the Family. It's the reason why I told Dom to keep this on the level. We could have handled this in a different way and made it look like an accident."

"What will you have me do, Ramesses?" Sin looked completely exasperated. She struggled to avoid the tears that would manifest whenever she was frustrated. "I can't just sit and do nothing."

"Mistress, I need you to do what you have been doing," tiger finally said, wrapping his arms around her waist. "This is not going to be an easy process. I need you."

"He's right, Sin. The defense attorney is going to pull out all stops on this," I told her before turning my attention back to tiger once we all sat down again. "Thank you for telling me what happened, all of it this time. The reason I needed you to tell me everything was based on a text that I received from Niki. They got tapes from that night, and a few others also."

The whole room got quiet…eerily quiet.

"She videotaped the damn thing?" Sin was absolutely beside herself. "I don't want those shown in open court, Dominic. The damage that could be done—"

"Wait, she was that stupid?" Ramesses raised an eyebrow. "I mean, really? She never struck me as the type to want to collect trophies like that. Do you know what that means?"

"Yes, she just fucked herself," I replied with a grin on my face. "She thought that she hid everything from officers when the original warrant was issued. But I got the ADAs to convince a judge to go back in."

"I don't want to know anything more." Sin stopped me dead in my tracks before I could say another word. "If this is how the bitch gets stopped, then let's do this."

"It's not that simple, Sin, and Ramesses can back me up on this," I told her, looking at tiger before I made my next statement. "You said something about another that hit you up by phone about you not being the only one, right?"

"As a matter of fact, I got an email from someone yesterday." tiger snapped his fingers like he'd meant to say something earlier. "I don't know if it's the same person that was on the phone, but he said that he was scared to say something to anyone when it happened to him, and if I came to the DA's office, he would come, too."

"Then we need to get that email," Ramesses said. "The more, the merrier, and the more time she can spend locked away."

TWENTY

"I need to talk to you, Sir."

This conversation was a couple of days in the making, and I was pissed with myself that it took this long to have it.

"What's on your mind, Dominic?" Ramesses asked after ending a call. He leaned forward on his desk, resting his elbows on the desktop. "You look conflicted about something."

"Conflicted" didn't even sound like the right word, but it was the closest thing that came to how I felt.

I wanted Ayanna, but I wanted to figure out why I wanted her so badly.

I couldn't stop thinking about her, having her again, even though I'd been with Niki and Natasha almost all week long, and I was beginning to think that I'd been losing my mind or something.

"Sir, it's about Ayanna," I began, trying to figure out where this anxiety was coming from. "We've been together, sexually speaking, recently. I'm a little at a loss as to what to make of what's going on with me. She's invaded my thoughts when I'm not with either of the girls, and I don't know what to make of it."

Ramesses raised an eyebrow, which put me on the defensive immediately. He leaned back in his chair and remarked, "Taliah told me something went down between you two. From the moans that she heard coming from your office, she did the math and came to her own conclusions."

I nodded, trying to mask the outright disturbance that I felt in the pit of my stomach. "Sir, I can explain—"

"Look, Dom, I'm the last person to give a fuck about who does who and for what, okay?" Ramesses flatly said. "I'm surprised that you hadn't figured out that Taliah has been in service to me, and not only as my executive assistant."

Now my mind was blown. "Ramesses, wait a minute, you and Taliah?"

He shook his head and chuckled. "Neferterri hand-picked her for the position because she wanted to make sure that anyone that works that closely with me needs to be someone that she can trust."

"Okay, now I really am confused," I admitted, leaning back in my chair this time.

"Okay, kid, let me hip you to things…the reason Taliah and Ayanna are here at our service in a professional capacity is that she knows that we are tremendous flirts, for starters," Ramesses continued. "She needed women here to look after us, in a manner of speaking, and what better way to do that than to have submissives handling those duties."

"So, you mean to tell me that Ayanna was hand-picked for me by Neferterri?" I asked, feeling a bit put off for a moment. "How the hell did she know that Ayanna would be a good fit for me?"

He laughed out loud at that statement, taking a sip of his water to try and calm down a little. "How do you think Taliah was such a good fit for me? Women know other women, just like men know other men, especially when it comes to this realm."

He leaned forward on his desk again, this time a little more serious before he spoke again. "I have a hard question for you. Are you collecting? Are there any other females that you are considering at this moment?"

Collecting, by consensus meaning within the BDSM community,

was when a Dominant added submissives to his or her charge without conscience or awareness of how they might mesh with the submissives already in his or her charge.

I folded my arms and huffed, "No, Sir, Ayanna means a lot more than that to me."

"Good man, I want to make sure that is the case, because I don't want Ayanna in a bad position, especially considering she lost her best friend," Ramesses made clear, which tripped my red flags. Did he know something more than what he originally let on?

He must have been reading my body language, because he said, "Relax, Dominic, your secret is safe with me, and for the record, your boy, the IT tech over at the DA's office, tipped me off to the emails between safi and Ayanna. Oh, and while we're at it, I know about the shit you pulled on behalf of your girl, Tori, the other day with that idiot, Vega. You're getting soft in your old age, aren't you? Usually I would have heard about you getting locked up or something."

I hated when he did that, but it's difficult to get anything past him; I should have figured that out by now.

But old age? He was older than me by a couple of years, so he was the last person to be calling someone old.

"I ought to take you inside the ring trying to call me out like that, Sir," I joked, trying to recover a little from the information purge that he'd dropped in my lap like I'd put a few over on him. I guess he was going to find out sooner or later anyway.

"I don't think you want all that, young'un," Ramesses laughed again. "Don't let the smooth and calm demeanor fool you. Remember, I wasn't always like this."

Yeah, I had to remember that, especially when we were teenagers and he had an itchy trigger finger and a temper to match it. I always wondered back then if he would ever calm down.

I guess growing up will do that to a man sometimes.

Marriage and kids would do that, too.

I still wanted some balance, so I took the opening that he gave me to begin my line of questioning.

"You said that you didn't know if you would have gone to the get-together that safi set up a few days ago." I set up the question that I wanted to ask. "I need to know, did you really have no clue that safi was not going to be in Atlanta? I have a hard time believing that of all the people we've kept surveillance on, she was the one to slip your eyes."

Ramesses's facial expression changed from disbelief to surrender in a matter of minutes. He rubbed his hands over his face as if it was about to be confession time. "The truth is…I did not know, and the reason I did not know is that I left a forty-eight-hour window open in which I did not check her emails, nor did I have anyone else do any follow-up."

"Why didn't you have me or one of the boys cover your lapse so there wouldn't be one?" I grew concerned over where this line of questioning was going to lead me.

"Because…she asked me to." He sighed, putting his face in his hands. "I trusted that the other surveillance protocols she didn't know about were still in place to catch up with her if she tried something, so I granted her request."

Damn. No wonder he'd been off-kilter.

"This is not on you, Kane," I stated matter-of-factly. "safi made her choice, and she got other people to bypass the protocols that we had in place. Why are you beating yourself up so badly over this?"

"Because I don't go against my gut like that, Dom," he replied as he lifted his head from his hands. He looked dejected and defeated. "safi always had a way about her. I mean, I wouldn't have relaxed my protocols, not even for my girls. Somehow, she convinced me that it would be okay just this once."

"Look, you and I have been friends for a long time, and I know when you've made bonehead mistakes," I explained to him to make a point. "You need to shake this off so we can get the fool that off'd her."

"You're right, young'un; I need to get back on the ball before we let this idiot slip through," Ramesses said as he stood from the desk and gave me pound. "I think we need a quick R&R tonight at NEBU. You have some things to work out with the girls."

Introducing the girls to Ayanna wasn't as bad as I thought it would be.

But then again, Niki tipped my hand a little bit.

Doing the introduction at NEBU had a lot to do with that being the case.

I sat at a table with Ramesses, Neferterri and a few other Dominants as we watched the submissives gather and chat among themselves and enjoying every minute of it.

I focused on Niki and Ayanna especially because Niki had more of a tendency to be possessive. Natasha had her moments, but she enjoyed the energy of watching Niki and being watched by Niki whenever we all got together.

Tonight would be different, however, because they would be watching Ayanna and me in a scene together. They wouldn't have the option of participating until after she'd been taken down from the spanking bench I'd planned to use for the scene.

Ayanna looked at peace around the other submissive women. That really made me take a step back and wonder if this was the place she was supposed to be the whole time. It was always fascinating to me to see someone who finally looked like they were finally comfortable in their element.

It's not like she wasn't that way at work, of course. I knew better than that.

I saw Ayanna and Niki seem to be getting along pretty smoothly, and I even saw a few laughs being shared between the two of them before Natasha jumped into the fray, and it became a party of three.

I didn't put too much stock into it because it would be a matter of time before things would be taken down to the dungeon area, and then we would see how chummy they would be with her.

The plan that Ramesses and I had hatched was something similar to what he and Neferterri did with Taliah about a year ago. He would allow sajira and shamise to get all gooey and shit with her during a party, and then when it was time to get to the dungeon, he basically had them give him the different toys that he would use on Taliah. It was a test of their training and loyalty not only to him and Neferterri, but to their service side within the House.

It sounded brilliant when he explained it all, and Taliah being with their girls was proof positive as to the success of that plan, but I wasn't so confident because shamise had been with them for at least four years, and sajira was comfortable with them from their swinging days before she crossed over.

I didn't have those things in my favor.

It didn't stop me from going ahead with the plan, though. I had confidence in the training that shamise and sajira put my girls through, and I figured that you only go through this life once, and mistakes will be made, so why not enjoy the mistakes and the successes, too?

"Ayanna, come here, please?" I called to her, breaking her connection with the rest of the women in the small group. She sheepishly walked over to me, kneeled at my feet and dropped her head so she would not meet my eyes.

I wasn't prepared for her to adapt to protocol, but I think she did it because she saw the other submissives adhering and she didn't want to look out of place.

"What is your command of me, Sir?" Ayanna asked, barely speaking above the music playing in the background.

"It's time for the two of us to perform a scene together, pet," I informed her as I stood. "I expect you to be in position on the spanking bench downstairs in the dungeon in the next five minutes."

"Yes, Sir, as you command," she replied. "Your command is my will."

The moment she left and hurried downstairs, I saw Niki and Natasha move toward me in unison. shamise and sajira took their places at Ramesses's and Neferterri's feet also, and once I sat down, the tension that I'd expected was ready to steep.

I felt the heat on Niki immediately.

Her eyes gave her away, but no one knew but me.

"Begging your pardon, Master," Niki began, clearly trying her best to keep her emotions in check. "You will be scening with Ayanna tonight?"

"That would be correct, Niki," I answered without hesitation, giving her a look that dared her to try to question me. Her eyes softened quickly, which made Ramesses smile slightly. I guess the "look" was having its effect after all. "I expect to have you and your sister to help keep the toys in place as we play."

"May I ask if you are interested in her, Master?" Natasha interjected, trying not to sound disappointed also. "She is fun to be around, but we got the feeling based on her grin after leaving you that there is more there than just your work relationship."

"You two are always so perceptive, and to answer your question, yes, I am interested in her, but not in the manner in which you think," I began to explain.

Niki seemed to develop selective hearing, as her body straightened up and she threw caution to the wind. "Are we not enough for you, Master?"

"Have you forgotten your place, Niki?" I asked sternly, a little disturbed that she would want to pick a time like this to show out. "Have I kept anything from you or Natasha the entire time that we have been together?"

"No, Master," Niki shed a small tear, realizing what she'd caused in front of the Dominants that were at the table. "You have been good to the both of us, but what is it that makes her special tonight?"

shamise silently looked up at Neferterri, who nodded her approval without a spoken word, and moved over to Niki. She placed a hand on her chest, moving around so that she could face her.

"No one ever said being a submissive or slave would be all peaches and cream, Niki." shamise looked over at sajira as she spoke. "There was a time when I thought my sis was trying to replace me, and after I got over that and accepted her, that was when Taliah entered the family."

"Family? What in the world are you talking about, shamise?" Natasha asked as her face twisted up like she didn't have a clue of what shamise was driving at.

Hell, it had me confused, too, so I couldn't blame either of them for the confusion. I continued to let shamise explain, though, because I pretty much knew I would screw it up.

"Taliah is a part of our Leather Family, Natasha. What that means is that while she does serve the House as a submissive, she does not belong to Daddy or Goddess," shamise continued.

sajira picked up where shamise left off. "She is entirely within her right to submit to another Dominant, if she chooses to, but she still belongs to the Family, and she is still one of our sister submissives. If Daddy or Goddess chooses, they can, and will, play with her when they feel like it. It doesn't mean they don't love us any less, but being Poly is not about the singular person; it's about the unit as the whole."

"So, what they are saying is that you are not trying to own her; is that right, Master?" Niki looked up at me with hopeful eyes like if my answer would make or break her universe as she knew it.

I knelt down and kissed them both. "I love you two to death, and I couldn't be happier with you. Ayanna is an integral part of what happens at work, and I couldn't be happier with her there, also. Ramesses explained to me that there was the Leather family invitation that I could extend to her, to keep everyone happy."

The smiles on their faces were more than I could have hoped for, and I did prepare for the worst-case scenario. I even saw a wink, which had me wondering what that was about. The next question out of Niki's mouth explained a lot, though.

"Have you fucked her, yet?" she asked, but not out of jealousy. I could read it in her body language. "If it pleases you, Master, I still have that fantasy that I told you about after that confrontation... the one of seeing you fuck someone in front of us?"

"Ah, I do remember you saying something about that." I nodded. Natasha looked like she'd missed the memo on that exchange, but she didn't give herself away too much more than that. "Perhaps we should make that fantasy a reality after all."

TWENTY-ONE

"I want to watch you fuck my Master."

Ayanna looked up at me with quizzical eyes, trying to make sense of what was happening around her. Niki's statement threw her, as she didn't expect to be put on display after such an intense scene.

"Are you sure it's okay?" she quietly asked me, her hands trembling against my skin. "I…I'm a little nervous."

"Don't be nervous, sexy." Natasha moved toward her, placing her fingers around my shaft. "We've been curious for a while to see Master enjoy himself for a change, and you are the perfect one to help with that."

I looked down on the two of them, and I could feel the urges on them both to have this happen. I grunted. "Do as Niki asked, Ayanna, and get my dick ready for me to fuck you."

"As you command, Sir," Ayanna replied quickly, moving with a determined skill to get my pants off. "Your command is my will."

Natasha kissed me deeply and whispered in my ear, "This brings back memories."

I'd almost forgotten about the foursome we'd had at the sex club last year. It was no wonder Natasha wasn't exactly upset about seeing this happen; it'd already happened before.

As Ayanna concentrated on getting me hard, Natasha moved back to where she lay on the couch with Niki and quickly spread her legs to enjoy her oral sex fixation.

I quickly lost myself in Ayanna's tongue as she kept bringing me closer to the edge of my first explosion. I closed my eyes to let my other senses take over, and I heard Niki moaning and gasping at the way her sis continued to suck and tease her clit, nearly yelling at her to keep fucking her with her tongue.

"That's it, Ayanna, suck him like a good girl should," Niki kept dictating, even though she was in the throes with Natasha the entire time. "Make him want to tear that pussy up."

Ayanna had me floating, and I wanted so badly to be inside her that I grabbed her by her hair and whipped her down on the carpet. Before she could get her bearings, I was deep inside her, grinning at her body shaking and trembling underneath mine.

"Damn, Daddy, you couldn't wait for it, could you?!?!" she moaned in my ear, loud enough for only my ears to hear it. *"Come on, Daddy, fuck me like you did in your office…I want it so bad right now!"*

"That's it! Fuck her like you own that pussy, Master!" Niki shouted out as Natasha made her come. *"Damn, Tasha, make me come all over your pretty face!"*

Hearing the girls going at it with each other kept me high, and Ayanna felt so good I didn't want to let up from the pounding that I gave her. Hearing her calling me Daddy was the liquor I needed to keep me drunk and craving her.

By the time I felt my body begin to tighten before the eruption made itself aware, I began to hear Natasha screaming to the heavens that Niki was giving her the business with a dildo that she had in her toy bag.

"Fuck me, Niki, fuck my pussy, baby…oh my God, you got me gushing!" Natasha kept screaming out, keeping her legs spread so Niki could get it in deep.

My senses were overloaded and my body was ripping me apart, so I gave in to my climax and clasped my fingers around Ayanna's throat to brace myself for the force that rumbled through me.

Ayanna's eyes widened as she took her fingers and tried with futile success in taking my fingers away. I felt her violently shake and give a strangled cry that she was coming again.

I never stopped, even though the flow blew through me, and Ayanna didn't complain a bit, urging me to keep pumping inside her, wrapping her legs around my back to keep me inside her.

I felt Niki's hands scratching my back, biting on my shoulder deeply. She cooed in my ear, "We want her too, Master; don't wear her out too much before we can have her, please? Can we have her now?"

I slowly pulled out of Ayanna, breaking our connection, and for the moment she reached out to me as if she wasn't ready to let go yet. She saw Natasha moving in on her and at first, she hesitated.

Natasha kissed her intensely, moving her fingers down to her pussy and began to finger fuck her before Ayanna could protest. "You liked the way Master fucked you, didn't you? I can tell you did; you're coming all over my fingers now."

Niki slid over to me, moving over my dick to get me going again, and it didn't take long for her to accomplish her mission. She kissed me, raking her nails down my chest, moaning as she felt the head of my shaft tapping against her clit.

"It's more than I ever dreamed it would be, Master," Niki uttered as she slipped my manhood inside without much effort at all. "I can't stop coming. Watching you fucking her was so erotic; my pussy is twitching with the images in my head."

She kept her eyes focused on me the entire time, not letting me see what Natasha and Ayanna were doing. She only let me listen as Ayanna begged to be fucked deeper and harder as Natasha grabbed the same dildo that Niki used on her to fuck Ayanna into oblivion.

"I love you, Master. Forgive my jealousy; I don't mean to be, ever," Niki whispered as her eyes locked and pleaded with mine. "I don't know what I would do without you."

I placed my fingers against her lips to quiet her as I grabbed her hips and made her ride me harder. I wanted her to come so hard that the thoughts she had would fade away.

Before long, Niki and I only heard the soothing oohs and ahhs from Natasha and Ayanna. They were completely sprawled out at the foot of the bed, and it looked like they'd worn each other out because neither wanted to move. I smiled as I watched them in their post-orgasmic comas and enjoyed the night for what it was.

There wasn't going to be much of a choice in the matter.

Once the morning came, it was back to the grind on these investigations. I'd only hoped that no other surprises were on the horizon.

I knew I was asking for a lot, but a man can dream, can't he?

TWENTY-TWO

FetLife was on fire.

The boards were ablaze with status messages, personal journals, and flame wars, as each side either sided with tiger or with Mistress Edge.

Kacie didn't waste time while we were enjoying our evening, basically calling the claims against her baseless and trying her best to paint tiger and the other "spineless pussies" as opportunists that were trying to give Dominant women a bad name all the way around.

Talk about a mess? The majority of the morning was spent helping Ramesses and Neferterri with damage control.

The trend that made things crazy was watching all the nut jobs that wanted their moment in the sun to bash people that they didn't even know. It had me wondering why people have the gall to do something like that, and then will be the first person crying foul when the tables are turned.

All we could do was consistently try to put as much correct information as we were allowed to try and stem the rhetoric and name-calling. It worked to some degree, but it was time-consuming and difficult, to say the least.

What was even more daunting was keeping Sin from taking matters into her own hands on behalf of her slave. To hear her tell it, all that was needed was space, opportunity and a pay-per-view ticket gate to watch the fireworks fly!

But of course, we couldn't let that happen because it would be more fodder for the discussion boards and for Kacie's lawyer. With the sub bois coming forward to testify—there were five so far that were willing—it had the makings of a sensational trial.

That, according to Ramesses, was something we absolutely needed to avoid at all costs. We battled back and forth for a couple of days on the feasibility of what he wanted to happen versus what the law will allow to happen. Yeah, my submissive was in the DA's office, but that didn't guarantee anything. She was still an officer of the court first, submissive second. There was always the hope that she could be persuasive in her argument with the DA to plea the case out, but that alone was a crapshoot.

Once the morning madness was over, we turned the watchdog duties over to Ayanna and Taliah to keep things as civil as possible.

The next order on the menu was heading over to the DA's office to speak with Niki and Jason to find out how the interviews were going with the victims that had been flooding our office with calls.

Why they hit us up? Well, technically speaking, they trusted us a little more.

Considering how Jason first reacted to the whole case in the beginning, I could definitely understand trying to go to a police precinct, only to have the officer taking the information down look at you like you were half a man. Whether it's a fucked-up perception or not, the fact is that reality bites.

Perhaps we could use this case to bite back.

We began making our way downtown and I got lost in my own thoughts as we drove. Ramesses worked from his laptop, trying to get more information on Kacie to see if we could use it against her if the case got pushed to trial.

We finally got to the building to see about Niki, and once we got into her office, she didn't even notice we were in the room. It was almost as if she were on automatic pilot.

"My God, Jason, how many more will there be?" she called out to the air as she continued to write notes. She must have assumed that we were Jason, coming in with another of the men that we passed by on the way into her office.

Wow, what in the world had we stumbled into?

Niki looked like she had been run through the torture rack with some of the notes that she scribbled down in shorthand to keep up with the pace of the men that had visited her office. Jason looked a bit unnerved also, a little more than I cared to admit, and I didn't know if I wanted to acknowledge that or not.

Being a cop, we tended to get used to dealing with the worst in people, almost to the point to where we look for it so often that we forget that there might be good in even the bad people we encounter. Jason, from what I could tell, went from law school straight to the DA's office, which meant he never had to deal with the grimy stuff the way Niki did.

Ramesses and I walked into her office and took a seat as Jason closed the door to deal with the last of the interviewees.

Once we were alone, she slipped quickly into protocol, almost like she needed it to get back into balance. "Master, the accounts that we have been hearing have been nearly overwhelming. I thought it was difficult dealing with women when it came to rape cases."

"What have you been hearing?" Ramesses asked. "Have they been that bad?"

"Yes, Sir, they have been." Niki shook her head. "Every interview has been similar in some instances, different in others, but the end result was Edge imposing her will and taking them by force before untying them and letting them leave."

"How many are willing to testify so far?" I asked, curious to find out what we were dealing with. "Do you think you will have enough to go to trial?"

"We originally had five, but two pulled out because they didn't want their families to know what happened," Niki answered, clearly frustrated by the whole ordeal. "I'm hoping to have at least one more to strengthen the case."

"I'm sure you will find the person you need, my dear," Ramesses calmly stated, hoping to put her mind at ease. "The fact that you have three that are willing is a good thing in and of itself. You said it yourself, these crimes rarely get reported."

"Yes, Sir, this is true, but it doesn't make it right," Niki explained. "These men are victims, and someone needs to bear witness to that victimization."

"Do you think that the three you have will be enough to force a plea deal?" Ramesses asked. "I don't mean to sound dismissive, but we don't want this type of publicity, even for a second."

"Master Ramesses, I understand your concerns, and they are duly noted, but I have to do what is best for the people of Fulton County…with all due respect, Sir." Niki's demeanor was sheepish, almost hesitant as she responded to his question. "I don't mean to sound ungrateful for your efforts, but I can't have the victims thinking that they got slighted when it comes to justice for the crimes committed against them."

"I do understand, Niki, and hopefully, it doesn't get to a point to where cameras will be involved," he replied, smiling just enough to put Niki at ease that a war of words wouldn't ensue between them. "But we will support whatever the office wants to do."

"Thank you, Sir. That means a lot coming from you." Niki smiled back.

Jason made his way into her office, and he still wore the pensive look on his face. Niki looked up at him, dismissing his expression and asked him, "Are there any more that need to be interviewed, Jason?"

"Yes…as a matter of fact, there is one more," Jason blurted out. "Me."

"Would you care to run that by me again?"

Hell, Niki sat with her mouth gaping open, and I was right there with her with the same "what the fuck is this?" look on my face, too.

Ramesses simply leaned back in his chair, his Poker face never giving him away for a moment. "So, that would explain all the bravado earlier in the week when this case first came to light. Hit you too close to home, huh?"

"Mr. Alexander, I never would have guessed that you all were involved in that world, and had I known that you were, I probably would have said something sooner to help you," Jason explained solemnly. "I tried to avoid pushing this case because it would have meant that I would have had to come forward, too, and I wasn't prepared to do that...at least, not on my own."

"I can understand why you felt you had to do what you had to do, Jason, but we're sworn to uphold the law when it's broken." Niki softened up, understanding the grief her colleague must have been feeling. "I know this won't be easy, but you are among friends."

"Thank you, that does make me feel better," Jason exhaled as he spoke. "I guess you've also figured out that I was the one that sent tiger the emails, too, Mr. Alexander?"

Ramesses tried not to look too smug as he looked at me. I shook my head wondering if he'd figured it out while we were on the ride over here and he was waiting for the proper moment to let us all in on the secret.

"To answer your question, counsel, yes, I figured it out." He leaned forward in his chair, wondering what we were all curious about. "The question is: why would you go through something like that and not tell anyone? I mean, there has to be someone...a close friend that could have helped you bear this burden?"

"I'm a transplant from Texas, and a lot of the friends I have are back home," Jason explained further. "They wouldn't...*get it*...if you know what I mean?"

Yeah, I understood the story all too well after being a part of things for the past year or so. Friends that began to look at you as a freak of nature, or strange as hell because you're not "normal" or something like that.

I remember a gay friend of mine on the force that gave me the side-eye because I was into spanking and other proclivities. Never mind the fact that he was a gay male on the fringes of the societal norms of sexuality, and he basically looked at me like I was the crazy one.

Go figure.

"Right now, we need to get to the heart of the matter and take this all down." Niki kicked right back into attorney-mode. "You know how this works, Jason, so have a seat and tell us how this all went down."

Jason sheepishly took a seat at the front of Niki's desk. He took a deep breath as if he were trying to convince himself that we could, in fact, be trusted with what he was about to say.

"I found Mistress Edge through another dude who turned me on to her services when we were at the conference up in D.C. about three months ago, remember?" Jason began to recount.

Niki nodded, acknowledging the trip that they were on for about a week.

"He said that she was good, and she was sexy, too, and that I should check her out. Her rates weren't too crazy, so, we set up a meeting at her house to do the scene," Jason continued to recall. His fingers tapped against his thigh, and I noticed his eyes darted all over the place, which was normally what happens when someone tries to remember things. "I made sure that I covered my own tracks. I paid in cash, I made sure I didn't withdraw too much money at one time to keep the paper trail from being too suspect, and I even gave her a fake name—Paul—so that I couldn't be traced back once we were done."

"Did you take your car when you met her?" Niki asked, still scribbling notes.

"I rented a car. I paid in cash for that, too," Jason answered quickly. "I had to give them my real name, though."

"Explain to us what happened when you got to the house." Niki started to ask the questions that would be more difficult to answer, emotionally speaking.

"At first, I was in awe of her beauty." Jason let a small smile escape and spread across his lips. "I've always been kinky, but most women…well, the ones who aren't into kinky stuff…have this thing about submissive men being weak and all, so when she came along, it was hard not to want to do anything for her."

"Tell us about the terms of your agreement." Niki continued with follow-up questions.

"I was there in a domestic capacity only. At the time, I was with someone, so sex was not on the menu," Jason stated flatly, and we all noticed a change in his demeanor once we got to the real matter. "I was naked the whole time, and she would grab my ass and make comments about how fine I was.

"I didn't have a problem with it because that was part of my kink; to be verbally humiliated and treated like a piece of meat," Jason explained further. "I was almost done with the kitchen when she just came at me out of the blue."

"What happened next?"

"She started kissing me, grabbed my dick and started to rub on it to get me hard," Jason answered as his eyes turned dark. "I don't know when she left me to put her strap-on on, but she had it on by the time she was on me, trying to get me to feel on her piece. I tore away from her, telling her that this wasn't a part of our agreement."

"Did she say anything else to you after you broke away from her?" Niki kept the flurry of questions going.

"She glared at me and said that I was going to pay for rejecting her," Jason replied, this time tears beginning to form. "I didn't care what she said. I was getting out of there, period."

"How did the attack happen?"

"I walked to where my clothes were, in the foyer by the door, stacked in a pile, just as instructed. I felt something hit the back of my knee, and I dropped to the floor in pain. Next thing I know, she grabbed my wrists and cuffed them behind my back." Jason's voice began to crack as he spoke about what happened next. "I was flat on the floor with my face crushed against the tile as she grabbed some lube and tore into me like she'd just got out of prison and needed some badly."

"Did she say anything during the rape?"

"She kept saying that I should have been glad she was fucking me, that I was a worthless piece of ass." Jason's tears rolled freely at that point. I don't think he cared that he was in the presence of other men by then. "She just kept growling and telling me how good a slut I was. That she was coming and squirting all over my ass as proof of how good I was."

Niki looked like she wanted to cry for him. She reached across the desk and grabbed his hand. "How on earth were you able to keep yourself together after something like that?"

"Honestly, I still don't know. I wanted to say something sooner, but I didn't know how you would react to it." Jason shrugged as he spoke. "I still don't know if I could do this on the record."

"If you want this woman to pay for what she did to you, you have to," Niki urged. "tiger is going through it, and we have two others also that are willing to step up with you."

"Look, Jason, this case that you're in right now is all about consent," I interjected a bit. "We've been trying to put all of these measures in place...the Rape Shield laws and such...to protect women who don't give consent. What's most important is, regardless of the gender, no means no. If someone overpowers you and forces themselves on you sexually, it's rape, period."

"I feel where you're coming from, but I have to protect my career, too," Jason objected again. "It's one thing to get caught up in a trial, but the details become public record. It will seal my fate as a prosecutor."

"Let me worry about the DA, Jason. I'm sure he will not object to keeping you on," Niki demanded.

"How are you so sure, Nikia? I mean, this is not your run-of-the-mill prostitution ring or something that can be easily swept under the rug," Jason insisted, still shaking from explaining everything. "If this goes to open court, you know the media will have a field day with it."

"Maybe this might help you change your mind," I said as I pulled out the discs and handed them over to Niki. "Edge completely fucked herself when she decided to keep the videos of every one of her encounters."

"Oh, for fuck's sake, she videotaped us, too?!?!" Jason cried out. "Okay, why in the fuck would she keep the shit?"

"I tried to tell you, Jason, it's all about consent, except this time, it's backfiring on her," I replied to him, letting a smirk spread across my lips. "She's been so used to keeping tapes in case a client tried to go after her that she fell victim to her own habits."

"Wait, wait, wait a minute." Jason kept the questions coming, as he really had no idea of what was happening. "Explain this to me, because now I'm a bit pissed that I was even caught on tape to begin with."

"Okay, here's the deal, Jason." Ramesses sat up in his chair to get into his familiar positioning when it was time to go to school. "Pros have been caught out there for years when it came to their clientele deciding that they had buyer's remorse. It became a he said-she said battle if it went to court, with the Pros ending up on the short end of the stick. So, they took extra steps without the clients ever knowing what went on, getting proof they were there."

"So, basically it still became a double-edged sword anyway." Jason's eyes lit up like the switch had been turned on in his mind. "If they were in the right, they basically didn't have to fight it out in court once the tapes were produced."

"Good man, now your legal mind is working again." Ramesses nodded. "Her lawyer might still want the tapes introduced in open court to embarrass you, but he would run the risk of watching his client, on tape, raping more than one man in the course of a year."

"Do you think he's that stupid to let her go through that?" Jason asked.

"If I know Edge, the way she's been behaving lately, I know he'll get pressured into it." I laughed as I said that. No one caught my joke, so I elaborated. "If you haven't noticed, he was already drooling over her before he informed her that he would be her lawyer. It wouldn't surprise me if he was one of her clients."

"Yeah, she tends to have that effect on men and women." Ramesses shook his head. "Once upon a time, she nearly had me wrapped around her finger as a young girl, before she decided to become a Pro. That was my breaking point with her. Otherwise, who knows what might have been?"

"Okay, enough with the fawning over this bitch, please?" Niki's envy began to rear its ugly head, especially considering she was the only woman in the room. "Right now, we simply need to concentrate on her being put behind bars so she can be somebody else's bitch for the next ten to fifteen."

"She's right, gentlemen. These tapes should be the death knell to keep this from going to trial," Ramesses stated. "But I think we all know that it really won't be that easy."

"No, nothing like this ever is easy, Sir," Niki replied, shaking off the attitude that she had a moment ago. "However, maybe she can be persuaded, woman to woman, to make a deal. She doesn't have much to lose, and she might not have a choice."

"Okay, we'll work this out to the best advantage that we can; that way you will have some leverage to use," Jason suggested. He exhaled before he finally said, "Even if you have to use me on the witness stand."

He and Ramesses left the office, leaving Niki and I alone for a moment.

Now was as good a time as any to figure out a lingering question in my mind.

"How long have you known about the ultimatum that the former DA shot at me?" I didn't feel like mincing words at that point.

Niki lowered her eyes as she tried to avoid looking in mine. "Right after I got settled into my office, former DA Barnes decided he needed to level with me, because he said he knew you wouldn't."

"Okay, so what happened?" I continued to query. "Lay it out."

"He told me that he tried to force you into the position because he felt that you would be the front man he needed to take care of some under-the-table business," she recounted. "He knew about your...in his words, proclivities...and thought it would be perfect timing to rid the city of that element."

I softly placed my hands on her shoulders as I saw her begin to tremble. I had no idea that Barnes had been so reckless, but the way she was explaining the story, I knew he had dropped all this in her lap.

Bastard...I ought to pay him a visit when this is all done.

"He put you in a no-win situation, and he knew it," Niki kept the story going. "He knew you wouldn't go for the witch hunts that he had in mind for you."

"So, why did he tell you everything?" I asked, still not making sense of the whole matter. "The Barnes I remembered didn't have much of a conscience; there had to be something in it for him."

"Wow, Sir, for someone that keeps tabs on damn near everyone, I'm surprised you didn't know about this one." Niki shook her head. "Barnes passed away a month after he retired…from cancer."

Now it began to make sense, and it also made sense why I didn't hear much from him after he retired. I honestly thought that I would have heard something from him, if not to rub it in one last time before disappearing for good.

Good riddance. Tell Saddam I said hello, and give bin Laden a pound while you're down there, you sonofabitch.

"I'm sorry you had to bear that all this time." I held her close for a moment, inhaling her scent. "You didn't have to say anything to Bryson about that, baby."

"Yes I did. He's a jackass, and I'm still trying to figure out why I ever dealt with him in the first place." Niki smiled as she wiped a tear from her cheek. "Besides, he doesn't hold a candle to you, my Master…as a lover, or a detective. If anything, he's been trying to do his best to outmaneuver you any way he can."

"You're right, baby, now that you mention it." I jerked as the answer to the one last question in my head finally revealed itself. "In fact, you may have helped me stop a leak."

"We can do this the hard way, or we can do this the easy way—your choice."

I was smack dab in the middle of my old precinct, having a dick-slinging contest with the man that took my place as the lead detective.

Detective Bryson was going to be a tough nut to crack, but I had

Ty do some work for me, and he'd come up with some interesting information for me to use against this dude.

I wasn't about to lose a case over some easy pussy, and that's exactly what he went for.

Damn, he could have at least gotten some money out of the deal or something?

"Say what you gotta say and let's be done with it," Bryson smugly stated, sipping on his coffee like he was top dog or something. "As you can see, some of us have real detective work to do?"

"Funny you should say that, Bryson, because I did a little real detective work, as you say, of my own, and you'd be amazed at what I found," I coldly countered, dropping a manila envelope on his desk.

"And what the fuck is this supposed to be, bitch?" Bryson huffed.

"Consider it motivation to do the right thing and come clean before innocent people get hurt," I scoffed.

He looked inside the envelope, which showed him outside of Kacie's condo, inside her condo, and a couple of juicy snapshots in some pretty compromising positions.

All while wearing his badge…and very little else.

Not to mention a DVD that accompanied those pictures.

"Who's the bitch now?" I rhetorically inquired, placing my index finger against my ear to try and hear something.

Detective Tanner walked into the standoff between us and it was clear he was completely oblivious to what was transpiring before his eyes.

"Detective Law, good to see you, bro," he said.

"Good to see you, Tanner." I kept things civil, even though the other officers gave me away as to the icy tension in the room. "I wish I could say this was a social call, but I'd be lying if I said it was."

"Did you find out anything new on the case?" he asked, trying to somehow deflect the conversation from whatever was going on.

"Yes, unfortunately I did." I couldn't sugarcoat any longer, and even Tanner could feel it on me. "I was hoping that your partner would want to do this in private, but he insisted on doing this the hard way."

"What the hell is he talking about, Ryan?" Tanner asked as he turned his attention to a now-dejected Detective Bryson. "What the fuck did you do, man?"

"I had no choice…don't you see that he's making a mockery of things?" Bryson protested. "I couldn't stand for it, so I had to do something."

"I think that's all I need to hear," my old captain solemnly spoke as he was flanked by two IAD officers. "Ryan, you've got to come clean to have a chance at saving your career."

I wasn't exactly happy, either, but it had to be done.

"This is bullshit!" Bryson yelled with his eyes wildly staring at me. "He's the fucking traitor, and you're arresting me?!?!"

"Don't make this any harder than you have to, Ryan." Tanner tried to calm him down.

"Think about your wife; you don't want to let her down, man."

That seemed to sober him up a little bit as the reality of the situation finally hit home. "Okay, look, I'll do whatever I have to do, all right? I love my job. I didn't plan for all of this to happen, I swear."

I watched as he walked into the captain's office to speak with IAD. Tanner shook his head, a disappointed look on his face. "Law, I don't know what to say; he's a good detective. I don't know what came over him."

As I slowly walked out of the place that I used to call home, I turned back and answered, "I do, and I honestly feel sorry for him. Some ghosts are hard to remove."

TWENTY-THREE

"Tell me you're not serious?"

Natasha was on the phone with the medical examiner's office, getting the final report on safi's cause of death. It was asphyxiation as we thought when we were at the crime scene, but something else more disturbing came to light.

Her neck was snapped like a twig after she died.

That made the murderer's motive all the more clear: it was a crime of passion, something extremely personal on a few levels.

That opened up the suspect list again, including almost everyone that might have had an ax to grind.

It was definitely no secret that safi was a flirt, a social butterfly, and extremely open with her sexuality. Regardless of gender, she left bodies and hearts in her wake, and with Dominants—once his or her heart is broken—there is a grudge that can last through the Ice Age.

"Is everything okay, Natasha?" I asked as we walked up to Domina Torina's front door. "You sound as if you didn't expect the ME's report to go down like that."

"No, Sir, it's not that, it's just..." Natasha commented as she slowed down for a moment. "safi didn't do anything to deserve this, Master. Yes, she broke some hearts, but are Dominants that cruel that they can't move on?"

I honestly couldn't answer her question because I didn't know the answer anymore. When you're used to hearing *yes* all the time as a Dominant, hearing the word *no* is like a shock to the system; you don't know how to react.

We reached Torina's front door, and when she opened the door, we all did a double-take at the sight before us.

This woman stood a good six feet one inch, and the heels didn't help with making her any shorter. She was dressed to kill, which said a lot considering it was three in the afternoon. Boned leather corset, leather skirt to match, five-inch platform ankle boots, and her long legs were shaved smoother than a baby's bottom.

To say this woman was fine was an understatement.

It would be a struggle to keep both Trish and Natasha from losing their professionalism…especially Natasha, considering that she had a weakness for taller women.

"Wow, I must be special. I get a three-on-one? You must really want what I have to give, huh?" Torina laughed as she welcomed us into her home.

As we sat down on the sofa, Natasha fell into protocol, even with Trish in the room, and took her place between my legs. I felt her trying to avoid being so conspicuous in her trembling, and tipping me off that Torina already had an effect on her.

I needed to make this interview go quickly before Torina caught the vibe that Natasha was giving off.

Trish was confused by Natasha's actions, but she quickly shrugged it off to begin asking Torina the questions that she wrote down. "What do you know about the events that happened that night, Torina?"

"I'm not telling you anything; I'm not in the proper mood for it." Torina scoffed as she crossed her legs. "Dom, where's that sexy-ass mentor of yours? I might be persuaded to *try* to talk if he were present."

"I don't have time for these bullshit games, Torina." I sneered, not the least bit amused by her need to deal with Ramesses. "Either tell us what we need to know or I'll—"

"You won't do anything, Dom." Torina smirked. "Ramesses won't allow it, especially if it's not in either of our best interests. So, tell you what, if you get Ramesses here, I might tell everything I know. But it will be on my terms because you're in need of the information that I know. Got it?"

"Do we really have to deal with this BS?" Trish was absolutely irritated. "I can have a subpoena here in the next twenty minutes."

"And you act like jail is something I'm actually scared of, detective?" Torina shot a look at her. "All a subpoena will do is piss me off and shut me down. Do you really want that?"

I flipped out my cell phone in the next moment, on the phone with Ramesses.

He didn't sound too thrilled about what he had to do. I honestly wasn't sure what it was he had to do.

"She's been after me for an interrogation scene for years, Dom; that's why she's being so hard about this," he told me. "Give me ten minutes, I'm not far from you. If a scene is what she wants, she'd better be careful of what she wishes for…and you're going to have to trust me—no matter what happens—trust me."

"I didn't think you would come."

Ramesses was dressed in a jet-black suit and a matching black shirt and boots. To say he looked like the Grim Reaper was putting it mildly. The icy look in his eyes made it clear that he was not to be trifled with today.

"I don't think I told you that you could speak," Ramesses uttered.

"I think you need a moment or two to take a look and gain a better appreciation of your situation."

"What the hell are you talking about, Ramesses? I'm not in any trouble here, but I know who is," Torina tried to speak out.

Ramesses stepped closer to her, causing Torina to quickly try to step back to create space between them. The closer he got to her, the more she tried to move away to keep him from getting so close to her.

"I don't think you realize just how much trouble you've asked for, slut." Ramesses's tone was different. He didn't even recognize any of us before entering the house. "And you *will* show me the proper respect that a Master of my caliber deserves."

She lowered her dark eyes quickly, I suspected because she knew he'd see the fear in them if she looked at him.

Ramesses towered over her, asking in a soft, but cold voice, "You know why you're in here with me; now don't you want to tell me all about it and go the easy route?"

Slowly, without neither looking up nor opening her mouth, Torina shook her head, her long, dark brown hair dancing side to side and curtaining her face from view. Finally, she defiantly stated, "No matter the pain you inflict, you're going to earn this confession, I promise you."

"But you assume I'm going to inflict pain, slut." Ramesses chuckled. "I already know that you're a pain slut, Torina, despite your trying to deter me otherwise. I can tell you this: before this is done, you're going to want me to ease your suffering, even beg for it, but I won't. I will, however, get what I want out of you."

Her body jerked suddenly as he grabbed her by the nape of her neck, tossing her easily across the room and onto her love seat. She hit the seat heavily, her eyes suddenly showing terror and confusion, but Ramesses gave her no time to react as he landed against her, his hands pressing against her lungs, taking the wind from her.

He straddled her stomach; his expression was that of pleasure as he watched her wince in pain from his weight on top of her, holding her in place with his size. He leaned down to whisper coldly into her ear, but loud enough for the rest of us to hear him. "You will tell me what I need to know, or this will hurt, bitch…a lot."

She groaned almost as much from the fear in her eyes as from the pain I knew she must have been feeling. Trish started to move forward, but Natasha laid a hand against her shoulder, firmly holding her in the spot that she stood. She silently shook her head to let Trish know that this was part of the scene.

Torina whimpered, "I…I don't know anything, Sir…please… don't hurt me."

It took everything I had to forget my academy training because this was way off the mark in terms of by-the-book interrogation methods. I knew she wanted the scene to go down like this, but the line between fantasy and reality was blurred beyond recognition. Despite my instincts, I had to trust Ramesses to know what he was doing.

Torina's eyes begged for release of his hands around her throat as she witnessed the cold, evil smile spread to the corner of his mouth. She continued to struggle underneath his weight, but at the same time, I saw her trying desperately to get her face close enough to his. If I didn't know any better, I would have sworn that she wanted to kiss him.

Ramesses must have realized it, too, because he squeezed her throat tighter, taking pleasure in the trembling of her body as she struggled for air. The laugh that bellowed from him was a frightening sound, and that's saying a lot coming from a cop. Finally, Ramesses backhanded her, again speaking softly, but the iciness came across as eerily as the first time. "There are no safe words in jail, slut. Obstruction is not a charge you want to have over you. Tell me what I want to know or I'll hurt you badly and I won't stop till I'm good and ready."

To emphasize his words, his long fingers clasped the hooks on her corset, ripping through it like it was made out of plastic. Torina's frightened chestnut-brown eyes widened and leapt up to meet his, gasping loudly as she tried to cover her nudity from her hulking interrogator.

I swear to God, I didn't recognize him at all at this point. It was like he was a completely different man altogether. A different persona that had been hidden so deeply that I didn't think Neferterri knew about it.

He leaned down, keeping her body pressed against the cushions of the small sofa. As his lips came nearer and nearer, her body reacted like she was dreaming. Her lush red lips parted, begging for a kiss. He laughed as he saw her reaction and veered off, sinking his teeth into the curve of her neck. Biting the tender flesh viciously, his body reacted to her scent, the fear surging from her in waves, the red fluid flowing as he drew blood, pushing her closer to the brink of orgasm. Her only reaction was self-preservation as she tried to bite him back, sinking her own teeth into his shoulder, unsuccessfully trying to hurt him through the heavy material of his dress shirt.

Gasping for air from the intensity of the bite as he lifted from her body, Ramesses's hand flashed across Torina's face, glaring at her as he wiped the droplets of blood from his lips.

She tried desperately to get up and get her balance, but her legs were like jelly and she slowly slid down the front of the love seat, unaware of the rough scrapes to the flesh of her now bare back. Ramesses grabbed her hair, dragging her across the room before picking her up and throwing her face down on the smooth wooden table. He ripped off the already torn corset from her body and lifted the skirt so that both her ass and her back were illuminated under the harsh light of the lamp.

Torina huffed, desperately trying to clear her head and get her breath back, but froze, her whole body tightening, as she felt his rugged palms caressing her body. Suddenly, his hands grabbed the cheeks of her ass, long strong fingers digging in to the soft skin before she heard the hard thud of the palm of his ass slamming into her tender flesh, sending pain that made her writhe and scream.

"Tell me what I want to know, Torina," Ramesses demanded. "Tell me, slut…dammit, you will tell me what you know or you'll think this is a party...I'll let Dominic have at you, too, and he's nowhere near as forgiving as I am...you'll be screaming all your secrets by the time we're done with you…*tell me!*"

"That's enough, Sir!" I had reached my boiling point, and I was going to stop him even if he didn't want to be stopped. "There's another way to get what we need."

"Oh, no, she's about to tell us everything we want to know, aren't you, bitch?" Ramesses's eyes were wild with aggression. "You killed her, didn't you? You were the one she was with before she died!"

He growled something into her ear that I couldn't make out, as he slid two fingers inside her pussy. Whatever it was that he told her combined with the finger-fucking that she endured, it brought her to tears. Her body shook violently as she wailed from the orgasm that gripped her body.

"I'll tell you what you want, I'll tell you everything! Have mercy, Ramesses!" Torina screamed out as she cried uncontrollably. She yelled and cursed at Ramesses, who walked away from her as if he didn't have a care in the world, a smug look on his face like he was pleased with himself.

Shaken to her core, Torina sobbed softly, her tears pooling onto the soft, smoothed wood of the table as she tried to compose herself.

As Torina spoke with Natasha and Cross, I bypassed Ramesses's exhausted state and demanded, "What in the hell was that about, Sir?"

"That…is why…I don't…do interrogation scenes." Ramesses was exhausted. He could barely catch his breath. "It brings out a darker side of me that cannot always be controlled."

Natasha came rushing to my side immediately, her eyes searching mine for permission to provide some care in the absence of Ramesses's submissives. I nodded my permission as she knelt next to Ramesses to find out if he needed anything to drink or something to eat to take the edge off from dealing with Torina.

He looked a complete wreck, but I didn't care. I was confused; I'd never seen him like that before. I was even more confused as I felt helpless to stop what was happening and at a loss for words as to how to proceed.

The looks on Natasha's and Trish's faces let me know I wasn't the only one in a state of shock.

"You could have hurt her; you know that, right?" I continued to admonish him. "What the hell made you think I would just sit and watch while you damn near raped that woman?"

"Dominic, I told you this was going to be intense when you called me, and I told you that you were going to have to trust me," Ramesses answered as Natasha brought a ginger ale out of his truck for him to drink. "Those scenes are some of the most intense and misunderstood within the BDSM world because they blur the lines between reality and fantasy."

I looked over at Torina, and she was still crying and shaking like she was literally in a traumatic state. "Sir, you can't be serious?"

Ramesses laughed it off. "I told her she might want to be careful what she wished for. What I do in demos and what I do for real are two different things. Don't worry, young'un, she's fine. Don't let the dramatic act fool you."

Almost on cue, Torina walked over to where we sat, dropped to her knees and kissed Ramesses on the back of his palm. "Thank you for the scene, m'Lord. I hope that the information that I have provided for your investigation leads to the conclusion you need."

Of course she would enjoy the whole damn thing. I shook my head, trying to make sense of the scene in front of me. That's what I get for thinking I had seen almost everything.

"Sir, Torina's told us what we need to know," Trish stated, a look of irritation washed over her face. "I don't think you or Mr. Alexander is going to like it."

TWENTY-FOUR

Het-hotep.

This whole time, it was him. He was behind safi's murder.

We sat as Torina recounted what she knew and what she saw after she and safi finished with their sexual interlude. Torina went to wash off and get dressed before she came back to bring safi out of her unconscious state when she saw Het-hotep over her body, glowering with a look of pure hatred on his face.

The next thing she saw was him grabbing her neck before hearing a snap. She freaked out and left the scene of the crime, but not before calling the cops.

Ramesses was sick to his stomach.

I was left wondering why the fuck would he kill someone he professed to love.

I'm surprised he didn't bolt. I know I would have if I killed someone. What the fuck am I sticking around for?

That's what made this all the more disturbing. He waited around this whole time. But, why would he?

I have to admit, I didn't exactly see this one coming.

I think it might have had something to do with the fact that we took him at his word and were too busy trying to make sure someone else did it that we didn't pay attention to the deception that set up camp right in our backyard.

So much for honor within the circle…

Torina was another matter; she was derelict in her duty as a citizen to report a crime when she saw one happening. Why didn't she cut all of this bullshit down to size when she had a chance? It wasn't like she was the one who murdered safi.

She got hers and kept on moving.

That in itself was a sad set of events. She could have at least pointed us in the right direction instead of putting Ramesses in the position to where he had to go to the extreme that he did.

All so she could get her rocks off again.

The more I thought about it, the more it pissed me off. I guess regardless of the community, the politics would always be there to play through.

At least I was my own boss now, or I would really be pissed. I still don't know how Ramesses has dealt with it this long.

I shrugged off my feelings on the matter; it was time to put this case to bed.

Natasha continued to tend to Ramesses as Trish and I spoke about what to do next.

"He has to be brought in for questioning, Law," she admitted. "The alibi checked out when we looked at the flight manifests. How in the hell did he get here and commit the murder, if what Torina says is true?"

"Look, I'm just as confused as you are, but think about it this way: what if someone else was on the commercial flight?" I posed the thesis. "He came in from overseas; who's to say that he didn't take a private jet while someone else took the commercial?"

"I'll go check the flight manifests at Peachtree-DeKalb Airport, since that's the closest strip that he lives by and see what turned up in the last few days," Trish replied, looking over at Ramesses for a moment. "When this is over, I really want to talk to you all about the things you're into. I'm still trying to figure out my feelings after watching Mr. Alexander with Torina. I don't know if I should be turned on or not."

We walked over to where Natasha and Ramesses were sitting with Torina, and I asked Ramesses, "Are you in decent shape to roll? We have a brother Dominant to see about."

Ramesses rose from his seat quickly, a look of determination mixed with trepidation in his eyes. "I believe we have answers that we need to get."

"Not without one of us present, Sir," Natasha protested, sounding like she was protecting Ramesses from his state of mind. "If you go over there without balancing, you may mess up the questioning and cause him to do something stupid if he thinks he's stuck in a corner."

"We're only going over there to stall him until you are done over at PDK, Natasha," I replied, trying to calm her concerns. "We'll have a social chat with him, off the record, until you get there, okay?"

Natasha's eyes narrowed as she tried to study my face to see if I was lying to her. I gave her the best Poker face in my arsenal, not giving her a single clue of whether I was being completely forthright with our intentions.

Her instincts were sound, but she couldn't prove it.

Finally, after a few seconds of finding what wasn't there, Natasha whispered, "I trust you, Master. But please be careful."

"I've been expecting you two."

That statement was not exactly what I wanted to hear when we got to Het-hotep's home.

My senses were on alert, trying to keep my outward appearance from giving us away. I scanned the living room area where we sat down for any clues as to what might have been going on before we got there.

The only thing that caught my immediate attention was the .44 Magnum revolver that sat on his right thigh when he sat down across from us.

That was enough to keep my attention the rest of the time we would be there.

Ramesses wasn't carrying, at least not to my knowledge, but that didn't mean that I wasn't. Being a cop, keeping a weapon on your person was as natural as putting on clothes. I didn't go anywhere without at least one of my SIG-Sauers on me at all times.

I took a good look at Het-hotep once we did get a chance to settle in and begin some sort of conversation. To say the man was completely lush out of his skull was putting it mildly. It wasn't until he took off his sunglasses that I saw the bloodshot eyes that really made me take note of anything else around him.

Sure enough, the bottle of Jack Daniel's was sitting on the coffee table in front of him, with a freshly poured glass next to it.

I reached inside my coat and unsnapped my gun free from its holster on my shoulder harness. I didn't want to take any chances, especially with a drunk man showing a weapon.

Dominant or no Dominant, I would not hesitate.

Ramesses started to talk to him, trying to gauge his state of mind. "How are you holding up? We wanted to come by and check on you to see how you were doing."

"No, I know the reason you're here, Ramesses," Het-hotep slurred as he took a sip of his liquid courage. "Don't think for a minute that I haven't figured out that you know that I had that bitch killed."

"You didn't have her killed…you killed her!"

That confession elicited a response from me, in the form of my gun being placed on the other side of the coffee table. I didn't keep it on me, as a show of faith that he wouldn't try to do anything stupid.

Het-hotep sneered at me like I'd disrespected him. He was right, too, and I returned his sneer with a glare of my own, daring him to say the words that would set things off.

"Do you really think that was really necessary, Dom?" His words were barely audible now, and I realized that things could get really ugly, really fast. "I could understand if I cocked the hammer back or something, but now you're just being rude."

In that same instant, I heard the familiar click of the hammer finding its place before the trigger could be squeezed.

I leaned forward, but Ramesses placed a hand on my shoulder, saying, "There is no need for things to get messy. Dominic has no interests in cutting you down, unless you give him a reason to, right, Dom?"

I nodded slowly, my eyes never leaving Het-hotep's.

"Good, because I do like him; he's done a lot of good in the last year or so," Het-hotep spoke again, taking his eyes down to concentrate on swirling his cocktail. "So, I'm assuming that you're here to find out why I did it, yes?"

He's too calm, I said to myself. *There's something not quite all there with him; I can feel it.*

The problem with most killers was that they tended to be simple. Crime of passion was the order of the day, and it usually involved someone else as the trigger for the crime of passion.

I needed to find who that trigger was attached to before the heavens erupted.

"Yes, do tell," I replied quickly, trying to keep him talking for as long as I could. I figured if I could keep him on his monologue, Ramesses would pick up on it and keep him going, too.

"She was always a handful, even when we first met," Het-hotep started, still sipping. "I was elated when she began focusing on me. After all, she was beautiful, trained as a submissive in service aspects, and she was a damn good fuck."

I felt Ramesses tense up, but I understood why he was feeling the way he did. Speaking ill of the dead was not a good look.

I kept the conversation rolling by asking, "So, if she was so good to you, why did you have her put to sleep?"

"I kept asking myself that same question, Dom." Het-hotep laughed a little to himself, as if he were in on his own private joke. "It kept fucking with me, even after I got home before I went through with it."

Ramesses was getting irritated, and Het-hotep could see it on his face. "Come on, Ramesses, you have to admit this is interesting banter going on. After all, you haven't had a chance to find out what I finally figured out."

"And what, exactly did you figure out, Het-hotep?" Ramesses tried to speak without letting his temper get to him. "Why did you kill a woman that was ready to commit to you?"

The alarms sounding off in my head would have given a normal person a headache. It wasn't hard to figure out what the trigger was anymore.

"Because she wasn't committed to *me*, Ramesses." Het-hotep's eyes grew wild with rage. "She was committed to *you*."

Things went from red-hot to white-hot quickly.

"You're imagining things, Sir." Ramesses leaned back in the chair he sat in. "safi made her choice: it was you. Putting this shit on me won't make you feel better about the act you committed."

Het-hotep's retort came in the form of a hard copy of the email that safi never got to send to Ramesses.

Fuck...I was gonna need to find an exit strategy as fast as possible or we'd both end up shot, or worse. He was growing more animated and enraged by the second, and there was no talking him off the ledge now.

"Do you still think I'm *imagining* things, Brother?" he boomed. "Are those words made up? They were on her computer when I got to it before I headed over to Inner Sanctum. The minute that I saw her with Torina, getting fucked like she didn't have a care in the world...she deserved what she got for betraying me!"

"I never got this email, Sir. I have no guilty conscience on this deal. I didn't find out about it until after she was murdered," Ramesses continued. "So, you killed a woman that was in love with you, and was ready to be with *you*, only for you to turn around and kill her because you thought she had a thing for me? How fucking high school is that shit?"

"Quit denying that she wanted you and that you wanted her, Ramesses; it's insulting as fuck." Het-hotep put his hands on the gun as he continued to slur his words. "How the fuck could you deceive and betray a fellow Brother of *Neb'net Maa'kheru*, Ramesses? Now I understand why you had to keep surveillance on her. You needed to know what to say to her to keep her under YOUR boot!"

"I never betrayed you! You knew full well why I had to have those measures in place! Not one time did you see an email from me! Not one time!"

This was going to end badly; there was no other way to slice it.

The conversation escalated faster than I needed it to, and eventually it was going to get personal. If I was honest with myself, I would have realized that it was personal the moment we found safi at the club. I didn't need that to happen, and I tried to find a way to calm things down before there was some action behind his purpose to have the gun in his hand.

Ramesses fucked that plan all to hell. "You deceived us all, you sonofabitch! You had us believing you were all broken up about your fiancée's death? Then quickly point the finger at someone else at the drop of a hat? Fuck me for not suspecting you in the first place!"

"You're right, Ramesses, fuck you! I killed the wrong person!" Het-hotep yelled. "I think I'll correct that oversight RIGHT NOW!"

My eyes widened as I moved quickly to grab my piece as Het-hotep picked up his gun and aimed right for Ramesses. I had to act with the quickness before anyone got hurt or worse.

Ramesses tried to duck out of the way before the gun went off, and he hit the other chair on the way down. I didn't have time to get to him to check and see if he was okay because Het-hotep had his sights on me in the next instant.

I fired before he had a chance to react, dropping him in his chair as the red spot in his chest began to grow.

I immediately grabbed a tablecloth from the dining room to try and help stop the bleeding, all the while watching as the life was draining from his body. I pulled him from the chair so I could perform CPR to keep his body breathing for as long as I could, but it was not working. After a few more furious minutes of trying that seemed like forever, I finally closed his eyes, conceding defeat.

Damn.

This was not the way I wanted it to go down.

I began checking on Ramesses as I heard Natasha and Trish racing through the front door. I guessed that they heard the gunshots and moved quickly.

"What happened, my Sir?" Natasha asked as she rushed to my side as I knelt over Het-hotep's body.

"I took Het-hotep out after he tried to shoot us," I replied, still trying to get my wits about me. "Ramesses took a bullet; I don't know where yet. I was trying to perform CPR on Het-hotep to keep him alive, but I was not successful."

I finally got to see where Ramesses landed, and I checked him for a pulse and I found a faint one. When I flipped him over, I saw a shot by his shoulder, but thankfully not in a fatal spot. He was unconscious, probably from the hit he took when he crashed into the furniture to get out of the way.

"Is he okay?" Trish asked as I heard Natasha calling for an ambulance over the police radio.

"He's fine, but the suspect has been killed," I answered matter-of-factly. "I guess we couldn't have a social conversation after all."

TWENTY-FIVE

Emory Medical Center.

I replayed the incident in my mind as many times as I could to figure out if there was a way out of that mess. I came up with nothing, not with two Alpha males who were intent on having the upper hand. Some things you can't help, and this was one of those things.

Neferterri's going to kill me for letting her husband get caught up in gun play. Again.

Technically, I could argue that we didn't expect Het-hotep to be strapped and ready to go out in a blaze of glory after he'd realized he'd been caught red-handed, but knowing her, she would have a counterpoint, and it would be on from there, with me being on the short end of the conversation.

Oh well, I could live with that for now. It's not like I was going to argue with my business partner about getting involved in a case. I was caught between a stubborn Kodiak bear and a very overprotective panther. I would have more success fighting Roy Jones, Jr. in his prime, and we all know he was the man back in the day.

I sat in the hospital suite that Ramesses was resting in when Neferterri, Taliah, shamise and sajira all showed up, ready to dote on the man in their lives.

It was interesting to watch all four of them working at once. It was a thing of beauty and precision. I was almost in awe.

Neferterri worked over the nurse's station, making sure that her husband had the proper medication and rotation schedule. Come to find out, Damian, the other submissive within the House, worked there as an RN, so he was the one that pulled the strings to get Ramesses the suite when we first arrived.

Taliah was by Ramesses's bedside, making sure he was taking his meds, eating and drinking, and not trying to move too much.

shamise and sajira kept the kids busy because they insisted on seeing their father. I figured that it would be that way with the three of them. They are Daddy's girls, every last one of them.

I felt a slight twinge of jealousy because I got to see the family—Leather and blood—in its entirety at one time. It was a shame that it had to be under these circumstances, but it's not like I didn't get the usual invitations to holiday get-togethers and such. I never got a chance to go because I was busy with Niki and Natasha.

"How are you holding up, partner?" I asked Ramesses as Taliah continued to dote upon her Sir. "You took a pretty good hit to your shoulder."

"Yeah, I forgot how much it hurt to get shot." Ramesses chuckled a little. He winced at the pain shooting through his arm from the vibrations. "I hope that my Beloved hasn't read you the riot act yet."

"No, I was saving that for you, darling." Neferterri chimed into the conversation at the right moment. "I told you that if you were going to get out into the field, the least you could do was get a vest."

"I did have my vest on, baby; he got me on the fly, hit a sweet spot outside of the vest," Ramesses protested, pointing at the cut-open vest that lay in the chair in the suite. "He didn't hit any vital organs, and I guess I still move pretty fast for an old man."

Neferterri kissed him on the forehead and replied, "Okay, old man, I forgive you this time, and the girls are good now that they know Daddy is okay, so we will leave you to relax a bit. I know you and Dom have some things to discuss."

Ramesses had a look on his face like he didn't know what she was talking about. I nodded in Neferterri's direction as the group left the room.

"Sir, I regret to inform you that Het-hotep is dead," I began, finding it surprisingly difficult to utter the words all of a sudden. "After he shot you, he turned the gun on me and I had to put him down."

I didn't know what to expect from him after getting that information out. I half-expected a lecture about preserving life at all costs, much like my old captain used to preach when we were out in the field.

Instead, Ramesses closed his eyes and seemed to mumble something that I couldn't make out for a few seconds before opening his eyes like he didn't have a care in the world. "You had to do what you needed to. He chose his fate when he pulled the trigger. Clean shoot, that's all that matters to me."

I nodded. There was no point in trying to discuss the matter further. If he could make peace with it, then I had to find a way to.

The next moment, he flipped back to investigator mode. "What is the status on the rape trials? Has Niki gotten everything and everyone she needed?"

"Yes, Sir, it looks like everything is a go," I replied. "They are going in later tomorrow for a last round of plea bargaining. If that doesn't work, they will be heading to trial."

"Good, that gives me some time to rest and get the fuck up out of here," Ramesses said as he tried to lift up in bed. He immediately grabbed his shoulder in pain and growled in his frustration.

"I think you will be hitting the sidelines for this particular case, Sir," I warned as he lay back down in bed. "Your Beloved will never forgive me if I allowed you to break doctor's orders."

"Yeah, yeah, it looks like I won't have a choice," Ramesses conceded, still holding his shoulder. "Take care of the trial details, Dom. I think you're more than capable of handling that. I'm only hoping that the verdict goes in our favor."

"Why do you say that?" I queried.

"Because if it doesn't, there will be hell to pay within the community." Ramesses shook his head. "That's something that we simply cannot afford."

"That's the deal, take it or leave it."

I sat in complete disbelief as Kacie's lawyer stonewalled every effort that Niki and the DA made to get a deal done before they went to trial. It wasn't like the evidence wasn't overwhelming against them.

Four victims ready to testify against her.

Fourteen counts of Rape…

Ten counts of Aggravated Sodomy…

Twelve counts of Aggravated sexual battery…

Fourteen counts of Prostitution…

Eleven counts of Keeping a house of prostitution…

I mean, the charges were buried on top of her so thick and high that if she were a male, the defense would be begging for a plea deal.

Not this idiot.

I don't know whether he was in awe of Mistress Edge or if she was greasing more than his bank account with the retainer fees and such, but every time Niki offered a deal that would lessen all of the charges down to do some jail time, regardless of the amount of time, he flat-out said no.

They started with the max of twenty-five years; he said no.

They rolled it back to fifteen years on all counts; he said no.

They rolled it back to ten years on half of the counts and probation on the rest of the counts; he said no.

If he kept this up, the jury would bury her for the rest of her life. The rape charges alone would give her twenty-five-to-life under the Seven Deadly Sins statute in Georgia. What, did she think that because she was pretty and sexy that the jury would take pity on her or something and not give her jail time even if she were convicted?

Not in this state.

I don't think her googly-eyed defense attorney was aware of the predicament he was putting her in, and she was as delusional as he was about her prospects.

"My client has done nothing wrong, counsel," Michael continued to repeat after each rebuttal from Niki. "These men are trying to get her. That's unfair; this is nothing more than a witch hunt."

"Your client was caught on tape on not one, but four separate occasions raping these men against their will," Niki insisted, completely exasperated by the behavior of the defense attorney. "If you really want to have the jury view that during a trial, your client will have no chance in hell of an acquittal."

I observed from the outside, listening in by earpiece with the mute activated as Niki had her cell phone on speaker, allowing me to hear everything that was going on.

I was frustrated for her and the DA.

Kacie kept smiling like she had a secret that she couldn't wait to tell.

Michael whispered something to Kacie after that statement, and then he scribbled something down on the legal pad in front of him. "My client is willing to do no more than two years in a minimum security facility. In return, she is willing to turn state's evidence against a colleague who has been operating as a madam in DeKalb County."

My body shook with that statement. Could she be talking about Tori?

"Why would we deal based on secondhand information?" Niki knew she could easily call Natasha and find out what was going on. "Your client is getting desperate, and we're not in the business of worrying about what DeKalb County does unless it affects Fulton County. No deal."

"Suit yourself, counsel." Michael tapped the table as if there was nothing left to discuss. "I guess we'll see you in court, then?"

"It's your funeral." Niki seethed.

I waited for them to come out to the waiting area, and Kacie gave me a look that left me wondering if she really wanted to leave the bargaining table.

"Kacie, don't throw your life away so recklessly. Despite what your lawyer is saying, you're caught dead to rights with all the evidence on you," I explained while right in front of Michael.

"Yeah, we'll see how that all comes out when they find out that you got that evidence illegally, Dom." Kacie smirked. "You violated my Fourth Amendment rights, according to my brilliant attorney."

"I don't know who told you that lie. The warrant was righteous, and I had probable cause." I balked, knowing good and fucking well that I knew what the fuck I was doing. "You got nothing."

"We'll see when the motion to suppress the evidence is heard tomorrow." Michael tried to sound all hard and shit. "The police never found the tapes in the initial warrant search, and you know that because you were there the first time around."

"That means nothing, Michael." I scoffed at him. I moved a slight bit toward him, and the first thing he tried to do was lift his briefcase in self-defense like I was going to hurt him.

You played yourself pussy; time to get fucked.

"You know, Kacie, you should pick better attorneys to give pussy payments to." I laughed as I walked away. "You're going to find out the hard way that the second warrant that was issued was righteous. Let me know what to put in your commissary when you get to North Georgia."

Kacie almost froze in her tracks. "How did you...?"

"You should take better precautions as to where and when you fuck your clients, Kacie." I tried to keep from laughing some more. "A holding cell is not the cleanest place to give an oral presentation, and the judge's chambers in the middle of the business day? Where the judge happens to be the one presiding over your trial? That wasn't the smartest move, either. I'm sure the prosecution would love to know how he ended up getting your case in the first place."

I waited for her expression to change, but I had to give her credit: she was going to stick to her guns until the bitter end.

Fine, you want to play, let's play.

Checkmate in one.

"Oh, and I found out who your informant was," I quietly whispered. "Detective Bryson will make a decent hostile witness, don't you think? I mean, considering all the dirt that he did for you in hiding the tapes in the first place?"

"You're bluffing, you sonofabitch," Kacie cursed. "Ryan wouldn't betray me. I've got him wrapped around my finger."

The self-satisfied look on her face was enough to make me want to slap her silly, and I didn't really advocate violence against a woman in that manner, but she was definitely asking for it.

"He would if he wanted to save his job...and his marriage," I retorted, waiting for her to hear the lack of a quaver in my tone.

She searched deep within the windows of my soul.

She saw that my ace in the hole was legit.

Her house of cards was crashing down around her.

I swear, she couldn't yell loudly enough.

"Wait! I want to go back! Get the ADA on the phone. I want to deal!" Kacie frantically screamed, ignoring Michael's pleas to keep quiet. "I don't want to go to jail for the rest of my life! It wasn't worth it!"

Niki and the DA rushed out into the hallway, trying to figure out what all the commotion was about. Niki's eyes were trained on mine, looking for some explanation. "What in the hell happened? What did you do to her?"

"I got her back into the negotiations again; that's all that matters." I smirked as I looked back at the arguing that client and counsel were going through. "She forgot to watch where she was doing business, and with whom she was doing business with."

"What do you mean?" the DA asked, confused.

"She thought she had you guys in a bind because the judge was supposed to be in her hip pocket," I explained, causing Niki to gasp slightly. "However, what Kacie forgot to figure out was who the judge's executive assistant was, and more importantly, who she knows."

The DA grinned as he began to put two and two together. "Thank you, I believe we have the leverage we need to get the plea deal done. Only this time, I won't be so gracious. By the way, I'm Jim Wariner, Fulton County District Attorney."

"Dominic Law, sir, it's a pleasure," I replied.

"That's right! I spoke to your business partner not too long ago," Jim told me. "I suspect that Mr. Alexander will be pleased with this turn of events."

I slipped a kiss on Niki's cheek as I got ready to go. I couldn't help but do that, considering the beaming proud look on her face gave her away. "Of course, Mr. Alexander will be pleased at the outcome; I'm sure of it. We were happy to be of service."

The DA grinned as he shook my hand firmly. "I have a feeling we might be able to use your services again in the future, Mr. Law."

"We would be happy to help in the future." I grinned at Niki as I grabbed the door to leave. "It's what we do."

EPILOGUE

"Damn, baby, get it…take that pussy!"

Tori had her ass on full display, assuming a doggie-style position, wet pussy and ass, for me to appreciate and penetrate.

It was a long-awaited reward for removing some unwanted "trash" from her front door.

Actually, I had the FBI to thank for that, but she didn't have to know all that.

I was ready, willing, and able to take all the credit, and the pussy, too.

"Is it good to you, baby?" she asked provocatively. She could feel my energy on her, pulsing through her, making her hornier by the second.

The answer came in the form of her pussy being penetrated balls deep. I felt her squirm to adjust to my girth, as I slowly slid in and out of her sex. She rotated her hips to get a better grip on me, and I couldn't help but growl at the heat that I felt between us.

Yeah, she'll make a good slut to use when I need her.

Although I needed her for more than that; she was my all-access pass to the underground network. If this was what was needed to keep that pass current, then she was going to get worn out six ways to Sunday for as long as my body could hold out.

Her moans became more primal, begging me to fuck her harder. She felt so slick, so wet, and yet she was so damn tight, it was crazy. It was almost euphoric, until another surprise came out of nowhere.

Tori felt slight stinging sensations across her ass cheeks and her lower back as I slowed down a bit. They didn't hurt, but they were definitely noticeable, even while being fucked.

"Relax, sexy, it's just wax," I told her as she looked back at me for reassurance. "Now work my dick while I drip it all over you."

"Damn, D, you know I like that freaky shit," she breathlessly replied, working her hips and trembling as each drop of wax from the candle I held in my hand landed all over her cappuccino-colored skin.

"Shit, you're gonna make me come…keep doing that…shit, yeah, keep doing that. I'm gonna come." Tori kept rolling her hips as the sensation became surreal for her.

I was near my own climax and I needed to delay it.

She wasn't getting away that easy. She needed to know who was in charge here.

I pulled her up close to him by the hair, this time angrily whispering in her ear, "Whose pussy is this, bitch?"

"It's yours, D, it's yours. Take it, D!!!!"

"Then come on my dick now, and you better not hold back. Make me want to fuck you again," I commanded.

"Ohhhhhhh fuck, I'm coming!!!! Oh, my God, I feel it…harder, D, please!!!" Her body tensed, and she buried her face into the rug and screamed as wave after wave began to sweep over her unmercifully.

Tori finally collapsed on the rug, still going through the aftershocks of the orgasm that she had just experienced.

But I wasn't done with her… yet.

I was just about to dive back in as I watched her ass wiggle and gyrate in the air, begging me to take her some more, when the familiar chime that let me know my partner was calling broke through the whimpers and coos escaping from Tori's lips.

"Yes, Sir, what can I do for you?" I asked as I tried to mask the shallowness in my breathing.

"I hate bothering you when you're otherwise engaged, especially on a pseudo day off, but we got a call from Niki." Ramesses sounded business-like as usual.

"Give me the rundown," I asked as my mood changed from casual to business in an instant.

"Okay, according to Niki's detectives, they were called to a scene by a convenience store owner, where the body of an unidentified black male was found dumped in the bushes behind the store. The description they have is he is wearing jeans, a black T-shirt, white socks and black leather work boots. She and Trish couldn't find any ID on him, but they are still searching the crime scene. Tire tracks and footprints can be seen in the dirt near his body."

"I don't get it, Sir. It sounds like routine homicide; why are they calling us in on this?" I inquired as I watched Tori continue to writhe and grind against her fingers, trying her best to distract me. "What's the angle?"

"Well, kid, the angle is the convenience store that the body was found is about a mile away from NEBU," Ramesses finally leveled with me. "This one's close to home this time, Dominic."

He wasn't kidding.

"I'll meet you at the scene in twenty minutes, Sir," I stated quickly. Tori was still waiting to be taken again, and if I was about to deal with a homicide, I needed my mind clear. "Better make that thirty; I have some business to finish."

ABOUT THE AUTHOR

Known for his mind-twisting plots and unique prose, Shakir Rashaan rolled onto the literary scene as a contributing writer to *Z-Rated: Chocolate Flava 3* in 2012. His raw, vivid, and uncut writing style captured the attention of the Queen of Erotica herself, Zane. A year later, Rashaan made his debut with *The Awakening*, opening to rave reviews and a "recommended read" accolade in *USA Today*'s "Happy Ever After" literary blog. The follow-up in the Nubian Underworld series, *Legacy*, has garnered even more success, and its third installment, *Tempest*, picked up yet another "recommended read" from *USA Today*'s "HEA" blog, making the series one of the most unique in the erotica genre.

Obsession was the first of the *Kink, P.I.* series, with the next installments, *Deception* and *Reckoning*, poised to add another exciting series to the mystery genre. A few new projects are also being developed under the pen name, P.K. Rashaan. With his prolific writing prowess and openness on his social media platforms, Rashaan has plans to be a mainstay within the erotica genre and beyond.

Shakir is a Phoenix, earning his Bachelor of Science degree in Criminal Justice/Communications from the University of Phoenix. He currently resides in suburban Atlanta with his wife and two children.

Follow the author on social media, or contact him.

Twitter: http://twitter.com/ShakirRashaan

Facebook: http://www.facebook.com/Shakir.Rashaan

Instagram: http://instagram.com/ShakirRashaan

Email: shakir@shakirrashaan.com

Blog: http://www.medium.com/@ShakirRashaan

WE'RE GLAD YOU ENJOYED "DECEPTION,"
BOOK TWO IN THE "KINK, P.I." SERIES.
BE SURE TO WATCH FOR BOOK THREE,

RECKONING

THE KINK, P.I. SERIES: BOOK 3

BY SHAKIR RASHAAN
COMING SOON FROM STREBOR BOOKS
Turn the page for a sneak preview.

PROLOGUE

"I didn't do it! I swear it wasn't me!!!"

He pleaded for his life in that moment, but mere moments ago, he shouted to the deity he prayed to as his pain-pleasure threshold was being pushed to levels never before realized. His play-partner-turned-captor waited patiently to flip the switch, realizing the time drew near to close the curtains on the scene…permanently.

Being a masochist, he didn't process the extreme pain and blood-letting as anything more than the orgasm-inducing experience he'd been looking forward to for the past month. His endorphins spiked to euphoric levels, providing the out-of-body experience he would brag about to the other masochists in the submissive male group he belonged to for at least the next upcoming months. He would be the envy of his peers, wearing more than a few badges of honor as vestiges of time well earned.

The last thing he suspected was the scene of his dreams turning into a nightmare of epic proportions.

"You're going to pay for the decision you made." The scowl on the face of his tormentor should have been enough to instill the genuine fear that washed over him, and it was in that moment that he realized the fantasy was over, but the reality was beyond any conscionable comprehension. "You took someone I loved more than anyone on this planet. I'm going to make you all pay."

The gravity of the situation weighed more than the chains that were originally used to tie and bind the so-called helpless victim. The fear of the unknown was palpable, but what had him paralyzed more than anything else was the lack of an answer to the scariest question of all: *Am I going to die tonight?*

Abraham Lincoln once said, "We all owe God a debt, and the debt that all men pay is death." He stared into the eyes of the debt collector, the person who would be the one who ensured he would never see another day of his life, to never see the next sunrise.

"I didn't do anything, all I did was what I am supposed to do. I'm an assistant district attorney, dammit! She broke the law!" If he was going to go, he wasn't about to go out like a scared little bitch, pleading for his life. As much as he tried, his mind was too far gone to process the wounds on his body as a credible threat to his life. It didn't stop him from voicing his anger over the cryptic turn of events. "I made the decision based on the evidence, motherfucker! I'll be damned if I let someone tell me I did differently!"

"You made your decision when you breached protocol to have my Domina incarcerated, and all over bullshit." The icy stare coming from his captor turned more menacing by the second.

"She didn't do anything that bitch boi didn't ask for, and you know it!"

"She raped me, too!" He blurted out the information he swore he would never tell another soul once Mistress Edge was sentenced and sent to prison. "I was not about to let her get away with it! Fuck you!"

The intensity increased once finely sharpened steel plunged into pliable flesh, leaving the victim in the position of not knowing whether to scream out in pain or ecstasy as his brain found it increasingly difficult to decipher between the two. His rational brain should have recognized the imminent threat, but the pleasure centers clouded that deduction. Even the sight of more blood than usual wasn't enough to activate the fight-or-flight mechanism.

Despite his cries, his tormentor treated them as nothing more than a dead man's final requests before he ended his life.

"Please don't kill me...please don't stop...I don't want to die!" The conflict flashed across his face as the words descended into unintelligible slurs, soon to be replaced by gurgles and the coughing of blood. His eyes conveyed the fear and confusion in his mind as he recognized the finality of his life being extinguished. He wasn't ready to go, but that choice was no longer his to make.

His killer took one look into the eyes of one of the people who had taken his Domina away from him. He remembered the frantic phone call he'd received while tending to business overseas. He remembered the fear in her tone as she'd told him she had been sentenced. Those sounds would haunt him the rest of his life.

"You're going to die, of that you can be sure." Tears flowed from his eyes as his thoughts moved to the phone call he received months later from the women's prison. The warden expressed her regrets as she informed him that his precious Domina had been killed in a cafeteria riot. He looked down at his helpless victim as he took stock of the life flowing out of the body he'd been torturing for hours. "An eye for an eye: isn't that what the 'good book' says?"

He didn't realize while he reminisced that the victim had already departed from this realm and journeyed to the next. Once aware of the expulsion, he shouted skyward in a symbolic gesture to his Domina. *He's on his way for You to torture, my Domina. More will be on the way soon.*

He stood there for a few moments as he contemplated his next move. Although they weren't far from where he wanted to stage the final scene, time worked against him. It wouldn't be perfect, but it would be enough. It was the first in a series of unfortunate events that would conclude with his final objective: taking everything from Dominic Law, including his very life.

He wouldn't rest until he dispatched everyone who had a hand in her death, but he would save Dominic for last. He wanted his new nemesis to feel what he felt when she was taken from him. Before it would be said and done, he would derive the ultimate pleasure in watching the hope drain from his eyes before he put him out of his misery.

It wouldn't bring her back to him, but it was one helluva start.

FOUR

"Daddy, there's someone on the line for you."

"Who is it, Ayanna?"

"She won't say, Sir. All she would tell me was that it's of the utmost importance. Should I patch her through?"

I was already on the phone, taking care of a minor issue up in the DMV with one of the compounds, Thebes, so I wasn't sure I wanted to take a blind call from someone that didn't want to identify herself to my executive assistant. My instincts told me not to entertain it until I had more information, but I couldn't take the chance. In this business, something like that could cost lives. "Patch her through, baby."

I waited for Ayanna to transfer the call, wondering who the mystery woman was on the other line, and more importantly, how she knew me. "This is Law."

"Detective Law, thank you for taking my call." The woman's voice sounded familiar, but I couldn't place her, nor could I picture her face. "I need to speak with you regarding a matter of some urgency."

"Time is money, Ms. …?"

"Ashton. Serena Ashton."

The last name had my immediate attention. The Ashtons were one of the many prominent black families in Atlanta. Along with the usual family names that got tongues wagging in this city, if anything happened of an ominous nature that could create negative press, it was a given that they would want to have this handled as discreetly as possible.

This wasn't about to be a normal case—that much was already certain—but the thing that had me baffled was how she knew me. I could understand if she knew Ramesses, but she didn't ask for him. "You will excuse me, but you have me at a bit of a disadvantage, Ms. Ashton. It's not like we run in the same circles or anything like that, so, at the risk of sounding tremendously blunt, how do you know me?"

"No, detective, we don't, but my half-sister, however, is a different story." Serena's voice sounded disturbed, almost like she didn't want to have the rest of the conversation. "You see, she also partakes in the proclivities of the lifestyle that you and Mr. Alexander enjoy. To put it more bluntly, Mr. Law, and to use your vernacular: she's a submissive. I also know she's been a regular at the place you run; I believe it's called NEBU, right?"

"And what is your half-sister's name, Serena?" I took out a pen and pad to write some information down. I had a feeling once I worked through the NEBU membership roster, I would find her name immediately. However, the minute she stressed the half-blood relationship to the woman in question, I realized that the search in the membership database wouldn't be as easy as I thought. "For that matter, what makes you think that she runs in those circles?"

"Her name is Kendyl Ashton, and I don't think she does; I know she does." Her tone suggested that I'd insulted her intelligence, but I wasn't about to apologize for my line of questioning, either. "I found your business card while going through her things in her condo. It says you guys specialize in cases of a sensitive nature when it comes to your lifestyle, is that right?"

"Yes, that's right, Ms. Ashton." Now I really needed to know what in the world was going on. Finding my business card was not a coincidence. "So, now that you have my attention, Ms. Ashton, what do you plan to do with it? Where is your sister?"

"That's what I'm hoping you will be able to help me with, detective," she acknowledged.

"Can we meet somewhere so that I can relay that information in person?"

"My office is secure and private enough for your needs, Ms. Ashton. Can you be here within the hour?"

She hesitated for a few moments before she spoke again. "It's a little past one right now, shall we say, two thirty? I have a few things in my schedule that I need to rearrange to make this happen."

"Two thirty it is. I will see you then." I hung up the phone, turning the recorder off with the intent of working through the information later tonight. I wasn't sure if I wanted to take on this case, especially with the affluent status of the families involved. The Ashtons had a habit of burying secrets when it suited them. I remembered dealing with a case when I was on the force regarding the Ashtons that got the police chief and the mayor involved every step of the way.

I could only hope the same thing didn't happen this time around.

"So, shall we get to the matter at hand?"

"I see that you don't like wasting time, detective."

"Hate me or love me, I get results, Ms. Ashton. I don't like having my time wasted, to be perfectly blunt with you."

"Fair enough, Detective Law, I'll get to the point." Serena shifted in the seat in my office, trying to find a way to develop a comfort level. I had designed my office for my comfort levels, not anyone else's. Even Ayanna had been able to adjust to the unique flavor of the space. "I think my sister is in trouble. She's been missing for the past twenty-four hours."

Who was she trying to fool? I needed to know the angle, so I pressed further for details. "That's hardly a problem that requires our services. Why haven't you alerted the authorities?"

"I need this handled with a degree of discretion that, quite frankly, would be difficult for APD to handle, considering our family's standing within the community." Serena began to fidget in her seat, a tell-tale sign that she was hiding something. I continued to observe, taking notes down to freestyle over later. Something was amiss; I could feel it. "I'm scared for her, detective. She said some things that I couldn't understand, and when I went to her apartment to check on her, the place was a mess. She was normally messy to begin with, but ever since she submitted to her Dominant, she had been meticulous in her duties, including the upkeep of her condo."

I stopped scribbling when she mentioned that clue. "You said she had a Dominant, yes? Do you know, or do you remember, his name?"

Serena closed her eyes, presumably to try and access her memories of whatever conversations she'd had with her sister. "She was in service to someone; I think that's what you call it. I think his name was Kraven or some crazy name like that."

"Master Kraven?" My senses were piqued, and not in a good way. Why in the hell do these new submissives always end up finding the ones that have a sketchy past? If it wasn't the sketchy, "bad boy" Dominants, it's the newbies that thought they knew it all. Kraven was a combination of both, which was saddening, but considering who he was away from the kink community…

Serena picked up on my sudden irritation and used the opening to pry. "So, you know him? Is there any way that you could find out from him where my sister is? Don't tell me, he's a bad boy, isn't he?"

I did what I could to calm myself, but the mere mention of Kraven was enough to get Ramesses's blood pressure up, and he rarely ever got irritated. "To answer your question, Ms. Ashton, yes, he is a bad boy, but he's harmless; trust me. He's not like your garden-variety thug on the streets, but he's nowhere near a saint, either."

"I understand, detective. What do you require to get started?"

She kept giving away mixed signals that continued to throw me off. One moment, she was uncomfortable, barely making eye contact with me, and in the next moment, she's ready to get down to business, her stare nearly piercing through me. If I didn't know any better, I'd swear she was a switch within the kink community, but there was no real way to be sure. Twenty-first century kink these days didn't require being out and about as much.

Nevertheless, something's up, there were no two ways about it.

I was already worried that she waited twenty-four hours and hadn't contacted the proper authorities to report her sister missing, so I needed to get with my girls and try to find a way to slip that under the radar to keep things above board. I needed to at least take the case, if for nothing else than to find this woman before she turned up harmed beyond recognition or worse. Missing person's cases hardly ever turned up positive, although there was a glimmer of hope if I reacted in enough time.

"Standard fees apply, a half-grand a day for surveillance; I'll be able to find out everything you need to know," I explained. A few clicks of the mouse sent the contract from the printer, and the virtual payment through Ayanna sealed the deal. "I should be able to give you an idea in the next forty-eight hours maximum. Our world is small by comparison, so it shouldn't take much to find her. I'll start with Kraven and work from there."

"Thank you, detective, and I can count on your discretion, yes?"

"You won't see anything in the public eye, unless there becomes reason to," I cautioned. "After that, all bets are off."